Augusten Burroughs

Augusten Burroughs is the *New York Times* bestselling author of *You Better Not Cry*, *A Wolf at the Table*, *Possible Side Effects*, *Magical Thinking*, *Dry*, and *Running with Scissors*. His work has been published in more than twenty-five countries. He lives in New York City.

Visit www.augusten.com.

also by augusten burroughs

You Better Not Cry
A Wolf at the Table
Possible Side Effects
Magical Thinking
Dry
Running with Scissors

sellevision

AUGUSTEN BURROUGHS

PICADOR

———

ST. MARTIN'S PRESS
NEW YORK

This novel is a work of fiction. The characters, companies, and television stations portrayed in this novel are entirely fictional, with the exception of certain actual persons, television stations, or companies that appear in the novel and are used fictitiously. All events and conversations depicted in the book, including those involving actual persons, television stations, or companies, are entirely the product of the author's imagination.

www.picadorusa.com

Design by Kathryn Parise

Picador® is a U.S. registered trademark and is used by St. Martin's Press under license from Pan Books Limited.

For information on Picador Reading Group Guides, please contact Picador.
E-mail: readinggroupguides@picadorusa.com

The Library of Congress has cataloged the St. Martin's Press edition as follows:

Burroughs, Augusten.
    Sellevision / Augusten Burroughs.
        p. cm.
    ISBN 978-0-312-26772-8
    1. Television personalities—Fiction. 2. Teleshopping—Fiction. 3. Scandals—Fiction. 4. Gay men—Fiction. I. Title.
  PS3552.U745S45   2003
  813'.6—dc21

                        2003040509

Second Picador ISBN 978-0-312-43007-8

First published in the United States by St. Martin's Press
First Picador Edition: June 2003
Second Picador Edition: October 2010

10 9 8 7 6 5 4 3 2 1

For Lawrence David

Acknowledgments

My deepest (and I *can* be deep) gratitude to Jennifer Enderlin and everyone at St. Martin's Press who laughed. Love and thanks to: Suzanne, Mark, Pick, Lona, Jon, Margaret, John Elder, Mary, Judy, John, and Jack. Special thanks to Christopher Schelling. In memory of Pighead.

sellevision

one

"You exposed your penis on national television, Max. What am I supposed to do?"

"I didn't expose it, Howard, it just sort of *peeked out*."

"It 'peeked out' during the Toys for Tots segment in front of twenty million viewers, many of whom were, not surprisingly, *children*. It's twenty-four hours later and we're still receiving faxes. The phone lines were so jammed last night that no one could get through to place orders. *Plus* I've got every mother in the country threatening child-abuse lawsuits."

Howard Toast, the executive producer of the Sellevision Retail Broadcasting Network, glared at the show host who was sitting in a black leather chair on the opposite side of his large glass desk. Behind Max and facing Howard, a bank of television monitors silently played live broadcasts of Sellevision, QVC, and the Home Shopping Network as well as broadcasts from the other three "B-class" networks.

Howard leaned forward and said quietly, "Jesus fucking Christ, Maxwell. This isn't the Playboy channel, it's *Sellevision*."

Max ran his fingers through his hair, a nervous habit. "Look, I was wearing a bathrobe, it was Slumber Sunday Sundown. We were *all* wearing bathrobes."

Howard's normally placid, waspy features contorted with frustration. A vein on his temple pulsed. "Max, the other hosts weren't *naked* under their bathrobes. It's just—well, there's no excuse—seven-year-old children and their mothers just should *not* know that you're uncircumcised." He took four Advil from the bottle on his desk and washed them down with cold coffee. "I mean, this could be worse than that Cuban raft-boy thing."

Max wiped his hands on his slacks. "Look, I'm sorry, it was an accident. I already told you, Miguel knocked my latte over onto my lap in the dressing room while he was doing my makeup. What was I supposed to do, wear soaking wet boxers? C'mon, man, I had less than *four* minutes before I had to go on air, I had no choice."

Howard straightened the stapler on his desk. "You should have borrowed Miguel's underwear," he said angrily.

"Miguel is *Hispanic*. He doesn't wear underwear. Besides, that's a disgusting thought, even if he did."

"Not as disgusting as showing your dick to families all across America while they're sitting down to eat dinner."

Max rolled his eyes. "Jesus, Howard, you make it sound like I did it on purpose. Like I'm some kind of *exhibitionist* or something."

Howard leaned back in his chair, sighed, and looked up at the ceiling. There was a silence between them, and Max glanced over at the executive golf-putting toy in the corner of the office. Howard leaned forward and placed both hands on the desk, palms up, like he had nothing left to offer. "Max, I'm very sorry this had to happen, but if I put you back on air, I'll lose my job, the station will be boycotted—as it is, you're just lucky your penis didn't make the cover of *USA Today*."

Max leaned in, blinking. "So what are you telling me? You're saying, what, that I'm fired? Is that what you're telling me?"

Howard nodded his head solemnly. "Yes, Max, I'm afraid

we're going to have to let you go. There's no way we can let you back on the air after this, just no way."

Max's hands flew up. "I can't believe you're firing me over this."

"I'm sorry, Max, I really am. I've got a few friends over at QVC and the Home Shopping Network, I could give them a call, see if they're looking for anybody. But you might have to start off doing the overnight. And if worse comes to worst, there's always"—he shifted his gaze toward one of the television monitors that was currently displaying an electric egg scrambler—"the E-Z Shop Channel."

"I can't fucking believe this," Max said, slumping in his chair, letting his mouth fall open.

"Max, America's *premier* retail broadcasting network simply cannot be associated with a controversy of this . . . *magnitude*."

"Oh, well, gee, I guess I should take that as a compliment," Max said sarcastically.

"It's not funny, Maxwell. It's sad, is what it is. It's very sad that you were so careless. You're a good host. But you crossed a line and, well, there are consequences."

Max left the office, mortified as security personnel accompanied him while he collected the possessions in his office, and then escorted him out of the building like a sex offender.

Peggy Jean Smythe sat in her office, reading an E-mail a viewer had sent her. Because of her high-profile time slots as a Sellevision host, she received dozens of E-mails each day. She normally responded with a standard forwarded thank-you letter. But if an E-mail was particularly flattering she would sometimes respond personally with one or two lines.

The reason viewers loved Peggy Jean was because they could relate to her. She often spoke of her three boys, "four if you count my hubby." She was a "working mom" and a good Christian woman who often hosted Jewelry of Faith programs, which featured crucifix cufflinks and Star of David money clips, both of which she presented with equal pride. She was attractive—blond hair worn in a short but full style, blue eyes, fair skin. Her roundish face seemed approachable and trustworthy. She was highly polished, yet friendly and accessible. Peggy Jean knew all of this to be true, because she had seen the consumer research. In fact, she had personally attended many of the focus groups.

"Peggy Jean, did you hear? About Max, I mean?" Amanda asked, standing in Peggy Jean's doorway.

Peggy Jean turned dramatically in her chair to face the young woman. "Of course I heard, and I think it's exactly the right thing to do."

"You don't think it's a little too severe? I mean, just dropping him like that?" asked the associate producer.

Peggy Jean smiled the exact smile she often wore for viewers while hosting a vacuum-cleaner showcase or one of the monthly Easy Wear 18K Gold specials. She touched the lapel of her jacket. "Well, of course I'm sorry for Max, as I would be for any human being facing an adverse situation. But when God closes a door, Amanda, He opens a window." Peggy Jean looked up at the suspended ceiling. "He must have other plans in store for our Max." Then the smile was gone. "And now, Amanda, if you don't mind . . . I have an awful lot to do."

Amanda shrugged. "Sure, I understand. I didn't mean to disturb you."

Peggy Jean returned her attention to the computer screen, listening to make sure Amanda actually had left. Then, almost biting the tip of her manicure, but stopping herself, Peggy Jean read the alarming E-mail for the third time:

To: PG_Smythe@Sellevision.com
Fr: Zoe@ProviderNet.com
Subject: Hi There!!

Hi Peggy Jean!

How exciting to be able to write you! I am a loyal Sellevision fan and have ordered everything from Crock Pots to jewelry. I am so pleased with the quality of the countless items I have purchased from Sellevision.

Peggy Jean, my ears always perk up when I hear your voice on Sellevision. You are my favorite host. You are so professional and friendly, and I just love your hair!!

Speaking of hair, I just want to tell you this, woman to woman: Peggy Jean, I have noticed many times in close-up pictures how very hairy your earlobes are. When I first noticed, it was a bit of a shock to see a beautiful earring on your ear, surrounded by all those hairs, which on my large-screen TV were each almost the size of a Vienna sausage!!

I wonder if you have considered using the *Lady Songbird Waxing Hair Removal System* that I have seen on Sellevision. It seems a painless, quick and easy way for you to be even more beautiful than you already are.

I bumped into (really!!) my friend Susan at the supermarket and we got to talking, you know, just catch-up stuff. Anyway, I mentioned Sellevision for some reason, I forget why. And before long, we were talking about the show and our favorite hosts and she said the very same thing I'm telling you now!!! Isn't that a hoot! (LOL) She said, "She's a very hairy lady." We both had a good chuckle out of it, but PLEASE understand it wasn't a chuckle AT you personally.

Well, I've talked on and on, so I'll stop here. May God bless you and your family. And you have my very best wishes.

Your friend,
Zoe :)

Peggy Jean pulled a small key from the inside pocket of her fuchsia DKNY blazer and unlocked the file cabinet beneath her desk. The drawer contained emergency nylons, a spare pair of simple black pumps, a few sets of earrings that could easily coordinate with most any outfit, and her purse. She pulled out her purse and removed her compact, peering into the small mirror, angling her head as much to the side as she could. She didn't *see* any hairs. But then, this was a small mirror, held at a distance. It certainly wasn't a macro shot from Camera One.

If there were, in fact, long blond hairs on her earlobes that were so obvious on camera as to be the subject of a fan's E-mail, Peggy Jean knew she would have to have them removed before going on air at four P.M. Yet, whom could she ask? If she did, in fact, have the hairs, whomever she asked would surely gossip— mention to somebody else, "Peggy Jean has hairy earlobes"— and word could easily spread all the way to her executive producer, Howard. The idea of being called into the refined, forty-five-year-old's office and being verbally confronted about the earlobe hairs, having to explain that the situation had been remedied—well, it was just unthinkable.

Peggy Jean remembered there was a large magnifying mirror in makeup, and that it was illuminated by a ring of small, round bulbs. Surely makeup would be empty now, between the hosts' shift change. Instinctively, she reached for the tube of Lancôme moisturizer on her desk and squeezed a dime-sized dollop onto the back of her hand. Then she quickly rubbed her hands together until they were soft and fragrant. Feminine.

She placed her purse back into the file cabinet, locked it, and pocketed the key. Leaving her office, she turned left and continued down the hall, passing Trish Mission along the way.

"Peggy Jean, you look wonderful, I *love* that jacket," Trish said, gently taking the cuff of the blazer between her thumb and forefinger, admiring the softness of the fabric.

"Well, thank you, I'm glad you like it. This is the first time

I've worn it in public. Took a little field trip to New York last Saturday with the hubby, and picked this up at Bloomingdale's."

Trish gave Peggy Jean a friendly nod. "Well, the color is just wonderful on you, it looks great with your eyes." And with that, Trish wished Peggy Jean good luck on that afternoon's Gem Fest and continued down the hall.

Was it Peggy Jean's imagination, or had Trish taken a quick look at her earlobes?

Trish was one of the "emerging" hosts of Sellevision. Her growing popularity was propelling her from the overnight slot where new hosts were groomed—presenting a Fashion Clearance or various kitchen implements—to the spot she currently occupied that, although varying, included the occasional prime-time appearance, most notably her recent trip to London where she hosted a British Bonanza.

How soon before the aging (thirty-eightish) hostess with a possible superfluous hair condition was replaced by the much younger, more beautiful, and fully waxed Trish Mission? There was a prized-racehorse quality about Trish that unsettled Peggy Jean. Tall, blond, and ambitious, Trish seemed to be growing more and more successful out of sheer entitlement.

Makeup was, thankfully, empty. Peggy Jean walked directly over to the small round mirror that sat on one of the dressing tables. She pressed a button on the side that caused the bulbs to flicker momentarily, then illuminate. She peered at her reflection, moving her ear as close to the mirror as possible, using the gleaming Frosted Cappuccino–painted nail of her index finger to move the lobe into the light. There they were: tiny hairs, faint and almost unnoticeable unless one were actively looking for them in an illuminated magnifying mirror, as she was doing at that moment.

Amanda, having noticed the light, paused and stood in the doorway, watching Peggy Jean examine her ear. "Peggy Jean?" she asked, concerned. "Is something the matter with your ear?"

■

Heading west on I-92, Max drove mostly in the passing lane, averaging a speed of seventy miles per hour. His favorite CD—the original cast recording of *Rent*—sat unplayed in his five-CD changer. "Stupid, stupid, fuck, *fuck*," was the mantra he repeated aloud to himself as he headed toward the Woodlands Mall to see if he could obtain a certain Beanie Baby named Peanuts for his almost-seven-year-old niece. As much as the Woodlands Mall was the exact last place Max wanted to be (Jake's Joint, a bar, being the first), he simply had no choice. His niece's birthday was the day after tomorrow and he had been unsuccessful locating the elusive plush toy on the Internet. Now he was forced to shop the old-fashioned way: in person.

Don, the Good Morning Show host and father of a fourteen-year-old girl, had told Max that the Toys R Us at the Woodlands Mall had a very extensive Beanie Baby selection. "That," he had said to Max, "would be your best bet—and I'm saying this as the father of a girl who wouldn't speak to me for a full week after I gave her Snort the Bull with that little red tag cut off." After wishing Max good luck in his search, Don had warned "Oh, and whatever you do—don't cut that stupid little tag off. It's *all* about the tag."

WOODLANDS MALL, NEXT EXIT, read the sign. "To think, unemployed . . . *me*?" Max said to the windshield. As he crossed over into the far-right lane, he resisted the temptation to aim the steering wheel into the cement guardrail, causing his top-heavy Ford Explorer to careen over the embankment, explode into flames, and kill him instantly. Instead, he decelerated down the exit ramp and wondered, What if I'm reduced to doing traffic reports? *On radio?*

At four in the afternoon on a Wednesday, the Toys R Us was thankfully empty. Cold, electronic renditions of children's songs played over the store's speakers: "The Itsy Bitsy Spider,"

"Old McDonald Had a Farm," even, oddly, "Kumbayah." Every few minutes, the Muzak was replaced with a loud chorus of children singing the haunting Toys R Us advertising jingle, *"I don't want to grow up, I'm a Toys R Us Kid . . ."* The store, as vast as a warehouse, was piled to the ceilings with urinating dolls, bikes, puzzles, Lego sets, action figures, colorful balls, teddy bears implanted with microchips that enabled them to shake hands, Just Like Mommy cell phones, board games, plastic machine guns, two-pound bags of M&Ms, and inflatable pool creatures. Max stalked the aisles, looking for the Beanie Babies, never more thankful for his homosexuality and the child-free life that went along with it.

At the rear of the store, Max saw a huge display of Beanie Babies. Hundreds, maybe thousands, maybe *millions* of Beanie Babies to chose from. And all Max had to go on was a name: Peanut. No description, nothing. To locate Peanut, Max would have to examine the name on every single little red tag.

Unless he asked the little girl who was standing at the Beanie Baby display along with her mother. Who better to ask than a child?

"Excuse me," Max said, approaching the little girl and her mother. The little girl spun around to look at the stranger talking to her. "I bet you can help me. I'm looking for a particular Beanie Baby named—"

The little girl's scream could be heard throughout the store, possibly the state. It was the sound of raw terror, as if Max were a ragged, scotch-stained Barney holding a machete. "It's him, Mommy, it's *him*, it's the pee-pee man from last night, *make him go away, make him go away*," she cried, clinging to her mother and burying her face in the fabric of her mother's skirt.

"It's okay, sweetie, it's okay," the mother reassured. Then to Max, "I'm terribly sorry, she's not herself today—Madeline saw"—she whispered—"a man's *penis* on the television last night and it really upset her."

Max stood dumbfounded, the shrillness of the little girl's cry stabbing his eardrums.

The little girl continued to sob into her mother's skirt. "It's him, Mommy, it's *him*." The mother examined Max more closely and a glint of recognition entered her eyes. She pointed at Max. "Oh my God, that really was you! You're Max Andrews from Sellevision! That *was* your penis!"

A store detective appeared before the three of them. "Is something the matter here?" he asked. "I'm in charge of security."

The little girl turned to the uniformed authority figure, and asked in awe, "Are you a policeman?"

The detective looked kindly at the girl, "No, honey. Well, sort of, I guess. I'm the police officer of the store, I suppose you could say."

The little girl pointed at Max, then burst into tears again. "He's a bad man, make him go away, I saw his thingie, he showed me his thingie."

The detective immediately turned to Max and glared.

The mother tried to calm her little girl by bending down and stroking her head, repeating, "It's okay, sweetie, there's nothing to be afraid of, it's okay."

The detective gripped Max's elbow firmly. "You are in *big* trouble, mister."

"Hi, and welcome to Sellevision. I'm your host, Peggy Jean Smythe, and you're watching Gem Fest." A small listening device, discreetly tucked into her left ear and hidden by her hair, allowed Peggy Jean's producer to communicate to her from Control Room 2 on the other side of the building. On the floor in front of Peggy Jean were two large color monitors. One was a live-feed, displaying the exact scene that the rest of America was watching. The other monitor displayed the next scene, be it a long shot of the set, a close-up of the model who sat in a chair off to the side, Peggy Jean herself, or simply a prerecorded "beauty shot" of the object she was presenting. At all times, there was a colored box on the left-hand side of the screen that contained the name of the item, the item number, and the price, along with the Sellevision telephone number. The color of the box varied and could be coordinated with the theme of the show. It could be yellow for the Good Morning Show, pink for a Hosiery Showcase, or blue for a Gem Fest. During the JFK Jr. Memorial Collection, the box was black. The Sellevision logo was always on the lower right-hand side of the screen, and never left.

At that moment, Peggy Jean was looking at the live-feed monitor, a medium shot of herself sitting behind a glossy, tan-and-black wooden table. Behind her was what appeared to be the evening skyline of an anonymous city. The windows of the "buildings" were illuminated and there was even a small, round moon in the sky, along with a smattering of stars. Very urban and upscale. The naked Barbie doll a key-grip had placed in one of the windows went entirely unnoticed by the viewing public.

All the Sellevision sets were spectacular—beautifully designed and of the highest quality. The kitchen set was like a charming farmhouse kitchen, with a delightful view of trees that could be seen through the window above the sink. The trees looked extraordinarily real, especially in the winter when the branches were covered with artificial snow by prop stylists. There was a bedroom set complete with dormer windows and wainscoting. And the living-room set had a working stone fireplace as well as an overstuffed sofa, comfortable chairs, and accent tables—everything a tasteful, upper-middle-class living room might include, even a bookcase filled with color-coordinated antique books. Sellevision was far superior to the other home-shopping networks and Peggy Jean felt proud to be a part of it.

"If you love amethyst, or maybe your birthday is in February, amethyst being the February birthstone, or you just love the comfort of lever-back earrings and the color purple and you are a woman who appreciates a real stone *presence*, my first item just might be for you."

The producers in the control room cut to a prerecorded beauty shot of the trillion-cut amethyst lever-back earrings.

Then they cut back to Peggy Jean who was smiling and holding a wooden ruler, the earrings displayed on a black velvet stand before her. "This is item number J-0415 and they are our trillion-cut amethyst lever-back earrings, priced at a very affordable forty-nine ninety-five. I just want to give you a measurement here," Peggy Jean said while she continued to smile broadly, placing the ruler against one of the gemstone earrings.

Cut to a macro shot, Camera One. On the monitor, Peggy Jean's fingers were each larger than a loaf of Wonder Bread as she positioned the ruler, displaying for the viewers at home that, "This is gonna measure about, well, a little more than eight-sixteenths of an inch across, and . . ." She measured the vertical. ". . . about one inch from top to bottom." Her manicure was absolutely flawless.

In her ear, Peggy Jean heard her producer saying, "Peggy, these sold out the last time they were presented which was on . . . lemme see here, okay, back in October."

Cut to medium shot of Peggy Jean. "Now, I just want to let you know, these earrings *did* sell out the last time they were presented, and that was way back in October. So it's taken us a good seven months to get them back in stock." Peggy Jean looked deep into the camera. "Keep in mind, the reason for this is because people actually have to go out and *find* the amethyst in nature, so that's something to consider." Gently tapping the stone with the tip of her nail, she informed the viewers, "These are absolutely beautiful earrings and they have a total gem weight of just over three carats, so that's about one and a half carats per ear. And that's a lot of stone."

"Peggy, the rings are already moving, this could be a sell-out, so push hard."

"Let me just tell you, these earrings are extremely popular tonight. We could become very limited, so if you want these earrings, I'm just warning you not to wait." A graphic appeared, counting the number of orders received. Quickly, it moved from 257 to over 500. The Teleprompter in front of Peggy Jean displayed: PHONE CALL. *Marilyn . . . New Mexico . . . Purchased.*

Off to the side of the Teleprompter, a gaffer scratched his crotch and took a sip from a can of Jolt cola.

"Let's go right to the phones and say hello to Marilyn from New Mexico. Hi, Marilyn, and welcome to Sellevision." Peggy Jean gazed pleasantly into the camera, as if she were sitting at a table across from a close friend. When no voice was heard, Peggy Jean tilted her head to the side and said, "Welcome, Marilyn. Are you there?"

"Oh yes, I'm here. Hello, Peggy Jean." It was the voice of an older woman.

"Well hi, and welcome. Are you picking these up tonight for yourself, or as a gift?" Peggy Jean asked.

"Oh, for myself, I need a little pick-me-up," the caller said, slightly down.

Peggy Jean beamed. "Well, *good* for you, sometimes we *all* need a little pick-me-up. Congratulations for ordering these beautiful, *beautiful* earrings. Do you have any idea where you're going to wear them?"

"Oh yes," the woman said, "I'm going to wear them"— silence, then—"I'm going to, my, well . . ." The woman was struggling and sounded on the verge of tears. "I've had a tragedy recently. I'm going to wear them to my son's funeral next Monday. My son Lawrence, that's his name. He killed himself."

Her producer's voice was suddenly in her left ear, unheard by the caller. "She's a fucking basket-case, get her off, get her off, Peggy Jean!" he shouted.

Completely unflustered, Peggy Jean adopted a sympathetic tone. "Oh, Marilyn, I'm so sorry to hear that. What a terrible tragedy. I have three boys of my own, and I cannot imagine what you must be going through, that is really just so terrible." Then brighter, "But I'm glad that you're being good to yourself by picking up these stunning trillion-cut amethyst lever-back earrings and I know you'll enjoy them for many years. And what a beautiful tribute to your son!"

"Excellent, Peggy, great segue," the producer said. "Now get rid of her."

"It's been nice speaking with you," Peggy Jean said instantly.

"I love you and all of the Sellevision hosts and I hope that none of you ever go through something like this. I pray for all of you each night." The older woman paused.

Peggy Jean leapt on the pause. "Thank you, Marilyn from New Mexico, and remember, because we ship UPS Two-Day Priority, your earrings will arrive in time for your son's funeral at no extra cost. Bye-bye and God bless."

"You are shameless," Bebe Friedman said to her television, positioned directly across from the cream-colored shabby-chic sofa on which she was curled. "Drop the earrings, Peggy Jean, this woman's son just killed himself." Bebe spooned one last bit of ice cream into her mouth, feeling not too guilty since it took her over a week to finish the pint.

Bebe was Sellevision's crown jewel. At forty-two, she was one of the original hosts when the network premiered eleven years ago. From day one, the self-deprecating, quick-witted, and very down-to-earth Bebe was a hit. And now she was on air only during the hottest of prime time. She had her own two-hour Dazzling Diamonelle show every Sunday night at ten, and she also hosted many special celebrity programs. Almost everything Bebe presented sold out.

While Peggy Jean, certainly number two behind Bebe, was a slave to product details, Bebe preferred to simply provide viewers with humorous sidebars, engaging stories about her mother who was retired in Needles, California, and tales of her permanently single life. She was also not above making fun of her own "very Jewish nose," or her "big mouth that gets me into trouble." Like all Sellevision hosts, Bebe was polished, but there was a certain realness to her that no amount of hairspray or liquid foundation could obscure.

On last Sunday's Dazzling Diamonelle, for example, Bebe was presenting a fourteen-karat white gold tennis bracelet that featured alternating marquise-cut and oval stones—fifteen-carat total simulated gemstone weight. And instead of taking the ruler and measuring the diameter of the tennis bracelet or talking about how Diamonelle is the world's finest simulated diamond, Bebe asked viewers to forgive her manicure, which had chipped while she was washing her Westie, Pepper. "I had to give her a bath, you know, because today at the park she felt this instinctive *doggy need* to go romp in the mud, and then roll around and, well, she was just a mess." Then Bebe added, "Now I personally own a couple Diamonelle tennis bracelets, and I wear one of them pretty much every day. But do you think I would wear an actual diamond tennis bracelet to drag my dog out of the mud? Give me a break. Of course, if you *are* going to be mud wrestling with your dog, it doesn't hurt to *appear* to be wearing a diamond bracelet while you do it."

The white gold Diamonelle tennis bracelet, item number J-1023, sold out instantly.

Chuckling to herself over Peggy Jean's ability to turn even

suicide back to the amethyst earrings, Bebe got up off the couch, placed the spoon in the dishwasher, then dropped the empty ice cream pint into the trash can, which she opened by stepping on the pedal with her bare foot.

Inside the trash can, a microchip alerted a small pump that the lid had just been opened, and the pump sent a small burst of liquid deodorant through a jet spray on the underside of the lid. Bebe had fallen in love with the trash can last year when it debuted, and purchased the clever item for herself.

Returning to the sofa, Bebe noticed the close-up shot of Peggy Jean's ear. A bevel-set peridot stud earring glinted beneath the studio lights. At first, she thought it was the lighting, but then she saw that no, in fact, Peggy Jean's earlobe *was* bright red—irritated. Almost as if, Bebe thought, she had just *waxed* it.

Having been distracted long enough, Bebe aimed the remote control at the television and turned it off. Then she refocused her attention on her mail-order catalogs.

She double-checked her orders. From Pottery Barn: the Nautical Rope Clock, the East Hampton Votive Candle Collection, and the Country Comfort Bathroom-Tissue Cozy. There wasn't much in the current Banana Republic catalog she was interested in, so she just picked out a few oversized sweaters and a man's belt she thought she could send to someone, sometime, for something. Highly unusual was the fact that she saw absolutely nothing in the Franklin Mint catalog, which always had some unusual little something. So she just ordered a small brass travel clock that looked like an ancient Greek coin.

"No, you still don't understand," Max told the Toys R Us store detective as they sat in a small room upstairs, off the sales floor. Unlike the colorful, toy-filled Toys R Us showroom, this room was decidedly more adult, featuring a large gray metal table, numerous folding chairs, an expansive one-way mirror, and a video camera mounted in the far corner. "Like I told you, I'm a Sellevision host—er, I mean, I *was*, until this morning. But anyway, we had this show last night called Slumber Sunday Sundown and I was wearing a robe and my penis slipped out momentarily." Just recounting the details was exasperating to Max; it was still so unreal. "So I guess what happened was, like I said, that little girl must have been watching and she saw the peek-out thing and, well, remembered me. And that's *all* there is to it. You can't detain me like this. I'll press charges."

The detective was taking notes.

"Ask her mother," Max said, angrily. "*Ask her.* I didn't flash her daughter, that little girl, I didn't—this is insane."

Once the event had been cleared up and Max was allowed to leave custody, he marched out of the store, Beanie Baby–less, certain he would never step foot in the Woodlands Mall again, for the rest of his life, for any reason. "Christ, John Wayne Bobbit doesn't know how lucky he was to have it chopped off," he said under his breath as he unlocked the door of his SUV.

two

"Is it hormonal? Do I have an estrogen imbalance?" Peggy Jean asked her general practitioner, Dr. Margaret Stewart. She had made the appointment with Dr. Stewart immediately after she had seen the hairs on her earlobes for herself.

"I really don't think it's anything, Peggy Jean," the doctor told her. "It's just natural. We all have hair on our earlobes—not just men but women, too."

Peggy Jean shifted uncomfortably in her chair.

"You could say it's left over from our caveman days. We all have faint, light hairs all over our bodies."

Peggy Jean did not believe in evolution, so her doctor's explanation sounded like rubbish to her. Peggy Jean believed the world was created in six days, and that God rested on the seventh. "Yes, but the blood work, that will tell you *for sure* if there's . . ." Peggy Jean paused, choosing the right words. ". . . a *female* problem going on?"

Dr. Stewart was amused by Peggy Jean. "Yes, the tests will show if, in fact, there is a problem—which I am certain there is not."

Peggy Jean was not so certain. Just that afternoon she'd received a *second* E-mail from Zoe, part of which read: *You*

*haven't taken up smoking, have you? The only reason I ask is because
your voice sounded a little husky the other night on Gem Fest. I hope
you're not smoking. It can kill you . . .*

"And no, Peggy Jean, your voice does not sound husky to
me. It sounds exactly like it always has," Dr. Stewart said.

That evening at home, Peggy Jean approached her husband,
John. He was in bed, reading. "Honey?" she said as she slipped
under the covers, her body sinking into the Cozy Nights
Feather Bed (item number H-3424), "Do you think we should
have another baby . . . while I still can?"

Her husband simply replied, "Um-hmm," absently turning
the pages of an Amy Fisher biography, which he was rereading
for the fourth time.

She rolled over on her side and reached for the glass of
Chardonnay she had brought to bed with her, something she
seldom did. But that night, that one time, she felt it was okay;
medicinal, even.

She thought about her visit to Dr. Stewart's office, wondering what she would do if the tests came back positive. And then
it hit her: the M word. Wasn't she too young to go through
menopause? But what if? What if she were suffering not merely
from a hormonal imbalance, but from the ultimate and final
hormonal imbalance? What if it was *already* too late to even
have another baby?

She set the glass down on the table and rolled back over, placing her arms around her husband. "Oh, John, hold me," she said.

"Jesus Christ, Peggy Jean," her husband cried, fanning her
breath away from his nose with the book. "Have you been
drinking?"

"Uncle Max? Why didn't you get me my Peanut like you said
you would?" his niece was saying into the answering
machine.

Max rolled over on his mattress, bumping against the sleeping man next to him whom he had known for a total of nine hours, the past seven of which were spent unconscious. "Shit," he said as he climbed out of bed, going into the bathroom to pee. As he looked at his penis, he said to it, "This is all your fault."

Judging from her message, his niece had not yet received the $350 McDonald's gift certificate he had FedExed to her. Enough money to purchase at least ten thousand grams of saturated fat and guarantee that she would be an overweight, unhappy teenager. Yet another life, aside from his own, that he had ruined.

"Hey, Mr. Handsome," called the body from the bed.

Max turned and saw a man probably ten years older than his own age of thirty-three. While six-foot-two Max sported thick, light brown hair, striking green eyes, and classic, all-American features that would not be out of place in a Banana Republic catalog, the man in the bed resembled a plump lawn gnome. Which was astonishing to Max, because only last night the man had resembled Mel Gibson.

"Up and about so early?" the lawn gnome asked.

Max needed the gnome to leave. As in, *immediately*. He made a mental note to never drink again.

According to his most recent automated telephone inquiry at Merchant's Bank, Max had $14,750 in his account, minus what he spent the previous night for drinks, which could easily have totaled over $100, maybe more. Max had calculated that he had approximately five months in which to secure a position as a host on one of the other shopping networks, five months until he would be forced to take whatever job was offered him, including, possibly, one on *radio*.

Max closed the bathrobe that he had slipped on immediately after exiting the bed occupied by the stranger. "Yeah, that's me, up and at it!" he chirped, his on-air personality taking over.

"And I need to get going, hop in the shower." *Hint, hint*, he thought, and scratched the cleft on his chin.

The gnome didn't take the hint, but instead patted the empty space beside him on the bed. "C'mere, baby. I know what you need."

On Fridays, the hosts gathered in a conference room for their weekly meeting with executive and associate producers to discuss any programming notes for the following week, as well as any other issues. Howard Toast was addressing the group. "As you folks know, Max Andrews has been released from his contract with us, due to an unfortunate incident during Slumber Sunday, the details of which I'm sure you're all familiar with."

A couple of the hosts exchanged glances. Trish Mission, who was never terribly fond of Max and all his air time, simply stared straight ahead. Peggy Jean hadn't seen the need for a homosexual show host in the first place.

"As a result, we find ourselves with a total of six hours of air time to fill each week," Howard said.

The slot Max had left behind included two hours every Sunday evening beginning at six P.M., two hours in the A.M. on Mondays (variable), and Wednesdays from noon to two P.M., all Eastern Standard Time.

"Therefore, I am pleased to announce that effective immediately, Leigh will be occupying the time slot previously held by Max."

The hosts broke into applause. Don from the Good Morning Show whistled. Bebe Friedman reached across the table and touched Leigh's hand. "You deserve it."

Leigh smiled sheepishly, "Thanks, everybody."

Previously a field reporter with WPBC in Philadelphia, Leigh Bushmoore had joined Sellevision two years ago, and had been hosting the overnight slot from two A.M. to five A.M., Monday through Friday. With the new slot, Leigh would have daytime exposure, even though she would be on air fewer hours. The exposure would no doubt boost the career of the intelligent and attractive twenty-nine-year-old. But because her new success was at the expense of her friend and former co-worker's career, the moment was not as exciting as it might have been under different circumstances.

Bob, the other overnight host, was to have his current five to seven A.M. hours extended to include the *entire* overnight slot, from two to seven A.M., an enormous windfall for the youngest Sellevision host. With twenty-five hours of total air time, it was ironic that the least experienced host now had the most on-air hours. Although viewership of Sellevision dropped nearly 85 percent during his hours, the experience in front of the camera was going to be invaluable. When Bob's new hours were announced, the room broke into another round of applause.

But Howard was quick with his caveat. "Now don't get a big head, fella, this is only temporary, until we've chosen a new host to split the overnight with you."

With this out of the way, it was time to discuss the following week's Today's Super Value, or TSV items. There were 364 TSVs a year (Sellevision suspended broadcasting on Christmas day). Sometimes a kitchen appliance or an air purifier, some-times a piece of jewelry, a TSV featured a very low price and its own bright red screen graphic. Many of the items, especially certain jewelry items, were in development for as much as nine months before their air date. A TSV was announced to viewers at midnight. Each of the hosts were required to be familiar with the TSV because it would be presented throughout the day, at prescribed intervals. If it was a piece of jewelry, all the female hosts were to wear it on air. The same was true of clothing. Often, a TSV would sell out before the next TSV could be introduced at midnight. In this event, the producers created a Just For Now Value to replace the TSV.

Amanda, the associate producer, passed around a six-page document detailing each TSV for the following six days. Peggy Jean noticed that on the day *she* would be introducing the TSV at midnight, it was not a Big 'N' Easy comfort shirt or a perfume sampler set. It was a HandiMan table saw. Something *just for the guys*. She frowned and fluffed the silk scarf around her neck.

Absent from the hosts' meeting because she was currently on air, Adele Oswald Crawley was stroking the cotton crotch of a pair of panties. "The moisture is literally whisked away, and that's why they're called Moisture Whik Control Panties. And as many viewers have told me on the air and in letters and E-mails, these are the most comfortable panties you can wear. As a matter of fact I have them on right now, and they really are truly comfortable." Cut to a medium shot of Adele sitting on a chair in the bedroom set with a display of panties on a table before her.

"Adele, double X just sold out," the producer said in her ear.

"Okay, my producer just told me that extra-extra large has just sold out. We still have small, medium, large and extra large available." Adele looked at the Teleprompter and saw that there was a caller, Lona from Connecticut, who ALREADY OWNS the panties. "Let's take a call and say hello to . . . Lona from Connecticut. Good afternoon, Lona, how are you today?" Adele said, fingering the crotch of the panties.

"Hello, Adele, it's so nice to speak with you."

"Thank you so much, Lona. I'm glad you could be a part of our show today. So you already own Moisture Whik Control Panties, is that right?"

"Yes, I do. And let me tell you, Adele, I'm a nurse so I'm always running around, working double shifts. And boy oh boy, do I feel fresh."

Adele smiled. "That's wonderful, Lona. So you feel fresh all day long?"

"Oh yes, I really do. I wouldn't wear any other panties—even if you paid me." The caller chuckled and continued. "And let me just say, the waistband is so comfortable. Because with some of the other panties I've tried, I sometimes get a rash because the elastic is really binding, but these are a treat."

"You bring up an excellent point, Lona, and I really should have mentioned that. The waistband of Moisture Whik Control Panties is a full inch in diameter, so it's wide and comfortable and doesn't pinch or bind. Thank you so much for calling, Lona, and you have a great, fresh day."

"I will, Adele, and you have a great day too. Can I say hello to my dog?"

Adele laughed. "Of course you can. What's your dog's name?"

"Her name is Nermal. Hi, Nermal, hi, baby," cooed the caller.

"Hello, Nermal," Adele chirped. "You be a good girl and stay off the sofa." Lona laughed.

"Adele, we're going to cut to the Di promo, mention the choker," the producer said.

"All right, and if you've been admiring this beautiful pearl choker I'm wearing"—Adele touched her necklace as Camera One zoomed in for a closeup—"you're gonna want to tune in to Sellevision this evening when Trish Mission hosts 'England's Rose: Jewelry Inspired by Princess Diana.' This particular piece is the Diana Triple Strand Simulated Pearl Choker, and it's item number J-5212. It's introductory-priced at just twenty-five ninety-nine. Take a look at this." The producers in Control

Room 2 cut away from Adele to a prerecorded thirty-second promotional commercial.

The commercial was a montage of footage featuring the Princess. The clips were purchased from various news services and stock-footage agencies and assembled by Sellevision editors. The spot featured shots of Diana exiting a limousine as flash bulbs fired, Diana smiling with her eyes lowered, Diana sitting at an official engagement, Diana hugging her two sons on a ski slope. The promo ended with the heartbreaking shot of the crumpled black Mercedes inside the Alma Tunnel in Paris.

Intercut with the footage of Diana were beauty shots of various pieces of fashion jewelry: a simulated-sapphire ring surrounded by faux diamonds, the choker that Adele was wearing, assorted bracelets, and a twenty-inch beaded necklace. There were also pins, a lariat, and the most affordable item in the showcase: a key fob.

A voice-over romanced the upcoming program. "She was England's most beautiful rose, Princess Diana. Loved by millions and suddenly, tragically, taken from us at the height of her beauty and freedom. Join Sellevision this Friday at eight P.M. Eastern Standard Time for a full hour of our first 'England's Rose: Jewelry Inspired by Princess Diana' showcase. This extraordinary show features beautiful fashion jewelry created in loving memory of the most famous princess the world has ever known. If you love Diana, this is your chance to add her legacy to your own jewelry wardrobe. Don't miss 'England's Rose,' this Friday evening, only on Sellevision."

Cut back to a medium shot of Adele and the Moisture Whik Control Panty display.

"Yes, please," Bebe told the waiter at Café Sonzero, when he asked if she would care for a sprinkling of freshly grated parmesan cheese on her Rhode Island field greens and grilled calamari salad. Bebe had taken Amtrak into Manhattan to do some shopping and have lunch with her friend, Amy, a children's book editor with Depretis Books. It was a beautiful Saturday afternoon, and after lunch the two friends would head uptown to shop on Fifth Avenue.

"I can't believe you, Bebe. What if you meet some psycho who tries to tie you up or something?"

Bebe laughed wickedly. "Who says I don't want to be tied up, huh?"

"I'm serious, you could meet a lunatic," Amy said firmly. "What on earth possessed you to write a personal ad and place it on the Internet?"

Bebe stabbed a piece of calamari with her fork. The emerald-cut Diamonelle on her ring finger sparkled as she lifted the morsel of deep-sea predator to her lips. "Amy, I know lots of people who have placed personal ads. You know Trish? Trish Mission from the show?"

Amy nodded, having just seen Trish on the England's Rose show. She'd even ordered the key fob.

"Well, she placed an ad last summer and yeah, she met a couple of bozos, but she also met her boyfriend, Steve. And believe me, he's no psycho, he's an analyst with Price Waterhouse."

Amy remained skeptical. "I don't know, Bebe, maybe I'm old fashioned, but I'd rather meet somebody through friends, or just by chance in the supermarket."

Bebe took a sip of wine. "Amy, the only people I meet at the supermarket are housewives who come up and show me all the Diamonelle they're wearing and ask for my autograph, while their kids whine and tug at their legs." She leaned in. "Look, I'm forty-two and single. This calls for desperate measures."

Amy smiled and rolled her eyes. "Fine. So what'd you say in your ad?"

Bebe rested her fork on the plate, clasped her hands in front of her on the table and recited: "Aging Jewish Princess, forty-two, seeks her prince, or at least a guy who walks upright. I'm attractive, successful, with a down-to-earth nature and an unfortunate passion for Rocky Road ice cream. Healthy, active, and fit, I enjoy the outdoors as well the occasional night on the town. I'm very spontaneous, and love to travel. You should be likewise. You should also be devastatingly handsome, filthy rich, outrageously funny, prone to extreme lapses of common sense, and humble. What else did I say? Oh yeah—the sense-of-humor impaired need not apply."

Amy clapped. "Well, well, well, you could make a living doing that."

The two laughed and Amy raised her glass in a toast: "May the princess meet her Homo-erectus."

Bebe smiled and they clinked glasses.

After lunch, the friends took a cab uptown to Henri Bendel. The store was filled with chic Manhattanites carrying dark green shopping bags from Gucci, trademark blue bags with Tiffany & Co. printed in glossy black ink, Banana Republic totes, and navy blue plastic drawstring Gap bags. "I really need a couple of new suits," Bebe said as they ascended the grand staircase. "I saw a darling Calvin Klein two-piece in *Vogue* last week—beige scoopneck with these wonderful, gigantic lapels."

As the two passed through *accessories*, Amy fell in love with, but simply could not afford, an Hermes scarf depicting mer-maids, starfish, and dolphins.

"Maybe you should splurge," Bebe suggested. Then she glanced at the tag in her fingers, read the $399 price, and added, "Or maybe not."

Amy sighed. "I'll have to wait until I'm a rich and famous children's book *author* instead of just a poor and invisible chil-dren's book *editor*."

Bebe tried on four different suits, took none of them, but instead left the store with a $1,400 sheer black cocktail dress by Michael Kors. "It's for Mr. Homo erectus," she said as the two stood on the curb. "You know, for our *second* date."

Amy raised her arm to hail a cab to take them to the train station, but Bebe quickly moved it back to her side. "I just need to do a little more shopping," she told her. "I feel like I'm forgetting something. I really ought to pick up a new bag; let's just run over to Coach."

Outside the CVS Pharmacy, John Smythe and the three Smythe boys sat in the Acura Legend waiting for Peggy Jean. Ricky, Robbie, and Richie, though not triplets, were dressed in identical outfits of jeans, long-sleeved blue-and-white striped shirts, and baseball caps, each featuring a *Family Circle* logo. The oldest Smythe boy at thirteen, Ricky was dividing the package of red licorice whips between himself and his brothers. John sat at the steering wheel, the sports section of the *Philadelphia Examiner* folded over in half, hiding his copy of *Tasty Teens* magazine.

Inside the store, Peggy Jean was selecting a calcium supplement with iron, because a commercial she saw the other night warned of the dangers women face as they mature, namely osteoporosis and bone loss. After choosing a supplement, Peggy Jean paused in the aisle and wondered if perhaps there was something homeopathic she could try in order to clear up her possible estrogen/superfluous hair condition. Recently she'd read an article that said a lot of Hollywood celebrities swore by homeopathic remedies.

Although the names were completely technical and unhelpful, she saw that each of the boxes displayed a visual illustration of what the remedy was for. One of the boxes featured a head with lightning bolts coming out of it: headache. Another box showed the lower back with jagged marks zigzagging across it: lower back pain. Then Peggy Jean saw a box with an illustration depicting a uterus, fallopian tubes, and two ovaries: *female troubles*.

She took this box off the shelf and headed for the checkout counter. A new issue of *Soap Opera Digest* was displayed on a rack next to the register, so Peggy Jean placed this on the counter along with her other purchases.

Ever since high school, she'd been a die-hard *Guiding Light* fan. Peggy Jean felt that *Guiding Light* had a wonderful spiritual subtext, unlike *The Young and The Restless*, which was just smut.

"Shoot!" Peggy Jean cried as her husband pulled out of the parking lot. "I forgot the Spray 'N' Wash."

Laurie Greenberg, of Greenberg, Kirshenbaum & Partners, enjoyed being a talent agent, especially when she had good news for one of her clients. And she had good news for Max. The E-Z Shop Channel was looking for a new host.

"It would mean leaving Philly and moving to Florida," she told him.

"I have no problem with that," he replied. "What do you think my chances are? Do they know about the . . . *incident?*"

"I spoke with Bob Shriber. He's the head of broadcast production. I told him that I represented you, that up until recently you were a host on Sellevision and that you were now open to new opportunities."

"Yeah, what'd he say?" Max asked impatiently.

"Well, he um, well . . ." Laurie hedged.

"C'mon, Laurie, what did he say? Tell me the truth."

"He said, and I quote, 'Has he started wearing underwear yet?' "

"Oh Christ, I'm fucked. I'm totally screwed, my career—"

"Hold on, hold on, I'm not finished," Laurie interrupted.

"He was just joking. He also said that he would be happy to meet you in person."

"He did?" Max asked, warily.

"Yes, Max, he did. He'd like to arrange something for next week. He's out of town all this week on vacation, but we're going to speak at the beginning of next week and set something up."

Max exhaled loudly into the phone, feeling great relief.

"But don't get your hopes set too high. They're meeting with a few other candidates, and there's a chance they might want to go with an Asian or an African American, so we'll just have to wait and see."

"No, I understand, it's just that, well, at least it's something. I really would hate to end up at Denny's as a waiter."

"Oh, Max, no matter what, you won't end up at Denny's," Laurie reassured him. "Discovery Channel is always looking for new people, and KRON in San Francisco might be looking for an entertainment correspondent, so don't panic quite yet."

"Thanks, Laurie, thanks for not dropping me immediately."

"Sweetie, I would never drop you. I'm your agent *and* friend, for better or for worse, through sickness and in health . . . with pants or without."

"Ha ha, very funny."

After she hung up, Laurie scribbled a note on Max's file: *Reevaluate in three months.*

three

"Knock knock," Leigh Bushmoore said, leaning in the doorway of Executive Producer Howard Toast's office.

Looking up from his desk and seeing Leigh standing there in her two-piece beige cashmere sweater and skirt (A TSV from last month), Howard smiled. "Knock knock right back at you. Care to, uh, join me on the casting couch?" He winked and glanced in the direction of the leather sofa against the wall.

Closing the door behind her and pushing the lock button on the doorknob, Leigh walked around Howard's desk and stood in front of him, smiling seductively and fingering the eighteen-inch strand of freshwater pearls around her neck. "Well, I guess I really should thank you for my recent promotion. Or is it Max I should be thanking?"

He rose from his chair, placed his arms around Leigh's trim waist, and whispered in her ear. "I don't think Max is the sort of man who would appreciate a thank-you like that."

She pressed her body into his and softly kissed his neck. "I've missed you," she said. *Constantly*, she didn't add.

After they made love on the throw rug, Leigh asked Howard, "When are we going to spend some *real* time together, not just these little afternoon escapades, but dinner or a movie? You

know, those things two people do together when they care
about each other?"

Leaning over to kiss her cheek, Howard assured her that as
soon as the divorce proceedings were set into motion, which
would be any week now, everything would be different between
them. She smiled, wanting to believe him.

He stood and zipped his fly. "But, sweetheart, you know that
it would be too risky for us to take chances right now. We need
to act responsibly. I promise you, it won't be like this forever."

"I know, I'm sorry," Leigh said. She hated herself for acting
like this. "I don't mean to pressure you, it's just that, oh, never
mind, I do understand, I really do."

Howard looked at her, her dark hair, tight ringlets of curls
that collected across her shoulders, her eyes a rich brown, "like
amber," he once told her. He studied her fine features, her long
neck and legs. "Don't forget your panties," he said, pointing
under the couch.

Leigh stood, slipped into the panties, then adjusted her top
and smoothed her skirt. "Well, I better be running along, I've
got some stuff I need to get caught up on."

"You do that. And don't you worry." He wagged his finger at
her. "I love you, and I just need you to be strong for me. For us."

Leigh nodded her head. "Well, thanks again," she said, then
added quickly, "I mean for the hours." Before turning to leave,
she paused. "They're not, you know . . ."

"No, Leigh, they're not," he said cutting her off. "You got
those hours because you worked for them. Business is business
and in this business, it all comes down to what the viewers like.
And they like you."

She smiled, walked to the door, and placed her hand on the
knob.

"And, Leigh?" he said.

She turned.

"*I* like you, too. I more than like you."

She left his office and returned to her own. The remainder of an apple she'd sliced in half and left next to her keyboard had turned brown, so she threw it in the trash. It hit the bottom of the can with a hollow *thunk*. She folded her arms on top of her desk and rested her chin on them. Was love supposed to feel like having your period without any Advil? Was this even love, or was it some sick obsession? One minute she wanted to hold him, and the next she wanted to spray Lysol in his face. It was all so *Fatal Attraction*. Would boiling the family pet be next? God, how could she have been so stupid? After all, she'd known Howard was married from the beginning.

She'd begun working at Sellevision right before the company Christmas party. And at the party, he had come over and started talking to her. Her, of all people. Not Peggy Jean, not Bebe, *her*. He told her he wanted to make sure his new host was happy, that she enjoyed her job, and she had told him yes, she was enjoying it very much.

She noticed the wedding band immediately. In fact, she made a point of looking, because she'd been attracted to him since her first interview. He was handsome, dignified—and, she hated to admit it, fatherly.

They'd talked for quite a while. And had quite a few drinks. He suggested they step outside for some fresh air. And they had. And then they had kissed. And the kiss turned into a romance. And the romance turned into a relationship. And the relationship turned Leigh's stomach into a constant knot.

She reached into the trash can and took the apple out. Just as she bit into it, she noticed a fresh, moist stain on her cashmere top.

To: PG_Smythe@Sellevision.com
Fr: Zoe@ProviderNet.com
Subject: Much better!

Dear Peggy Jean,
      I'm delighted that you took my suggestion and addressed your
hairy earlobe problem so swiftly. I must say you looked absolutely
radiant on Tuesday's Big Bold Gold, and I even purchased those
stunning Domed Swirl 14K gold button earrings that you were
wearing. After I sent you that note, I told my good friend Cheryl,
golly, I hope I didn't hurt her feelings. Cheryl told me that she was
sure you'd appreciate having this pointed out to you, as sometimes
we can't see ourselves as clearly as others can. Have you thought
about trying that nicotine gum to help you stop smoking?

                              Your friend,
                              Zoe :)

After reading the letter, Peggy Jean clicked the Reply button
on her mail screen and forwarded her standard E-mail. As she
clicked the Send Now button she muttered, "I don't smoke."

To: Zoe@ProviderNet.com
FR: PG_Smythe@Sellevision.com
Subject: Re: Much better!

      While Peggy Jean does read all of her E-mail, it's impossible for
her to reply personally to each and every person. Therefore, she
has asked me to write you on her behalf and thank you for your kind
words and for taking the time to write. Peggy Jean hopes that you
continue to enjoy Sellevision and she looks forward to shopping
with you in the future.

Checking her flexible bangle bracelet two-tone watch with
genuine quartz movement, Peggy Jean saw that she had less
than fifty minutes before going on air. Just enough time to pick
up a decaf from the hosts' kitchenette and introduce herself to

the special guest who would be joining her on that evening's Celebrity Doll Showcase.

"You Light Up My Life" had always been one of Peggy Jean's favorite songs. She considered it a beautiful and powerful love song to God, and she found herself actually quite thrilled that she was about to meet Debby Boone in person. That evening marked the debut of Dolls by Debby, and she very much looked forward to spending an enjoyable two hours presenting the (adorable) collectible porcelain dolls and showing video clip highlights of Ms. Boone's extraordinary career.

As Peggy Jean was leaving the cantina, she saw Trish Mission leaning over the water fountain in the hallway. "Trish, I just wanted to tell you how *stunning* that Royal Crystal tiara looked on you the other night during your England's Rose show. It didn't surprise me a bit that it sold immediately."

Trish rose from the water fountain and a drop of water fell from her lower lip. "Thank you so much, Peggy. I know, wasn't it terrific! Everything except the 'Always Wear a Seat Belt' glitter brooch sold out, so it looks like I might do it again in a few months."

"Let's keep our fingers crossed," Peggy Jean called back as she walked down the hall.

That was one show that she, herself, would have enjoyed hosting. Peggy Jean felt a special kinship toward the princess, as both women lived very public lives yet were successful mothers. They even shared a similar hairstyle. Although Diana had been divorced, Peggy Jean didn't blame her in the least. It was perfectly clear to the world that her husband was an adulterer. And the princess had done all she could to keep the marriage alive, for the sake of the children. One had to respect that.

"Debby?" she said, walking into the guest's lounge.

Debby Boone looked up from her Patricia Cornwell novel.

Peggy Jean extended her hand and beamed. "Hi, I'm Peggy Jean Smythe and I'm going to be joining you on this evening's show. I just wanted to welcome you to Sellevision and let you know what a huge fan of yours I am!"

"*Amy, you were right, I must be losing my marbles,*" Bebe said to herself as she sat at her computer, reading the responses to the personal ad she placed last week on America Online. Occasionally laughing out loud or shaking her head in disbelief, Bebe was slowly resigning herself to the fact that maybe this computer-dating thing hadn't been such a great idea after all.

One of the men had asked Bebe if she was capable of multiple orgasms. Another said that although he was a big man (385 pounds) he was still a very good person who deserved to be loved. Some guy even sent a nude picture of himself in the form of a JPEG file. Bebe had to admit that although that man did have an excellent body, there was no way she would ever consider meeting somebody who would send such a picture to a stranger.

Rising from her chair and stretching, Bebe brought her coffee mug into the kitchen and made herself another cup of Lemon Zinger tea. Then it was back to the computer to read the last of her responses.

Occasionally, Bebe would glance up from the computer and over to the small Sony Trinitron she kept on a bookshelf near her desk. Bebe had no less than five television sets in her condominium, and most were usually tuned to Sellevision, often— like now—with the sound muted.

Peggy Jean was on with Debby Boone. She was laughing and placing her hand on Debby's shoulder. The two seemed to really be hitting it off.

More than ten men had responded to her personal ad, and out of these, so far exactly zero were contenders.

Pepper walked into the room and Bebe reached down to scratch the dog's back. "Looks like it's just you and me, kiddo." The dog licked her hand.

Then Bebe read the last of the replies. The letter was from a man named Eliot who lived close by in Philly, forty-two, never married, the owner of a chain of dry cleaning establishments. When Bebe read this, she chuckled to herself, "How perfect for me, now I can dribble all the pasta sauce I want over myself and not have to worry about it." As Bebe continued reading Eliot's letter, she began to think that maybe she should write the guy back.

At least on paper, he had a great sense of humor: "I assure you, I'm not a psycho who pulled the legs off ants as a child, nor do I have any outstanding arrest warrants. At least in this state."

Plus, they seemed to like some of the same things. "I've been known to get a little teary-eyed at sappy movies, scream my lungs out at football games, and once in a blue moon put on a tux, head to Manhattan, and listen to fat people sing in a language I don't understand: i.e., opera. I treat common sense as a spice and I love to travel."

"He's probably married or really short or has very bad breath." And with that, Bebe set about writing him a little note in return.

Afterward, she logged on to Ebay to see if any of her bids had been accepted for the classic Leica M3 rangefinder camera, the antique silver hairbrush, or the bronze swan garden loveseat.

"Moist towellette?" the flight attendant asked Max, presenting him with a plastic tray piled with steaming, freshly microwaved cloths.

"Uh, yeah, sure, thanks," he said, taking one of the towels, unfolding it, and pressing it against his face. It smelled fresh, like lemon. Like new things about to happen. Beneath the cloth, he was smiling. He still couldn't believe he was actually en route to an interview with the E-Z Shop Channel.

His agent, Laurie, had called two days ago to ask him if he'd seen the current issue of *The National Enquirer*.

Sarcastically, he'd answered, "Yeah, it's sitting right here on top of my *Scientific American*, I just haven't gotten around to reading it yet."

Laurie then went on to inform him that on page four there was a large color picture of him from the Slumber Sunday incident, a black box over his crotch and a headline that read SELLE-VISION HOST SLIPS OUT, GETS OUSTED.

Yet despite the tabloid article, E-Z Shop Channel was *still* interested in meeting him. After all, they were paying for the flight, the hotel room, even his meals.

"As a matter of fact," Laurie had told him, "I think it might even work in your favor. They need all the publicity they can get."

So be it. If his penis was responsible for getting him fired in the first place, it was only fair that it should help him secure a new and better job. Besides, E-Z Shop was located in Florida. And he had to admit, Florida wasn't such a bad place to live. There was South Beach, after all. And he almost had the abs for it. Plus, he wouldn't have to deal with those frigid northern winters anymore. And maybe he'd finally meet somebody, settle down. A nice, sun-bleached Florida guy who was really sweet and wholesome. And didn't read *The National Enquirer*. Sure, the E-Z Shop wasn't as classy as Sellevision, but then again, it beat the hell out of *radio*.

"Ladies and Gentlemen, in preparation for landing, please make sure that your tray table is stowed and that your seat back is in its upright position." The flight attendant looked directly at Max when he said this.

He tightened the belt around his lap and peered out the window. The plane seemed to hover just above the tops of palm trees as it came in for the landing.

As he exited the aircraft, Max noticed that the forty-some-
thing pilot did a double take when he saw him. The pilot stared
for a moment and then glanced at Max's crotch before smiling
and whispering something into the copilot's ear. Max assumed
he was being paranoid, but after stepping onto the exit ramp, he
turned around. The pilot, copilot, and flight attendant were all
looking at him, smirking. The obviously gay male flight attendant was at least covering his grin with his fingers.

To: PG_Smythe@Sellevision.com
Fr: Zoe@ProviderNet.com
Subject: Gee, thanks.

Peggy Jean,
    I know you're a busy woman with a demanding career and
three young children who no doubt receives more than her fair
share of "fan mail" but I have to tell you that I was a little hurt that
you couldn't find the time to send me even a brief personal note,
especially considering I took the time out of my own busy life to
inform you of your hairy earlobe problem, not to mention express-
ing my concern over your health in terms of smoking.

                          Zoe :|

After reading the letter, Peggy Jean once again sent her
standard reply in return, making no apology and adding not a
single personal comment. She then phoned her husband at his
office and asked if he wouldn't mind picking up a can of cream
of celery soup on his way home. She thought she'd try out a
new recipe for canned salmon casserole she'd clipped from the
back of *Soap Opera Digest*. Peggy Jean then opened the box of
homeopathic medicine she'd purchased, pushed one of the pills
through the foil backing, and placed it under her tongue, letting it dissolve.

four

"Ta da!" Trish sang, extending her finger so that Leigh and Peggy Jean could admire the gigantic diamond engagement ring.

"Oh, Trish, congratulations—he finally asked, you are just . . ." Peggy Jean stopped midsentence, rendered speechless as her eyes fell on the *rock*.

Leigh simply gasped. Then, taking Trish's hand in her own and bringing it closer to her face, she said, "Trish, this stone is *enormous*, it must be like seven carats. How . . . ? I mean . . . ?"

"Seven point five," Trish said gleefully, *"but who's counting!"* She squealed and stamped both little feet.

Peggy Jean discreetly turned her own diamond engagement ring around so that the small stone faced the inside of her hand.

"I had no idea your fiancé was so, well, loaded," Leigh said. "This ring must have cost him a fortune."

Trish tilted her hand slightly from side to side, dazzled by how the ring just soaked up all the light in the room. "Huh?" she said, looking up. "Who?"

"Your *fiancé*," Leigh said again. "This must have broken the bank."

"Oh, *him!*" Trish laughed. "This didn't cost *him* a penny."

And it was true.

When Trish's Price Waterhouse boyfriend had presented her with the *original* engagement ring, it had been in front of Trish's father, Walter Mission III. Trish and her boyfriend had flown to Dallas to celebrate his sixtieth birthday, an event Trish would not have missed for the world.

As the only child, Trish was not only the apple of her father's eye, but also the sole heiress to the entire FlushKing Toilet Bowl and Urinal fortune.

"Daddy!" Trish cried the moment she saw him, running to the front door of the estate toward her beaming father's out-stretched arms. Her boyfriend was left behind to collect the luggage from the trunk of the rental car.

"My baby princess!" he gushed, scooping the girl into his arms and giving her a great big bear hug. He was a large man, in every way. Even his white eyebrows seemed twice as thick as an ordinary man's. And he didn't speak, he boomed.

"Oh Daddy! Happy birthday, happy, *happy* birthday."

Porcelain, the white Maltese, scampered to the door and began yapping.

Trish's boyfriend arrived and set the luggage on the flag-stone steps.

Mr. Mission released his daughter and extended his beefy hand for the boyfriend to shake. "Hello, Stan," he said.

"*Steve,*" Steve corrected, shaking Mr. Mission's hand. Mr. Mission squeezed *hard* and Steve winced.

Trish playfully slapped her father on the arm. "Oh Daddy, stop teasing him. You know his name." Then she bent down and scooped the little lap dog into her arms. "I missed you, too," she said, laughing as it licked her face.

It was after dinner when Trish's boyfriend presented her with the engagement ring and asked for her hand in marriage. He had placed the simple one-carat ring on Trish's finger, and she said, yes.

Trish then leapt up off the mahogany leather sofa and dashed to her father, who was seated in a matching wing chair. "Look, Daddy," she cried, "isn't it pretty?"

Her father placed his reading glasses on the bridge of his nose and peered at the ring. He leaned closer and his nostrils flared.

"You call this an engagement ring?!" he bellowed. "It's a chip, nothing but a chip." Trish frowned and looked at the ring.

Mr. Mission glared at Steve, who was sitting on the couch in a fresh state of shock. "Where the hell did you say you work?"

"Price Waterhouse," Steve replied.

"Well, that explains everything," he hollered. "You'll never amount to anything as long as you work for someone else."

"Oh, Daddy, don't be hateful," Trish whined. "Steve has a good job. He makes almost half a million dollars a year."

"Half a million dollars a what?" he demanded. "A year?" He got up and stormed toward the doorway. "Gunther!" he yelled.

The servant appeared almost instantly.

"Get Jim Lewis on the phone and tell him to open the store immediately. We're coming over now. And get the car started." Then he stomped angrily over to his daughter and said, "Give me that thing," pointing to her finger.

Reluctantly, she slipped the ring off her finger and set it in her father's outstretched hand. He made a fist around it and abruptly shoved it into his pocket before walking to the minibar and pouring himself a tumbler of scotch.

Steve looked at Trish, who gave him a shrug and mouthed the words, *That's Daddy*.

Then, at just after midnight, the three of them, along with Gunther, went to Tiffany & Co., where her father demanded to see the best and largest diamond in the store. When the seven-and-a-half carat stone was delivered to him on a black velvet cushion, he took the original engagement ring out of his pocket and plunked it next to the diamond.

"We want to trade up," he barked.

Jim Lewis, the store's senior manager, inspected the engagement ring. He recognized it immediately for what it was—a good quality stone worth approximately $4,000. Then he looked at Mr. Mission. "Well, sir," he began, "I'm afraid the difference in cost will be quite substantial."

"Surprise, surprise. Let's get this over with. I want to go back home and get some sleep." He pulled his checkbook out from his breast pocket.

"Absolutely, Mr. Mission," Mr. Lewis said. He then retrieved a sales form and a calculator from beneath the counter. He subtracted the price of the original engagement ring from that of the rare, perfect quality seven-and-a-half carat stone. "Here you are, Mr. Mission," he said, sliding the completed form in front of the impatient millionaire.

"What the hell is this?" he grumbled. "I don't have my reading glasses. Just tell me how much the damn thing is so I can write a check and we can all get out of here. This is taking far too long. Time is money."

Mr. Lewis cleared his throat. "Yes, sir. That will be one million, four hundred thousand dollars."

At hearing the price of the stone, Steve's jaw unhinged.

Trish left his side and ran to her father, kissing him on the cheek.

Mr. Mission filled in the check, scrawled his signature at the bottom and turned to his daughter. "See, my little princess? One and a half million, just like that." He snapped his fingers in the air.

Gunther's head instinctively turned.

"Nothing is too good for you." He kissed his daughter on the forehead. Then he looked at Steve and glared. "And *you*," he warned, "better not go shopping in a Cracker Jack box ever again."

■

"Hi everybody, welcome to Sellevision. I'm your host this evening, Leigh Bushmoore, and for the next hour I invite you to kick off your shoes, get into a cozy pair of your favorite pajamas, and join me for Slumber Sunday Sundown," she said, standing in the bedroom set.

Cut to Slumber Sunday seven-second intro.

Leigh took a quick sip of water from a bottle that was hidden out of sight of the camera and sat on the edge of the bed.

Smiling broadly into the camera, Leigh asked viewers if they shared her frustration at "always forgetting to moisturize your hands, so you end up with dry, cracked skin? Well, guess what? You don't ever have to think about it again. Take a look at this." And she presented an item called RemoteControLotion, a universal remote control unit that not only operated most televisions, VCRs, and stereo systems, but dispensed moisturizing hand lotion through tiny pores on each of the buttons. To demonstrate the unit, Leigh aimed the device at the television directly across from the bed, which instantly popped to life, displaying a Sellevision logo. "I've just pressed 'on' and already, lotion has been released onto my fingers."

Cut to a close up of Leigh rubbing lotion between her thumb and index finger. "See?" she asked viewers.

Cut to medium shot. "Now, I can have soft, smooth skin by doing nothing more than being the couch potato that I already am."

Within two minutes, RemoteControLotion sold out and Leigh crossed her pajama-clad legs and moved on to the next product. "How many of you have ever dreamed of owning a hand-crafted cuckoo clock but thought you could never afford one?"

After her Slumber Sunday show, Leigh headed back to her office. She picked up her phone and dialed Max's number. His machine answered. "Hi Max, it's Leigh. I'm just calling to wish you good luck in case you check your messages before the interview. I'm sure you'll do great. Call me when it's over and let me know how it went."

Then Leigh caught up on her E-mail.

"Boys, make sure you wear your red ties," Peggy Jean called down the hallway toward her sons' rooms. Then, to her husband who was in the process of knotting a blue tie around his neck, "Sweetheart, *please*," she said, touching him on the elbow with her Honey Desert fingernail. "The boys are wearing *their* red ties. Wear your red tie, too. I like us to look like a *family*." Peggy Jean was wearing a simple navy suit with a red scarf tied loosely around the neck.

Her husband sighed loudly. "Fine," he grumbled and unknotted the tie, tossed it onto the bed, and walked to the closet to retrieve the red tie.

Peggy Jean adored Sundays because dressing up and going to church gave her family the chance to be together and do something wholesome that everyone enjoyed. And that particular Sunday was especially important, given her medical problems. The fact that she had not yet heard back from her doctor worried her. There was something her doctor was not telling her, she just knew it. "Shoot!" she cried. She brought her finger to her mouth and began sucking on it. "I pricked myself with my crucifixion pin. See what happens when I get worried? You'd think I would have heard *something* from the doctor by now."

John slid his eyes over toward his wife and smirked as he secured the red tie in place. "You're overreacting."

"Overreacting?" she shrieked. "I most certainly am not *overreacting*. This could be a serious medical condition, I may need *hormone therapy*."

"Whatever," he mumbled.

In the car, with her husband driving and the three boys in the backseat, Peggy Jean quizzed them on last week's sermon.

"Do you boys remember what nice Father Quigley spoke of last week, hmmmmm?"

The boys looked at each other, then at their mother's face, which was reflected in the vanity mirror on the visor. They said nothing.

"You remember. He spoke of how important it is to forgive people, even when we feel that they have done or said something we don't feel we can forgive," she said, picking a small clump of mascara from an eyelash. Then she glanced back at her sons. "Don't you boys think that's an important thing to remember?"

They nodded their heads in unison, as if on cue.

"I think it's important, too," she said, snapping the cover of the vanity mirror closed and putting the visor back in place. She turned to her husband. "Sweetheart, there's no need to drive so fast, we have plenty of time."

He glanced at the speedometer. "I'm only going forty-three miles an hour."

"Yes, but the speed limit is only *forty* miles an hour. We don't need to be speed-freaks, especially when we've got the boys in the car on the way to church."

He depressed the brake ever so slightly and the car slowed to thirty-nine miles per hour.

Peggy Jean smiled and gave his knee a little pat.

The Divinity Center was a nice, clean, contemporary church with colorful stained glass windows depicting various saints and uplifting words such as "hope," "joy," "peace," and "love." It had a modern P.A. system so one wasn't forced to strain in order to hear the sermon. And *this* church didn't make the boys sneeze like the musty old church they used to attend.

At first, Peggy Jean had been angry with the boys, believing their sneezing was deliberate and mischievous. Then she took them to see an allergist who determined, after many needle pricks, that the boys were, indeed, allergic to certain molds. As soon as they changed churches, the sneezing stopped. But Peggy Jean insisted they still have booster shots on a monthly basis, as prevention.

This Sunday's sermon was about separating "needs" from "wants," and how important it was that needs were met and wants were curbed. While Peggy Jean sat with a pleasant smile on her face, hands folded on her lap, listening to Father Quigley, her husband was looking two pews ahead and slightly to the left, at his neighbor's seventeen-year-old daughter, Nikki.

He was thinking that Nikki would make an excellent baby-sitter for the boys. He was also thinking her hair was exactly the color of honey. At one point, the girl turned around to adjust her bra strap. She spotted Mr. Smythe looking at her and gave him a shy smile before looking away.

After church, the family walked to the McDonald's next door, a favorite Sunday ritual. The boys were each allowed one Happy Meal. Peggy Jean ordered a Filet-O-Fish with extra tarter sauce. And her husband had a double Quarter Pounder, despite the fact that Peggy Jean thought a half pound was just too much meat. After carrying the red plastic tray over to a table, the family sat down and joined hands. Peggy Jean closed her eyes and led the family in a small prayer. "Dear Lord, we are so grateful for this food and for our good health. We know we are blessed and take pity on those less fortunate than our-selves. Amen."

"I got a machine gun!" the middle Smythe boy cried when he opened his Happy Meal.

The youngest boy tore into his meal. "Mine's an axe!"

Ricky, the oldest, rolled his eyes and frowned, tossing his toy plastic gas mask on the table. He felt way too old to be at McDonald's with his parents, eating a Happy Meal.

After the family had finished eating and were preparing to leave, the youngest boy noticed a dirty man in ragged clothes standing in front of the restaurant. "Look, Mom, it's a bag man."

Peggy Jean bent down so that she was at his eye level. "We don't call them 'bag men' anymore, sweetheart. They're called *The Homeless*." Peggy Jean opened her purse and pulled out a quarter from the change compartment of her wallet. "And we need to help The Homeless whenever we can."

As the family left the restaurant, the man held out his hand and said, "Help me get something to eat?"

Peggy Jean smiled and placed the quarter in the man's hand, saying "You're welcome" as she did.

The family began to walk toward the car, but the man cried out after her, "One lousy fucking quarter? What the hell am I supposed to get with one lousy fucking quarter, you bitch?"

Peggy Jean quickened her pace. All three boys turned around to look at the man, who was waving the quarter in the air above his head and shouting.

"Cunt!" he screamed. "Whore!" He threw the quarter at her.

"*Don't* look back at him," she scolded her boys.

Inside the car, the youngest Smythe boy asked his mother, "What's cunt? What's whore?"

Peggy Jean unfastened the seatbelt she had just fastened and turned around to face her boys. She pointed a finger at her youngest. "Those are the words of the Devil. You must never, *ever* say those words again, or even think them. God will be very angry with you if you do." Then, calmer, she said, "Another thing, the next time we encounter one of The Homeless, we will not look at him, we will just mind our own business and pretend he doesn't exist. Is that clear?"

The boys nodded.

"Good. From now on, we can't see The Homeless."

Then she turned around, fastened her seatbelt, and stared straight ahead out the windshield. As the car moved out of the parking lot and onto the street, Peggy Jean tried to put the image of the screaming man out of her mind by thinking of a field of poppies. She allowed her mind to zoom in on a drop of dew that graced one of the gentle petals.

As he steered the car, John wondered if Nikki trimmed and shaped her pubic hair. He decided that she did, and that she left just a small little patch at the top. Probably a little triangle.

Bebe's Dazzling Diamonelle show on Sunday night was, as always, a hit. Historically, Bebe's weekly ten to twelve P.M. show earned the highest ratings of the week. In fact, the only other programs that could challenge the ratings of this Sunday night show were also hosted by Bebe. But as "on" as Bebe always seemed to be, this Sunday night she was even better than usual. Within the course of two hours, nearly every product sold out; almost one and a half million dollars in inventory was moved, making every single minute Bebe was on air laughing, talking about giving Pepper a flea bath, or wishing out loud that her thighs would stop screaming for "more ice cream!" worth over eight thousand dollars.

What Sellevision management and the millions of viewers watching at home could have no way of knowing was that if Bebe was in fact having an exceptionally great night, the reason was due largely to a man who had never even heard of Sellevision. A man who had never met Bebe in person and was named Michael Klein, though he preferred to be called by his middle name, Eliot. Already they'd spoken on the phone for nearly two hours, and tomorrow night she would meet him for drinks at a bar called Changes.

"Bebe, you were so funny tonight. I was feeling a little blue before we went on, but a couple times I really had to bite my cheek to stop myself from laughing." The compliment came from Hoshi, the beautiful Japanese-American model who sat ten feet to Bebe's left for the duration of Dazzling Diamonelle.

"Hoshi, what a sweet thing to say, thank you so much. But I'll tell you something, I'd trade my big fat mouth for your beauty any day."

Hoshi smiled.

And then before leaving the set, Bebe turned to her. "Oh, Hoshi, by the way, do you know if the Woodlands Mall is still open twenty-four hours a day on Sundays?"

five

"My father's dead and my mother wishes she were."

Bob Shriber, head of broadcast production for the E-Z Shop Channel, laughed at Max's answer to the question he'd just asked: "How did your parents take the whole penis thing?"

Max noticed that Bob's suit had a sheen to it. And one stray hair extended out of his left nostril. He also noticed that the office was not nearly as posh as Howard's. Clearly, this was a rung down on the ladder of success.

"I know you must be sick and tired of defending yourself—but you gotta admit, it's a pretty unusual way to lose your job."

"Yeah, actually, I do admit it. But it was a pretty unusual job to begin with, so in a sense it's like this perfect cosmic thing." Immediately regretting the Southern California overtones of what he just said, Max changed the subject. "So it seems like a lot of people play golf down here. I mean, I saw a lot of golf courses on the drive from the hotel."

Bob gave Max a puzzled look.

"Well, the only reason I mention it is because my old boss, Howard Toast, he had this executive golf-putting toy in his office, and I'd always whack a few balls around whenever I went to see him. I mean, except for the last time."

"I see," said Bob. "So, how does your wife feel about the prospect of moving to Florida? I mean, if it came to that."

Max shifted uncomfortably in his seat and ran his fingers through his hair. "Actually, I'm not married. Still single."

"No girlfriend, even?"

Max smiled. "Nope."

Bob studied him for a moment, then shrugged. "So, you catch the game last night?"

"Are you kidding?!" Max laughed with relief. "I wouldn't have missed it for the world. I'm totally addicted."

Bob chuckled. "Oh man, last night was a close one, huh?"

Max rolled his eyes. "I couldn't believe he blew it! I mean, everyone knows "The Wind Beneath My Wings" is from *Beaches*. What a dork."

Bob's smile fell. "What?"

"I just about knocked my wine over with that one! *Evita*? What was he thinking?" Max said, shaking his head.

"What are you talking about?"

"What do you mean? Last night's game. *Who Wants to Be a Millionaire*?"

"I wasn't talking about *that*," Bob said sourly. "I was talking about the *game* game. The Mets versus the Cardinals. Not some *game show*."

Max's face turned red. He ran his fingers through his hair again.

Bob looked annoyed. "You do that a lot."

"What?" Max asked, swallowing.

Bob mimicked the gesture. "Run your fingers through your hair. My ex-wife was always doing that and it drove me crazy."

"Oh, sorry. I guess I wasn't really aware that I do it."

"You don't do it *on air*, do you?"

Max bit his lower lip. "I don't think so. I mean, not that I'm aware of. No, I'm pretty sure I don't."

"Because, you know, little *tics* can be very distracting to the viewers. We once had this host, Tabby something, Clearwater, I think. Yeah, that was her name, Tabby Clearwater. Anyway, she did this *thing* with her eyes." Bob twitched his left eye repeatedly, causing the corner of his mouth to spasm.

"Wow, yeah, I can see how that would be distracting."

"I mean, this is the South. We're very laid back down here, very easy-going. All these twitches and fingers-through-the-hair stuff might be fine in the North; the pace is a lot quicker up there."

Max discreetly tucked his hands under his thighs.

"Say, what's that on your chin, is that dirt?" he asked, pointing to the center of his own chin.

Max placed his index finger on his chin, felt his cleft. "You mean this?"

"Yeah, that. What is it?" He was frowning now.

"It's just, you know, a cleft."

Bob leaned in closer and narrowed his eyes. "That could be a lighting problem."

After the interview, Max climbed into his rented beige Kia and drove two miles to the Shangri-La. He opened the minibar and took some booze from the inside-door shelf, grabbing a bag of Kettle Crisps Vinegar and Salt potato chips at the last second. Then he took the square ice bucket and walked down the hall, filled it with ice and returned to his room. He lifted the sanitary paper hat off one of the plastic glasses in the bathroom and mixed himself a stiff drink.

Max then realized that alcohol alone was not the answer. He would also need television. He took the remote and aimed it at the screen. Of all the possible channels, on popped Sellevision.

Forty children with Down's syndrome were standing on the set, dressed in purple choir uniforms and ringing colorful bells. Some of the children rang red bells and some rang yellow bells.

When the conductor held up a blue flashcard, only those children with blue bells rang them. The other children pressed their bells firmly against their chests to keep them silent. When the conductor held up a green flashcard, the green children rang their bells. In this method, a barely recognizable version of "People" was being played, very slowly.

A screen graphic read *Bell Ringers*, and listed the item number as S-6884. Peggy Jean had tears in her eyes as she said, "They are just too precious and I don't personally know the words to tell you what it's like to be in this room with these very special children. So let's go straight to the phones and say hello to Roxy in Tulsa. Hi, Roxy!"

"Hi, Peggy Jean! I can't believe what I'm seeing, it's like a miracle!"

"I know, Roxy, isn't it beautiful? Let me ask, what moved you to call in this evening?"

"Well, for years my husband and I have tried to have children of our own, but that's turned out not to be an option for us."

Peggy Jean gave a nod of understanding.

"And you wouldn't *believe* all the paperwork involved with adoption. So when I saw these little Bell Ringers, I screamed out for my husband, I said 'Put that aluminum siding down and come inside, you've got to see what Sellevision has on, you just won't believe it—it's the Baby Jesus at work.' "

One of the yellow bell ringers accidentally rang her bell while the reds were ringing. Peggy Jean smiled at the charming blunder, which only made the Bell Ringers' rendition of "People" even more adorable.

Roxy continued. "But I don't see a price on the screen. How much are they?"

Peggy Jean gave a quizzical smile to the camera. "I'm not sure I understand your question, Roxy."

"Well, that little boy in the first row, the third one from the left—the one with the bangs—he's just as cute as a bug. How much would *he* cost?"

Suddenly understanding what the caller was asking, Peggy Jean tried to hide her shock behind a pleasant expression. "Oh, Roxy, you misunderstand. These children are not for sale, you can't *buy* these children. You can sponsor them."

"What do you mean? They've got an item number."

"Well, yes, but that's so you can make a contribution to the organization they're a part of, So Very Special Children. So how much would you like to contribute, Roxy?"

Max slammed his fist down on the hotel room desk. "They stole my idea! Those bastards stole my concept!"

A few months before he was "let go" Max had made a suggestion to producers. "Let's do a show called Hospice Hounds, where people call in and they can sponsor a dog from a shelter to be adopted, trained, and placed with someone who is in the terminal stages of disease." But the producers had dismissed the idea, saying the Humane Society would never allow them to auction off dogs on live television, no matter how good the cause.

When Max looked back at the television, the Bell Ringers were gone and Peggy Jean was smiling into the camera, introducing the next show. "If you love deep-fried foods—like me—but you don't love the calories, stay tuned for our very first Fried-But-Fat-Free Olestra Showcase with Adele Oswald Crawley. It's coming up next."

"Hi, Nikki. How are you?"

"Hi, Mr. Smythe. I'm okay, just trying to get some sun."

John had spotted Nikki from his living room window. The girl was lying on a Pokémon towel in her front yard, her firm, young body glistening with suntan lotion. He immediately went into the bathroom to brush his hair and then casually walked outside, pretending to be interested in his driveway. "Better not stay out too long, you don't want to get sunburned," he said, sweating slightly, not from the heat.

"Ah, it's okay, I'm wearing number thirty," Nikki said, shielding her eyes from the sun with her hand. John walked over to the edge of Nikki's towel. She smiled up at him.

"Say, Nikki, I was wondering if you might be able to baby-sit sometime soon?"

Sitting up, Nikki said, "Sure, Mr. Smythe, I'd be happy to. Except Wednesdays are bad for me, because I have gymnastics until eight o'clock in the evening."

Something, John thought, he would truly enjoy witnessing.

"Ah, no, I was thinking maybe"—he pulled a date out of thin air—"next Thursday. I'm taking Peggy Jean out for dinner, a surprise."

"Oh, how sweet and romantic," Nikki said. "My parents never do anything romantic."

"So Thursday's okay with you, then?"

"Sure, Thursday is great."

John shoved his hands in his pockets. "Well, then it's settled. Thanks a lot, Nikki. I'll see you then, on Thursday."

"Sure thing, Mr. Smythe. And thanks for thinking of me."

If only you knew how much I think of you, he thought. "Don't burn," he warned with a smile.

"I won't," she said.

John waved, nodded his head, and returned to his own yard, his manhood pressed hard against the zipper on his jeans. Then he turned back. "Oh, and it was nice seeing you in church the other week."

Of course, the trick now was how to get rid of Peggy Jean on Thursday so that when Nikki arrived, he could say that something came up with his wife, and she didn't have to baby-sit after all. Then maybe he could engage her in a little conversation, offer her a cookie or a glass of Pepsi, and hopefully be able to just talk to her a little.

Inside, he rang his wife at work.

"This is Peggy Jean Smythe," she answered confidently on the first ring.

"Hi, Peggy."

"Hello, darling, what a pleasant surprise. Is everything okay?" Then with a slightly worried edge in her voice, "Nothing's happened to the boys, I hope?"

John wiped his forehead with a quilted Bounty paper towel. "No, the boys are fine. They're up in their rooms, doing some reading for Bible study."

"Oh, that's wonderful. I'm so glad that they're putting their little summer vacation to constructive, good use."

"Yeah, well anyway, are you working next Thursday night?"

He heard the pages of her day planner turning. "It appears I'm off Thursday. Why, is there something you had in mind? Something special you'd like to do?" She smiled and twisted her wedding band around on her finger.

"Well, I have to work Thursday night. We've got a client coming in and I promised the boys I'd take them to the movies, but since I can't, I was wondering if you would."

Silence, then, "Oh."

"So can you?"

"Well, John, I suppose I have no choice, do I?"

"Great, thanks, hon, see you later." He hung up the phone and bounded up the stairs. "Boys?" he called out.

They appeared at their doorways.

"Your mom's taking you to the movies on Thursday night," he announced, so happy he almost laughed.

They exchanged curious glances at each other. "Why?" asked Ricky, the oldest.

"What do you mean, 'why'? Because she's your mother and she loves you."

The three boys looked at him and then Ricky said, "Oh."

"Well, you boys get back to your studies. I just wanted to let you know the good news."

John walked into his office and turned on his computer. Sitting at his desk waiting for the computer to come to life, he thought of Nikki in her little bikini, all fragrant and moist. He opened the file drawer of his desk and under NONREIM-BURSABLE BUSINESS EXPENSES removed the latest issue of *Jane* magazine. He thumbed through the pages until he found the article (with pictures) "Bikini Waxing Wisdom," an article he had not been able to stop thinking about. After his computer was on, his thoughts drifted back to Nikki. "Christ, she's just a kid," he told himself as he logged on to America Online. Then he typed in an Internet address, http://www.preteentwat.com, and waited for the familiar images of nude young girls with moist lips to fill his computer screen.

After hanging up with her husband, Peggy Jean made a note in her day planner about the movie. She also made a note reminding herself to make a personal and tax-deductible donation to the So Very Special Children Fund, as the show had moved her emotionally. She also realized that she could probably deduct the movie from her taxes, as it was part of her job to be modern and in-touch with popular culture.

Then Peggy Jean read her E-mail messages. A few of them asked about the watch she was wearing on a recent broadcast. A couple of them were book recommendations, one of which she made a note of (she'd always been a sucker for Western romance novels). And one of the E-mails was from Zoe.

To: PG_Smythe@Sellevision.com
Fr: Zoe@ProviderNet.com
Subject:Too good for me, huh?

I get it, Peggy Jean. I'm no fool. Go ahead and hide behind your hairspray and your clumpy mascara. But make no mistake: your utter selfishness has not gone unnoticed. And sure, while the hair on your earlobes may be gone, you are still a HAIRY BITCH with a mustache—and the only reason I didn't mention the mustache thing to you before is because I, unlike you, am a person who cares about the feelings of another person.

You snotty, fake woman: You just wait: That "hubby" of yours is going to open his eyes one morning very soon and see this bleach-blond, artificial cow sleeping next to him and he's going to go out and find himself a REAL woman who UNDERSTANDS THE CON-CEPT OF BODILY MAINTENANCE, who doesn't require a complete stranger to tell her to pull herself together. And who doesn't sound like a logger. Fuck you and your screwy hormones.

Go to hell,

Zoe :(

"A mustache?" Peggy Jean cried, then immediately retrieved the compact from her purse and checked her reflection. What she saw was shocking: faint—but present—hairs along her upper lip. She snapped the compact shut and tossed it back into her purse.

How could she have missed them?

Oh, and the awful, putrid tone of that letter! How could this Zoe person say such horrible things? And *yet*, she'd been right about the mustache. And what was that about sounding like a logger? Peggy Jean had sung soprano in high school. Was her voice actually changing, becoming deeper? Was Zoe right about *that*, too? Peggy Jean immediately picked up the telephone and dialed her physician. Something was definitely wrong.

"Dr. Stewart's office, may I help you?" said the voice on the other end of the line.

"Yes, I need to speak with Dr. Stewart." Peggy Jean drummed her fingers on her desktop.

"I'm sorry, she's with a patient right now. May I take a message?"

"This is *an emergency*," Peggy Jean exploded. *"Please."*

The receptionist sighed and placed Peggy Jean on hold.

A few moments later, Dr. Stewart came on the line. "Is something the matter Peggy Jean? Are you okay?"

"Dr. Stewart, did you get my test results back yet?"

"Test results?" the doctor asked.

"Yes, my test results, you know, for my hormonal condition, my *female problems?*"

The doctor chuckled. "Oh, now I remember. Yes, of course I got the results back. I told you that I'd call you if anything was the matter, and everything is, of course, perfectly fine, so I didn't call."

"But it can't be fine, something's wrong!" Peggy Jean's voice cracked with panic. "I have an actual mustache now, it's spread from my ears to my face."

"Peggy Jean, I really can't speak right now, I have a patient. But let me assure you that everything is normal with your blood work, there's nothing hormonal the matter with you."

In other words, Peggy Jean thought, whatever was wrong with her was going to remain untreated, left to take its own disastrous course. "Well, what am I supposed to do? I'm not imagining this, you know? My fans are noticing, I'm getting *letters* from them."

"Peggy Jean, I've already explained this to you; we *all* have little hairs. I have little hairs, *you* have little hairs, even movie stars like Kathy Bates have little hairs. It's just part of being human. Now good-bye, I must go."

Dear God, was she as hairy as Kathy Bates? "Wait, Dr. Stewart?" Peggy Jean pleaded. "Please, then, at least give me a little something to calm my nerves. I'm just very confused and upset."

"Peggy Jean, please. Take up yoga or get a massage. Now if you don't mind . . ."

"I can't take up yoga!" Peggy Jean cried into the phone. "I'm on live television *constantly;* I don't have time. Please, I can't be anxious on *television.*"

The doctor was silent for a moment. "Okay, Peggy, here's what I'll do: I'll phone in a prescription—just a small one—for Valium, and you can pick it up at CVS, okay? And remember, they're just for anxiety attacks."

She was flooded with relief and gratitude. "Yes, yes, good, thank you. All right then, good-bye, Doctor." After Peggy Jean hung up, she replied to the hateful E-mail.

To: Zoe@ProviderNet.com
Fr: PG_Smythe@Sellevision.com
Subject: Re: Too good for me, huh?

   While Peggy Jean does read all of her E-mail, it's impossible for her to reply personally to each and every person. Therefore, she has asked me to write you on her behalf and thank you for your kind words and for taking the time to write. Peggy Jean hopes that you continue to enjoy Sellevision and she looks forward to shopping with you in the future.

It then occurred to her that Zoe might not be a stranger at all, but one of the other hosts. A disgruntled host. Perhaps a host who had been recently fired?

Max had always acted strange around her. What was it about

him? He was so . . . *happy*. Happy-go-lucky Max. Peggy Jean bit her lip. It made sense. Max *was* homosexual, after all. And those homosexuals were constantly holding angry marches or demonstrations and carrying picket signs. Not to mention those red ribbons they always wore. *Blood*-red ribbons. They were so confrontational. Peggy Jean shivered as a chill went down her spine. The sad but true fact of life was that not everybody was a good Christian. She would have to give this Max/Zoe thing some more thought.

"What the hell are you telling me, Howard? Hmmm?" Leigh was blinking back tears, arms folded tightly across her chest, bold Stampato bracelet layered on her arm with a sterling Greek Key two-inch-wide cuff.

Howard, sitting at his desk, was trying to explain the meaninglessness of the two American Airlines round-trip tickets from Philadelphia to St. Barts that the travel department had just delivered to him. The skin on his face was smooth and moisturized from an afternoon facial. Explaining the trip he was taking with his wife had turned out to be more complicated than he had anticipated. But what did he think? That Leigh would wrap her arms around him and say, "I understand, darling"?

"Leigh—honey—it's not what it seems like. I swear—I'm going to bring up the divorce the moment we get back, maybe even on the plane ride home."

Leigh was still standing across from him with her eyes trained on the ceiling.

"Look, Leigh, I love you, it's *you* that I love. It's just that if I don't take this trip with her, it'll make everything worse. She's liable to explode and contest the divorce. But giving her a chance to relax, beforehand—it's a strategy, Leigh, that's all it is—a strategy."

"This is just so . . ." Leigh was struggling to maintain her composure, struggling hard not to simply pick the onyx-handled letter opener up off his desk and plunge it into his neck. ". . . I feel, I don't know, *used*. This is just not what I want for myself."

Rising from his chair and going over to Leigh, Howard—gently, slowly—placed his hands on her shoulders.

She looked away from him.

"Leigh, I mean it when I tell you that this is for the best, it's for us. Trust me, please? Don't give up on us, Leigh."

"So how long are you going to be away?"

"It's just for a week, baby, that's all—a week."

"And you swear that you'll tell her after?"

Wrapping Leigh in his arms, he held her tight. "Yes, yes, I promise with all my heart . . . a heart that no longer belongs to me."

She relaxed against him.

He made a mental note to ask his personal trainer about the whole fiber vs. carbohydrate issue, and what it really meant in terms of fat.

D on, the Good Morning Show host, was angrily storming down the hallway in Peggy Jean's direction.

"Don, what's the matter? Are you okay? What is it?"

"Oh, hi Peggy Jean, no, I'm fine, it's just that . . ." Flustered, he made the gesture of a handgun with his index finger and thumb, aimed it at his temple, fired. *"Pow."*

"Now don't even joke about that, Don."

"Sorry. Anyway, I'm in the kitchen set doing a Creative Cooking thing, right? And I'm in the middle of presenting that nineteen-inch Stick-Not frying pan, and the omelet that I'm making, which is supposed to like, *glide* out of the skillet, sticks, and then starts to burn and it's all black and smoking and I'm scraping at it. Then the plastic handle catches fire. It was just a disaster; they had to cut away to a Yanni promo."

Peggy Jean sighed. "Oh, Dan, I'm sorry, how frustrating. It's happened to all of us." Though nothing like this had ever happened to her *personally*.

"My *mother* was watching!"

"Well, I'm sure she'll understand. Live television doesn't always go smoothly," she said. Then she noticed that the bald spot on top of Don's head was shiny. She thought it must create a hot spot on camera. But now was not the time to mention it and perhaps suggest Propecia.

"No, she won't understand. Ever since Nancy left me for her personal trainer, my mother has been convinced that my daughter is malnourished. Now she has her proof that I can't cook and am an unfit parent."

Peggy Jean touched the sleeve of Don's shirt reassuringly.

"I'm not kidding, Peggy Jean. I guarantee you my mother will be on the next plane out here."

"Oh, Don—all I can think to tell you is, let go and let God."

"Gee, thanks, Peggy Jean," Don said sarcastically, shaking his head.

"You're welcome," Peggy Jean said earnestly.

As she turned and walked away she thought to herself that helping other people, even if only to give advice, really did lift one's own spirits. And when she reached her office, she was smiling.

Until she sat at her computer and saw that she had received yet another E-mail from Zoe.

To: PG_Smythe@Sellevision.com
Fr: Zoe@ProviderNet.com
Subject: Re: Re: Too good for me, huh?

I'm getting a little sick and tired of your fucking form letters. You treat me like shit, I treat you like shit. Deal? Deal. It's called having a taste of your own lousy medicine. Mustache cunt.

Zoe

Peggy Jean immediately looked away from the computer screen, horrified, and checked her watch. Less than an hour had passed between this E-mail and the last. *Less than an hour.* Her finger trembled as she brought it to her upper lip, touching, feeling the *hairs.* Thank God she'd phoned Dr. Stewart.

Peggy Jean sent her standard reply and then drove straight to the CVS pharmacy. She picked up her prescription and a bottle of Jolen Creme Bleach.

six

"How wonderful to see you, Peggy Jean. Just take a seat and I'll let Claude know you're here."

Peggy Jean made herself comfortable in one of the black leather petite Le Corbusier chairs of the salon. The air was filled with the scent of narcissus blossoms and ammonia-free semipermanent hair coloring. Setting her emerald green faux crocodile handbag on the floor beside her, Peggy Jean picked up one of the magazines off the glass-topped table in front of her and began leafing through the pages.

A moment later Claude's assistant, Mia, arrived with a tray on which was a tiny cup of espresso, some milk, and two little blue packets of Nutrasweet.

"Oh, Mia! You're a doll, thank you so, so much," Peggy Jean gushed.

Mia set the tray down on the table. "He'll just be a few more minutes, he's finishing up a comb-out."

Peggy Jean tore open one of the blue Nutrasweet packets and sprinkled half of it into her espresso. Then she added just the smallest drop of milk. She thumbed through the magazine, pausing occasionally to smell the scent-strips attached to the perfume ads. She enjoyed many of the fragrances, especially

Gucci's Envy, but her own Giorgio was still her favorite. Coming across a picture of Michelle Pfeiffer in the magazine, Peggy Jean wondered if she should maybe have reverse-highlights instead.

"Peggy Jean Smythe, how *dare* you step foot in this salon looking so ravishing. You're going to make all the other customers feel self-conscious," Claude announced as he appeared before her. She rose from her chair smiling and blushing and Claude kissed the air on both sides of her cheeks. "I love those slingbacks—Prada?" he asked, pointing at Peggy Jean's feet.

Peggy Jean laughed modestly. "Good heavens, no, these are just plain old Nine Wests."

Claude handed Peggy Jean a cotton/poly smock and instructed her to change out of her top and into the smock, guiding her to a small dressing room. Peggy Jean did so, belting it tightly around her waist. She returned to Claude's station, setting her purse on the shelf below the mirror.

Claude gave the chair three quick pumps with his foot, and then waved Peggy Jean into it. Standing behind her, placing both hands on her shoulders and looking at her reflection in the mirror, Claude asked, "Same as always?"

A slightly mischievous look crossed Peggy Jean's face. "Claude? I was thinking, wondering, if maybe I could do reverse highlights?"

Claude looked down at Peggy Jean's blond hair and ran his fingers through it, feeling the texture, evaluating the color as well as the existing level of damage. "You mean, sort of a Michelle Pfeiffer thing?" he asked, and then answered his own question, "I think we could do that, yeah. As a matter of fact I think it could be fabulous."

"Oh, well, wonderful then, let's be bold and try something new," Peggy Jean said. Then she casually fingered the sterling silver Omega necklace around her neck. "I'm flying to Milan for a special live broadcast, and I just want to look my best."

"Milan? How glamorous! You television people, I *swear.* Now don't you move a muscle," Claude instructed. He disappeared momentarily to get the color cart, but paused briefly in the changing room to snort a little crystal-meth. When he reappeared, wheeling the white plastic cart in front of him, he was humming the latest Ricky Martin single. Claude looked back down at Peggy Jean's shoes. "I can't believe those are just Nine Wests."

Snapping the plastic top off the colorant, Claude opened the fixative and poured it into the bottle of colorant, placing his index finger over the opening and giving the mixture a shake. He then placed a protective cape over Peggy Jean's smock, fastening it tightly at the nape of her neck.

"Guess who came in the other day for a cellophane?" he asked.

Peggy Jean *adored* Claude. "Who, tell me, *who?*"

"I'll give you a hint," he said, humming a few bars from the theme to *Maude*.

"Bea *Arthur?*"

"Better. Adrienne Barbeau."

"Adrienne Barbeau? Goodness, I haven't heard a peep about her in years."

"Darling, stop moving your head so much," Claude said, steadying her head with his hands. "Anyway, as I was saying, get this: She just had twins . . . at fifty one!"

"Claude, you can't be serious."

"Not only that, she looked wonderful. And she's as nice as can be. Though the poor thing *was* a little distraught over an infomercial deal that went sour."

"Oh, well that's a shame, but I'm sure another infomercial will come along. With twins, she could do a Beech-Nut thing." She scratched her elbow. "Connie Chung doesn't still do Beech-Nut commercials, does she?"

Claude put one hand on his hip and wagged the applicator brush at Peggy Jean. "Joan Lunden does Beech-Nut, girl. Connie Chung does Maury Povich. Get your news-divas straight."

Peggy Jean loved the way he always called her *girl*.

After brushing the color on Peggy Jean's hair, he wrapped each section in a square of aluminum foil.

"How's your *roommate?*" Peggy Jean asked, a modern, politically correct woman. Although she did lower her voice when saying the word "roommate."

"*Please* . . . he's driving me absolutely crazy. His latest delusional fantasy is that he's going be a food stylist, you know, for photo shoots?"

Peggy Jean nodded into the mirror.

"I came home the other day and he was rubbing shoe polish all over the outside of a raw turkey to make it look already cooked."

Peggy Jean scrunched up her face. "Yuck."

"It's been a nightmare. You try living with somebody who uses the blowdrier to melt cheese on top of nacho chips."

Peggy Jean couldn't *imagine*.

"You don't know the half of it. I caught him adding grill marks to a steak with my best curling iron," he said, all faux exasperation and rolling eyes.

For the next twenty minutes, Peggy Jean sat under a blow-drier, thumbing through *Elle* and wishing she had longer legs. Then, scolding herself for such a vain wish, she silently thanked God for her three beautiful, handsome boys and her loving husband.

After Claude checked her hair and decided she was done, he sent her over to the shampoo sink where Sonja rinsed, then shampooed and conditioned.

Back in Claude's chair, Peggy Jean's newly reverse-high-lighted hair was blowdried and styled with a circular vent brush. Standing back to admire his work, Claude said, "That was a marvelous idea. I love what it does for your features. It gives you angles."

Then Claude caught a glimpse of something in the mirror and leaned around Peggy Jean to look at her face. "Honey, we should really bleach those little hairs on your upper lip. You just sit right there and I'll be back with something in a flash."

But I did bleach them, Peggy Jean thought. Had she grown more of them? In the space of only a couple of days? She could do nothing except sit there, stricken, and stare at her reflection in the mirror, wondering, *What's happening to me?*

Then Peggy Jean reached into her purse and retrieved a Valium, which she swallowed dry.

"No, Max, I promise, he did *not* think you were a flake," Laurie was saying to her agitated client. As Max paced back and forth in his living room, Laurie attempted to offer him hope. "Next steps: First I'll contact Discovery Channel. And we'll go ahead and fax your résumé and bio over to Lifetime. I'll put out my feelers and see what's going on."

"Don't bother, nobody is going to ever hire me again. My career is over." Max knew he blew the interview with E-Z Shop the instant he mentioned the game show.

"Maxwell, you can't take this personally. They had to go with an *Asian*, they just didn't have a choice. They don't want to get involved in some hundred-million-dollar discrimination case like the Buy-a-thon Network."

As much as he hated to admit it, he could understand. Rebecca Chow's recent lawsuit against Buy-a-thon sent shock waves throughout the industry. She claimed that the network discriminated against her because she was relegated to the overnight position, while only the *white* hosts were allowed on during the daylight hours.

Even Sellevision had sent out a memo asking all their hosts if any of them had any "Hispanic, Asian, African American, or American Indian ancestry." It turned out Irish-Catholic Adele Oswald Crawley's great-great-grandmother on her father's side had some Navaho blood. So within a month, Adele was dressed in a little suede dress with fringe and given her own turquoise jewelry showcase called Indian Expressions, complete with potted cactus trees and a tepee. An old black-and-white photograph of Adele as a little girl wearing an Indian headdress at a birthday party was enlarged and hung behind her. Prop stylists added Navaho throw rugs around the living room set, but the deerskin was pulled at the last moment because of the lawyers. After the show, Howard had made it clear, "This is just a Band-Aid on the situation. We've got to get an ethnic in here immediately."

"When do you think you'll hear something?" Max asked Laurie.

"Any day, just be patient and don't panic."

"Don't panic, *don't panic*," Max told himself after hanging up with Laurie. "Don't panic, don't panic," he said walking from empty room to empty room, having no idea what to do with himself, wishing he had a dog that he could take for a walk or a boyfriend who could reassure him that everything would be all right. He couldn't call any of his friends because they, unlike him, were all at work. And if he went to a movie, the theater would only be filled with retirees and other unemployed losers like himself and he would only become even more depressed than he already was.

What scared Max the most was that in his heart of hearts, he felt almost certain that neither Discovery Channel nor Lifetime—nor any other network—would hire him. The sad fact was that he was only comfortable in front of the camera. And it just didn't seem like any camera was going to be aimed at him any time soon. "I'm heading *straight* for radio," he said, hands on hips, head pressed against the living room wall.

■

Changes was the current *it* bar and restaurant in Philly. Located on Twenty-sixth and Poplar, Changes attracted an upscale, hip clientele. Bebe was to meet Eliot at the bar at eight P.M. Although she had never seen him before, he'd given her a pretty good visual description: six-foot-one, 185 pounds, salt-and-pepper hair ("Yes, a full head," he'd laughed). She was to "look for the nervous guy at the bar wearing gray slacks and a red sweater with five or six empty martini glasses in front of him." At least on the telephone, he had been charming.

Bebe had tried on three different outfits before finally deciding on the new black slacks, the new black silk shell, and the coral cashmere jacket she bought two weeks ago, but hadn't worn. Around her neck she wore an eighteen-inch fourteen-karat white gold rolo chain, at the end of which was a Diamonelle Glitter Ball slide. For earrings, she went with simple fourteen-karat white gold demi hoops. She wore a tasteful Diamonelle tennis bracelet in fourteen-karat yellow gold, but you really didn't notice the yellow so much as the stones. But even if you did, it was perfectly okay to mix your white metals with your yellow. On the ring finger of her right hand, Bebe slipped a two-carat princess-cut Diamonelle simulated sapphire ring with two twenty-five-point channel-set trillian-cut stones on either side. But then she slipped it off, fearing that it might look like an old engagement ring she refused to return. She decided to leave her fingers ringless.

The first thing Bebe noticed as she stepped into Changes was the beautiful arrangement of lilacs atop the bar. The vase itself was filled with clear glass marbles in water. The second thing she noticed was a man in a red sweater. He was sitting at the bar, speaking with the bartender, when the bartender suddenly caught her eye and stopped talking midsentence. The

man in the red sweater tracked the bartender's eye-line, which
led him directly to Bebe.

He stood immediately and Bebe approached him, extending
her hand. He took her hand in his and gently guided her to a
chair at the bar, which he pulled out for her. "You must be
Bebe," he said. "I'm Eliot, as I suppose you've figured out by
now, unless you're an extremely well-dressed and friendly
meter maid and I forgot to put money in the meter."

Bebe laughed and sat on the tall stool next to Eliot, exhaling
and admitting that she was "kind-of slightly sort-of nervous."

Eliot suggested they remedy that situation at once and asked
Bebe what she would like to drink.

"Oh, a glass of white wine, I suppose." The bartender nodded and walked to the opposite side of the bar.

"You lied to me," Eliot said with a completely straight face.

"How did I lie to you? I told you I'd probably be wearing
something black."

"You also said you weren't beautiful—to use your exact
words, 'just slightly over average.' And that, Bebe, is a bald lie."

"Okay, that's it, I love you."

They both laughed.

As the bartender set the glass of wine before Bebe, he paused
and then said "I'm terribly sorry to interrupt you, but I just had
to ask: Aren't you Bebe Friedman from Sellevision?"

Bebe smiled and admitted that yes, indeed, it was she.

"I gotta tell you, my girlfriend started watching you and
then she got me hooked—you are so hilarious."

"Well, thank you so much!" Then motioning with her head
toward Eliot, "So how much did he pay you?"

The bartender laughed, excusing himself.

"I feel terrible that I'm not familiar with your work," Eliot said.

Actually, it was a relief to Bebe. At least she knew that he
didn't like her just because she was a semicelebrity. And was it

just the lighting, or did Eliot actually look like George Clooney?

"So tell me about the dry-cleaning business. I feel I have a right to know considering I subsidize the entire industry."

"You?" Eliot asked. "You're the epitome of elegance."

"You haven't seen me operate a fork yet."

He gave her a playfully doubtful look, then affected an air of elitism. "Dry cleaning is my life's passion," he told her. He took a sip of the martini before him and added, "Just teasing. It was my father's business."

After half a glass of wine, Bebe began to relax. Actually, it probably wasn't the wine, but Eliot himself. He seemed so easy-going, so quick to smile and laugh. She sensed a real warmth from him. Then, there was that George Clooney thing.

"So, Bebe, have you, ah, met any interesting men from your ad?" It was an awkward question to ask, but he made it sound as casual as possible. Like a weather question.

Bebe swallowed her sip of wine. "Yes, actually, one. One man."

A small bubble deflated in him. He gave her a smile that showed his teeth, "Yeah, so what was he like?"

Nonchalantly, Bebe looked up to the left, like she was think-ing of how to describe him, then looked directly back at Eliot. "Well, so far he seems like a pretty great guy."

It took him just a fraction of a second to get it.

For a while, they just sat there looking at each other, smil-ing. A moment later, the maître d' introduced himself and informed them that their table was ready. The maître d' had to repeat himself.

L eigh read what she'd written so far:

Dear Howard,
I'm writing you this letter because I can't speak to you in per-

son until next Thursday when you're back from St. Barts. I know I've been really demanding in terms of "us." I haven't exactly been patient. It's just difficult, because I love you so much and want to be with you. Of course, then I torture myself by imagining you with your wife on some beautiful beach and I end up making myself completely crazy.

I wish you could hold me right this minute and tell me everything is going to work out wonderfully, that the gap between us will soon be closed. I'll do my best

Leigh slammed the pen down on the table, crumpled up the note, and threw it into the wicker wastebasket beside her desk. *You are so stupid for falling in love with a married man who also happens to be your boss!* She stomped into the kitchen and yanked open the refrigerator. Yogurt, skim milk, tomatoes. "Yuck," she said, closing the door. "Where's the cheesecake when you really need it?"

She decided that a glass of red wine would have to suffice. She uncorked the nearly full bottle on her counter, took a long-stemmed wineglass from the cupboard, and poured herself half a glass. She looked at the glass and filled it to the top. Then she leaned back against the kitchen counter and took a sip. It tasted dry, but also like flowers and grapes. Like something to be shared with someone else.

A movie played in her head: Howard and his wife walking hand-in-hand at sunset along the beach on St. Barts, their thirteen-year marriage rekindled, passion rediscovered. In the movie, Howard confesses to his wife about Leigh, calls it a brief affair, and swears to end the fling the moment he gets back. Maybe they kiss right there, or maybe she slips her dress over her head and seductively dives into the bathtub-warm water, beckoning him to join her, while a wave . . . "*Stop!*" Leigh ordered herself.

Bringing her wine into the living room, Leigh decided that she simply could not be trusted with her own thoughts at the present time and chose to park herself on the sofa in front of the TV and pray that Lifetime, Television for Women, had a drama on about teenage pregnancy, codependency, or maybe alcoholism. Or maybe all three in one.

Later, sitting back on her sofa and nursing a second glass of wine, Leigh was utterly consumed by the Valerie Bertinelli thriller. In the movie, Valerie's sister was beaten to the point of near-death. And Valerie was sure that it was her sister's husband who was guilty. But he blamed it on robbers, and of course the sister had no memory.

Big-time melodrama, the kind that really sucks you in. And everything was fine until Valerie's character had a baby. And this dislodged something in the everything-is-fine section of Leigh's brain, and she found herself suddenly sobbing, clicking off the TV and burying her face in a pillow so that her upstairs neighbors didn't hear her sobs and think their downstairs single neighbor was being attacked.

seven

Aboard an evening Omega Airlines flight bound for Newark International Airport from Milan, Peggy Jean sat in her luxurious Connoisseur Class recliner. Her slingbacks were off because her feet tended to swell. She read the in-flight magazine, displaying her usual willpower over the cheese-plate appetizer on the tray table before her. *One water cracker, one wedge of brie—and that's all*, she told herself.

"Excuse me, but is something the matter with your cheese plate? Shall I get you something else instead?" the slim male flight attendant asked.

Peggy Jean looked up from the article on public payphone bacteria. "Oh, it's lovely, I had a bit of the cheese." She coyly glanced at her lap. "But television adds ten pounds, so I have to be very careful."

"*Oh my God*," the flight attendant exclaimed, clearly impressed, "are you a news anchor? Do you know *Stone Phillips?* He was on my flight just last week! He's so nice in person, just like you'd think he'd be. I mean you really feel like—"

Peggy Jean cut him off. "No, actually I'm not in news, and you can take the cheese plate away."

"Are you on a sitcom?" he persisted, the diamond stud in his ear sparkling from her overhead reading light.

Peggy Jean smiled pleasantly. "I don't believe in sitcoms. I feel that they trivialize relationships and life in general."

The flight attendant nodded, shifting his weight onto one leg. "I know what you mean. I don't watch them myself, except I do like some of the old re-runs, like *Mary Tyler Moore* and *Phyllis*. I've always loved Mary's apartment—that big 'M' she had on the wall." He made quote marks with his fingers in the air.

Peggy Jean remembered the M.

"Anyway, whatever you do, I love your hair."

She smiled demurely and touched her hair. "Oh, I haven't done a *thing* with it. I just got off the air hours ago, and, well, it must be a wreck by now."

"God no, it's wonderful. I love the fact that it's fashionably short, yet you still manage to get some *height* to it."

Peggy Jean knew exactly what he meant. She leaned forward and whispered as if confiding to a dear friend. "The secret is a vent brush, and to go from hot to cold and hot to cold with the blowdrier, always ending on cold."

The flight attendant's eyes widened. "I'll have to remember that." Then curious, much too curious *not* to know, he asked, "So you said you were in Milan doing, what? A *live broadcast?*"

"Yes, I'm a Sellevision host. You know, America's leading retail broadcasting network? We were doing an Earrings by Italian Artisans show."

The flight attendant's mouth opened, eyes flashing recognition. "I've heard of Sellevision. Oh my God, I think I just saw something about this recently . . . isn't that the one where they had a host and he, you know, flashed his *you-know-what* on live TV?"

Peggy Jean cringed and pressed her lips firmly together. She looked at the cheese plate and suddenly felt very crowded by it. "It wasn't quite like that," she said coldly.

"Well, anyway, yeah, I just read about it. Gosh. I can't imagine." Then, assuming the demeanor of a professionally trained flight-crew member, he added, "But I hope you enjoy the rest of your flight, and if you need anything, just give me a little wave." He waved his hand in the air and turned to leave, but remembered the cheese plate. "Oh, and did you say you were finished with this?" He rested his fingers on the rim of the plate.

She noticed he wore clear varnish on his nails. "Yes," Peggy Jean said, her eyes back on the magazine article. "Quite finished," she told him, without looking up.

As Peggy Jean read the in-flight magazine article, she was alarmed by the real dangers that payphone bacteria posed. As if ear, nose, and throat infections weren't bad enough, the germs could easily transfer from finger to eye and from person to person. So even if you didn't personally use a public payphone, you were still at risk if someone who did touched you.

Why don't people care? Why aren't public payphones banned? she wondered. She could understand the need for them would outweigh the health risks in underdeveloped countries such as India or New Zealand. But in America? Everyone she knew owned a cell phone, most of them digital.

Peggy Jean closed the magazine and placed it in the seatback pocket in front of her. It caught on the lip of the airsickness bag, which *reminded* her. She looked to make sure that the man directly across the aisle from her was still sleeping, and then she reached over and gently removed the airsickness bag from *his* pouch and placed it into hers, tucking both out of sight. Airsickness bags, she had found, made handy shoe bags for travel. She wore a size five, so it was a perfect, snug fit.

Reclining, she thought back to last winter when she and her

neighbor Tina were in Peggy Jean's kitchen making nativity cookies for the church bake sale. If Tina could only read this bacteria article, she'd understand how silly her comment back then had been, how uninformed.

They'd been sitting at the kitchen table while the last batch of Baby Jesus sugar cookies baked. It was a tricky thing, because the halo sometimes broke off into pieces, or just part of the halo would break away, leaving something that resembled a horn behind. And that you *didn't* want.

"Peggy Jean, I know how much you adore your boys, but it's funny—I don't think I've ever seen you, well, touch them," Tina had said.

The comment had taken Peggy Jean by surprise. Why had Tina noticed something so personal? And then *commented* on it, on something that was a *family* matter? As if the delicate balance of good parenting could only be achieved through the combined efforts of family and stray neighborhood acquaintances.

"Tina, let me explain something to you," Peggy Jean had said, clasping her hands together on the table in front of her, her smile of broadcast quality. "All day long I deal with *media people*, producers, wardrobe, and makeup personnel. People are *constantly* touching me." She took a sip from her Lemon Zinger tea and continued. "Fans touch me in supermarkets. They send me little crafts and knickknacks made from Popsicle sticks. Stuffed animals they've made out of scraps of unwashed fabric."

Peggy Jean paused to dab her pinky beneath her eye. "Lord knows I *want* to touch my boys, just all the time, but I don't have the luxury that *ordinary* mothers have."

Peggy Jean stood to check on the cookies, peering through the glass of the oven door. Then she went to the sink and gave the flowered ceramic dispenser two quick pumps with her wrist, dispensing an amber pool of Dial antibacterial soap.

"*Touch* is how germs are spread, Tina."

She rinsed her hands under the scalding hot water, dried

them on a fresh Bounty paper towel, and turned to her friend. "And my boys have always been very sensitive to germs. I just can't expose them. Did you know Staphylococcus can live for *hours* outside the body? *Hours*," Peggy Jean had informed her.

She was startled out of her memory by sudden turbulence. The plane bumped through the air like a speedboat across choppy water. The formerly sleeping man across the aisle from her awakened, gripped both armrests with his hands, and stared straight ahead. Peggy Jean, a seasoned international traveler, turned to him and leaned over. "This always happens when you pass over Greenland. It's thermo-something, has to do with all their volcanoes, I think."

"I think I'm going to be sick," the man said, and reached into his seatback pocket for the airsickness bag. Not feeling it, he leaned forward and peered into the empty pouch.

Peggy Jean turned away and looked out her window.

The man made a gurgling sound in his throat, his cheeks plumped out, and he leapt from his seat, dashing up the aisle toward the lavatory.

A moment later, after the turbulence had passed, the male flight attendant appeared and knelt beside her. "Well, hello again," he said. "I just wanted to let you know that we can serve you your specially ordered kosher meal anytime you're ready."

Peggy Jean gasped. "My *what?*"

"Your kosher meal. We have it all ready for you," He smiled. "If you like, we can serve it to you in courses, like the other passengers, or we can give it to you all at once."

"I, I didn't order a . . ." she lowered her voice and spat, "*a kosher meal.*"

The flight attendant looked at the notepad he was carrying. "You didn't?" He ran the point of his pen down the list, stopped at a name, and circled it. "Peggy Jean Smythe, seat 12D." Then he stood up and double-checked her seat number. "Yup, 12D, Peggy Jean Smythe, that's you."

"But I didn't order it, I don't want it," she hissed. "I'm not . . ." she turned her head to the window, imagined every passenger on the plane glaring at her, then looked back at the flight attendant. "I'm not *Jewish*. Not that there's anything *wrong* with being Jewish, it's just that I'm not."

The mere thought of a potential borscht stain made her anxious. After all, she was wearing a white silk pantsuit with palazzo pants and a sheer white chiffon blouse.

"Goodness, well, I'm terribly sorry," the flight attendant said, brushing the crease out of his pants as he stood. "There must have been some sort of computer error. So have you had a chance to look at the menu?" he asked, pointing to the enormous leather bound volume that contained a single page.

"Yes, as a matter of fact I have," she said simply.

"I'm sorry, Mrs. Smythe, what can we get for you this evening?"

Regaining her composure, Peggy Jean touched the simple ribbed hoop white gold earring on her left earlobe and then gave a small, polite laugh. "Well, actually, I was thinking I might enjoy having the chicken Kiev."

He smiled, his head cocked to the side. "The chicken Kiev it is, then."

Then a look of concern spread across her face. "Where is *Kiev*, anyway?"

The flight attendant paused, placed the tip of the pen between his lips. He thought for a moment, brow furrowed in concentration. "Let me ask the captain," he said finally. Then before turning away he added, "I'm sorry for the special-meal confusion."

"It's perfectly fine, I was just a little, you know, surprised. Because, I mean, I'm Christian." Then, smiling, "Of course I don't suppose a computer would have any way of knowing that."

He smiled back at her. "No, I suppose not. We're just not that sophisticated yet."

To get the whole incident out of her mind, Peggy Jean took a Valium from the One-A-Day vitamin bottle she stored them in. The Valium pills, she had found, came in quite handy.

Hours later, after dinner and the in-flight movie, Peggy Jean decided to freshen up in the lavatory. She unfastened her seat-belt and stood in the aisle, enjoying the brief stretch. She opened the overhead compartment and retrieved her hard-shell American Tourister cosmetics case, then made her way down the narrow aisle to the lavatory door. But before she reached the lavatory, she noticed the flight attendant's beverage cart parked in the little kitchenette nook behind the bulkhead. All three of the Connoisseur Class flight attendants were napping, as were most of the passengers.

Gently, she slid the metal drawer out and saw all the pretty little bottles; Grand Marnier, Drambuie, Crème de Menthe, and thought, *Why not? Why not take a few of the little bottles home, as gifts?* After all, it wasn't like she was stealing. Lord, no. Beverages were complimentary in Connoisseur Class. Her ticket *had* cost Sellevision well over five thousand dollars and *certainly for that amount of money, well . . .*

Carefully, she lifted out a little bottle of Grand Marnier. As a young girl, she'd loved oranges.

Of course, the problem was she was still holding the cosmetics case in her other hand. So she glanced around, just to make sure she wasn't creating a distraction. Then she set the case on the floor and snapped it open. She took the little bottle and plopped it inside, right next to her Aqua-Net. Then she reached for another little bottle. She started to close the case, but it occurred to her that if she gave only *two* friends the adorable little bottles, her other friends might feel hurt.

So, very quietly she slid the shelf of the beverage cart all the way out, just ever so gently. And she slipped an additional five little bottles into the case. *I could tie a pretty bow around these and attach them to the outside of wrapped presents,* she thought.

One by one, she slipped more of the little bottles into her case, eventually leaving only the heavy amber scotches and bourbons (for the men). There was no longer enough room for the Aqua-Net, so she left this in the cart also. *When opportunity knocks*, she thought to herself.

Max realized it was futile to try and fight his depression, so he decided instead to feed it. Turning on Sellevision at two in the afternoon, he was surprised to see a closeup shot of Bebe Friedman. Normally, Bebe only hosted the most glamorous shows, during the most premium hours. But as soon as the camera pulled out to a wide shot, he saw that Bebe was sitting alongside Joyce DeWitt, from *Three's Company*. Of course, that's why Bebe was on in the middle of the afternoon—it was a celebrity program. Max un-muted the television and listened to the show.

". . . and I realized there was no skin regime for women my age; everything was geared toward twenty- and thirty-year-olds," Joyce was saying.

"You know, that is so true. Mature women like ourselves, we end up wandering the aisles of the department stores and thinking, maybe I'm supposed to use dishwashing soap on my face or something."

Joyce laughed and interjected, "That's exactly it, Bebe. And that's exactly why I created Joyce's Choice, because I was fed-up with skin care products that ignore the needs of my over-thirty skin."

"Joyce, let's take a phone call. Let's say hello to Michelle from San Francisco. Hi, Michelle, thanks for calling in. Meet Joyce DeWitt."

"Hi, Bebe, hi, Joyce."

"Hi, Michelle," Joyce said into the camera.

"Bebe, you are my favorite host, and I've been trying to talk to you on the phone for years!"

"Aw, that's very kind of you to say, Michelle. I can't imagine anybody waiting years to speak with me on the phone, but I'll take your word for it."

"And Joyce, I just am so excited by your products! I ordered the Get Started Kit, and I can't wait to try it, because I have tried everything out there and I'm thirty-six and nothing works on my skin. Did you say it was okay for sensitive skin? Because I have very sensitive skin."

"Oh absolutely, Michelle. That's what's so great about Joyce's Choice. I worked really hard with the technicians to make sure that my products were perfect for every skin type. And believe me, your skin can't be more sensitive than mine."

"Oh, well that's so good to know. I really can't wait to try them. Joyce, can I ask you a question?"

Bebe cut in. "Let me interrupt here for one minute—I'm sorry, Joyce and Michelle—but I just need to let everyone know that quantities of the Get Started Kit are becoming very limited now. We started off with twelve hundred of them and now we have less than three hundred to go around. Again, it's item number F-9450 and it's twenty-four ninety-seven. Okay, I'm sorry, go ahead."

"Um, okay, so like, Joyce, I just wanted to tell you how much I loved you on *Three's Company* and I think you're a really great actress and I was just wondering if you have any plans to return to TV?"

"Aren't you sweet, Michelle, thank you so much. To answer your question, Joyce's Choice is keeping me pretty busy. However, I'm about to start shooting a drama for the Lifetime network about toxic shock syndrome, which I think is important because it hasn't gone away. So that's gonna air sometime next year . . . keep your eyes open."

"Oh thank you, Joyce, I will. I can't wait!"

"Okay, we're down to less than one hundred kits now, so they're really moving fast. If you can, please use Automatic

Tele-Order by calling the alternate number you see on your screen. The phone lines are very busy right now," Bebe said.

On her producer's cue, she said, "Michelle, we're just about to sell out, so we're going to have to say good-bye, but thank you so much for calling and sharing with us today."

"Thanks for having me," Michelle said. "I hope you both have a wonderful, um, *life*, I guess. Okay, good-bye."

"Bye-bye," Bebe and Joyce said in unison, just as a SOLD OUT graphic appeared over the Joyce's Choice Get Started Kit banner on the far lefthand side of the screen.

"That item *has* sold out, so congratulations to everyone who purchased it. I think you'll be very happy. Up next: Joyce's Choice Crows Away! under-eye gel. But first, coming up on Sunday, Don from the Good Morning Show will be talking with author and trend forecaster Faith Popcorn about her brand-new programmable popcorn popper that lets you pop tomorrow's popcorn today! If you're a busy snacker, you won't want to miss this presentation."

Both Joyce and Bebe smiled into the camera, waiting for the cutaway to the FuturePop Popcorn Popper.

"God, I have a pathetic existence," Max said as he watched Don demonstrate the appliance. Enough was enough. As he turned off the television and went to his hall closet for his leather bomber jacket, Max made a promise to himself: In two weeks he would either have a great new job or a great new boyfriend. Max had believed in Creative Visualization ever since they did Shakti Gawain incense holders on the show and she had made an appearance.

He wondered if Shakti did personal consultations.

Checking the hosts' schedule for the week, Trish noticed that she had mostly midday slots and only a few prime-time jewelry showcases. Peggy Jean was still hogging the limelight. And Leigh certainly wasn't hurting for hours.

At first, she had believed that her trip to London was just the beginning of her rise within Sellevision. Now it seemed things had reached a plateau. *Things*, she thought, were just not moving fast enough.

In her office, Trish checked her E-mail. She was not pleased to see that she had fifty-seven E-mails from viewers. Eight less than she had received after her last on-air appearance two days before. Fewer quality hours, fewer E-mails. Even her Price Waterhouse fiancé now seemed like a compromise. Maybe her father was right, maybe Steve *was* too short, too meek, too poor, and too, well, *ordinary* for her. Maybe she was *settling*.

After reading her E-mail, Trish decided to give a quick call to Peggy Jean at home. One of Peggy's little boys answered, and Trish said, "Hi, is your mom home?"

The little boy dropped the phone on a tabletop and screamed, "Mom, telephone, I'm going outside."

A moment later, Peggy Jean picked up the receiver. "Hello?"

"Hi, Peggy Jean, it's Trish."

"Oh, hi, Trish, how are you?"

"I'm fine. Listen, I just wanted to ask you something. I'm at the office and I was just reading over my E-mails, and I got a kind of a weird one."

Silence, then, "Go on . . ."

"Well, what was that person's name? The one who was sending you all those nasty notes?"

"Zoe, her name was Zoe. Why, Trish, tell me—did you get one too?"

"Shoot, that's what her name was. I knew it was a Z name. No, mine is from some person named Zonda."

"Oh, no. Mine is Zoe, definitely Zoe."

"All right, I just couldn't remember the name, that's all. Anyway, it's nothing, it's not offensive or anything, just a little strange. Sorry to bother you at home."

"No problem," Peggy Jean said.

"By the way, you were wonderful in Milan. Did you get any sight-seeing in?"

"Heavens, no. You know how draining international travel is. I'm still quite jet-lagged."

"Well, just try to relax as much as you can before you come back to the office."

"Yes, I will. And thanks for calling, Trish," she said and hung up.

Odd, Peggy Jean thought. Why would Trish call her at home? Trish had never phoned her before. She bit into a vanilla Slim Fast bar. It didn't seem normal for Trish to act so caring toward her. Could *Trish* be Zoe? Was she capable of such evil? Peggy Jean chewed slowly as she contemplated. Then she threw the wrapper in the trash. The strawberry Slim Fasts were much better than the vanilla, that much she knew for sure.

After speaking with Peggy Jean, Trish went to the host's lounge to get a cup of tea, a smile fixed on her face.

"Sparkling diamonds, that's what this is going to look like on your finger." Peggy Jean was on air, midway through Rings of Romance. "Six stones with a total gem weight of just over one carat, so this, ladies, is a very believable ring. It's a lot of sparkle, a lot of glimmer. And it has a wonderful diamond presence, but because it's Diamonelle, you're paying a fraction of what you would pay if this ring were set with real diamonds."

Cut to closeup, Camera One of Peggy Jean's finger showing the ring. "Fifty-three dollars and ninety-four cents is our introductory price on this ring, and it's item number J-6866. And ladies, let me remind you that you always have a thirty-day, unconditional, money-back guarantee here at Sellevision."

Cut to medium shot, Camera Three of Peggy Jean. "And that means that for any reason—maybe it's the wrong size, or maybe you just decide, 'You know, this really isn't me'—you can send the ring back to us and we'll give you a full refund. So if you've never tried Sellevision before, this ring could be a really good way for you to discover the quality and the, well, really the *beauty* of our jewelry."

The Teleprompter in front of Peggy Jean alerted her to the fact that there was a caller on the line. Zoe, from California.

For a beat, Peggy Jean ignored the message until her producer said into her earphone, "Peggy Jean, we've got a caller. Something wrong with the Teleprompter? Her name is Zoe from California and she's purchasing."

Peggy Jean smiled into the camera. "And we've got a caller. Let's welcome Zoe from California. Hi, Zoe."

"Hi, Peggy Jean. It's exciting to speak with you."

The caller's voice sounded muffled. Peggy Jean imagined a filthy dishtowel being held over the mouthpiece.

"It's nice to speak with you, too. Is this your first piece of Diamonelle jewelry?"

"Oh no, I own many pieces. I just love Diamonelle, I get more compliments than you could even imagine."

Peggy Jean continued to smile broadly. "That's great to hear, Zoe. Now let me ask you: What was it about this *particular* Diamonelle ring that caught your eye?"

"Well, I think it was the fact that, like you said, it's got a lot of glamour to it, but it's also really believable because it's not so big that people would think it's a fake."

"Exactly," Peggy Jean confirmed. "This is a very beautiful, very believable ring." *So far, so good*, Peggy Jean thought. *Maybe it's a different Zoe.*

"Oh yes, I'm looking forward to wearing it. I think I'm

really gonna love it. Especially because I, unlike you, am not a bitch with hairy knuckles, so the ring will look much bet—"

"Shit, Peggy Jean, we're going to disconnect the caller, stand by."

The caller was cut off midsentence with a squelch and then a click.

Peggy Jean began to tremble, visibly. She stared blankly into the camera, mouth open.

"Peggy Jean, are you okay? Peggy Jean?" When her producer got no response, he called out to an engineer, "Get her off, cut to a promo, *now!*"

eight

"My God, she humiliated me on live television, in front of *millions and millions* of viewers," Peggy Jean said, holding back the tears. She and Trish were sitting in Peggy Jean's Acura in the employee parking lot of Sellevision. Peggy Jean had run to her car immediately after the show when she realized she'd left her purse, which contained her pills, on the front seat.

Struggling to not ruin her eye makeup, Peggy Jean confided to Trish, "I'm really scared. *I'm being stalked.*"

Trish placed her hand on Peggy Jean's shoulder pad. "Look, she's just some crazy person who sent you a couple of letters and then got on the air, that's all there is to it. She won't get on the air again and I promise you, it's all going to go away."

"But it's not just a *couple* of letters, it's *many* letters, sometimes less than an hour apart. And now phone calls!" Peggy Jean wailed. The Valium hadn't kicked in yet.

"I know, it's scary, real people *are* scary, but that's the price we pay for being in the public eye. We've all received our share of letters from nutcases—a month from now, you won't even remember this Zoo person."

"Zoe, it's Zoe," Peggy Jean corrected.

"Well, maybe 'Zoo' is more appropriate."

"I don't know. Maybe you're right, Trish. I mean, maybe this is just the price we pay for our celebrity."

"It is, I'm telling you. Of course there is one thing you should be worried about," Trish said.

"*What*?" Peggy Jean said with alarm.

"Look over there," Trish said, pointing across the street at a Krispy Kreme sign being lowered by crane into place on the new store front.

Peggy Jean smiled, relieved. "Actually, that comforts me. It means there will be police officers around."

"Honestly, Peggy Jean, you have no need for police officers. Now come on, let's go back inside."

She had one new E-mail.

To: PG_Smythe@Sellevision.com
Fr: Zoe@ProviderNet.com
Subject: Cut, Cut

You cut me off mid-sentance on live television?
That's how you treat your FRIENDS???
Oh, nice try with the new frosting job, but sweetheart, let me tell you something: it DOESN'T work. Neither do your hairy knuckles. You are nothing but a RAT.
But I do know what would work for you:
Cut, Cut.

Peggy Jean gasped as she read the last two words: *Cut, Cut.* Was it a threat? A threat of physical harm? Had this Zoe person finally gone over some edge? "And I *don't* have hairy knuckles, you madwoman!" Peggy Jean said through gritted teeth as she tapped the "send" key on her computer. As she did this, she looked down at the knuckles of her right hand, turning them in the light to catch the profiles of hairs.

Yes, hairs.

She took another Valium, washing it down with one of the little bottles of peppermint schnapps from her flight.

After that week's third Joyce's Choice program ended and Adele Oswald Crawley's Indian Pride Fry Bread Extravaganza special came on, Bebe walked back to her office and, upon opening the door, came very close to fainting.

> B—
> *I was trying to remember how many times you blushed over dinner. I lost track after twelve, but figured a "baker's dozen" might get the idea across. You know, "an eye for an eye."*
> *~~Looking forward to seeing you again,~~*
> *~~Hoping to see you soon,~~*
> *~~Do you believe at love at first sight?~~*
> *~~Yours truly,~~*
> *Unable to stop thinking about you and praying you feel the same,*
> *Eliot*

The handwritten card was the most romantic thing Bebe had ever held in her hands. It completely overpowered the thirteen long white boxes, each filled with a dozen red roses, that were stacked on a pile atop her desk. One hundred and fifty-six roses altogether. It was completely overboard. The first thing Bebe did was phone her mother, Rose, in California.

"Mom, I really think I might have met somebody," she said.

"Oh, dear, that's wonderful! Did you meet him out shopping?" her mother asked.

Bebe hadn't thought of exactly what to tell her mother in terms of how they met. She improvised. "We've only had one date, but it's like I made a list of everything I wanted in somebody and he arrived, mail-order."

"Is he a doctor?" her mother asked. "An executive?"

"He owns a business, a chain of stores."

Her mother gave a small, delighted gasp. "A *chain* of stores? Imagine that, a whole chain, how wonderful. Do we have any of his stores down here?"

"It's a dry-cleaning business, actually. But that's not the point. The point is that he's handsome and smart and funny and, I don't know, I just have a really good feeling about him."

"Well, everybody needs clean clothes," her mother said, trying to sound upbeat. "Of course, there's no reason he couldn't branch out in the future."

After Bebe hung up with her mother, she looked over at the mound of boxes, the top box opened. It reminded her of a story her mother told her.

When Bebe was five, she lived with her mother and father in Brooklyn. Her father was a police officer with the NYPD. He worked a lot of nights, and one of those nights was Bebe's mother's thirtieth birthday. Because Dad frequently missed holidays, the family often celebrated them later or earlier. But on this particular birthday, a box arrived. Inside the box were three dozen roses. Why, out of all their nine years of marriage, had he chosen this birthday to have a special delivery of roses sent?

It was almost as if he somehow knew that he would be killed that night, in the line of duty.

Bebe didn't remember her father. But she did remember her mother's grief, because it lasted for years. And it was only when Bebe was ten that her mother told her of Bebe's brother, a brother she'd never known because he'd been given up for adoption at birth. Bebe's parents were newly married and hadn't expected a baby so soon, when they had so little money. It had been a difficult decision, but one they felt was best for the baby.

To this day, Bebe's mother still talked about the roses. And she still said the one regret in her life was letting that baby go and losing that piece of her husband. Of course, her other large regret in life was that her daughter was forty-two and not married.

Roses had never been just roses to Bebe. Roses had always been some sort of *message* from a father that she couldn't even remember.

At the Barnes & Noble superstore five miles from his condo, Max walked the aisles, glancing at books, but truly hunting for a prospective boyfriend. *What better place to shop for a smart man than a bookstore?* he reasoned.

He saw a handsome young guy in the Fiction and Literature section. Khaki slacks, blue oxford shirt, gold wire-frame glasses. Max paused, leaned forward, and took a book from the shelf, pretending to read as he peered over the top. The young man was engrossed in his own reading. Max studied the man's face, trying to determine if he could visualize the stranger at some future point in time throwing a Frisbee in the park for the not-yet-born golden retriever puppy the two would have obtained from a reputable breeder in upstate New York. The stranger, perhaps sensing that he was being scrutinized, glanced up from his book and caught Max's eye. The man smiled at Max, then looked back down at his book. Max managed to glimpse the title: *The Bell Jar.*

Immediately, Max replaced his prop-book on the shelf and continued down the aisle, walking past the man and making a sharp right.

Pausing in the neutral zone of Books for Young Readers, Max realized he was likely to encounter another *Bell Jar* reader unless he devised a strategy. Science Fiction? No, Max did not want a Trekkie boyfriend with a calculator wristwatch. Movies and Television? Just the thought of sitting home on Friday night watching a scratchy old copy of *A Streetcar Named Desire* with some guy who knew all of Blanche Dubois's lines made Max feel depressed. Sports? No towel-snapping ex–frat boys, thank you. Photography? Too pretentious. History? Science? Computers? No, no, no.

After eliminating Travel by reason of his own abandonment issues, Max decided that the only two sections of Barnes & Noble that were appropriate for boyfriend shopping were Self-Improvement and Pets.

While pretending to read *Feeling Good: The New Mood Therapy*, Max spotted a beefy, jockish-looking fellow. The guy had very large biceps, which could come in quite handy when it came time to haul firewood inside. The man scanned the titles of the books and then plucked a copy of *Codependent No More* from the shelf.

A codependent bodybuilder did not sound unappealing. Except then Max saw that the man was wearing a wedding band. This meant he probably had a wife who suffered from low self-esteem, who was needy and clingy and assumed that every time her husband went to the gym he was really visiting a secret girlfriend. He imagined the wife at home that very moment, wondering where her husband was, doing frantic sit-ups on the living room carpet in an effort to become more attractive to her ripped husband, thus staving off the divorce she feared was almost inevitable.

Or maybe he was gay. Gay men often wore wedding bands, trying to pass. But then the guy walked away, without so much as a glance.

Max read *The Right Dog for You* in the Pets section. He was surprised to learn that Chow Chows had black tongues and Basenjis didn't bark. Max had always assumed *all* dogs had pink tongues and barked. What other of his assumptions, he wondered, were untrue? Most? All? Until only recently, he had assumed he would continue with Sellevision, eventually rising to the ranks of Peggy Jean or Bebe. Perhaps even one day having his very own show, Max's Choice, which could have featured a collection of Max's personal favorites from the vast Sellevision inventory.

How quickly one's life could change, fall apart. If Max hadn't insisted on a preshow latte, it never would have spilled into his lap in the first place, thus setting into motion the chain of events that led to his subsequent misery, whereby he was left with no options except boyfriend shopping in the late afternoon at a suburban Philadelphia book retailer, where instead of a boyfriend he gained only knowledge of Chow Chow tongues.

Replacing *The Right Dog for You* on the shelf, Max made his way to the Philosophy & Spirituality section.

As Leigh headed for the checkout counter, a copy of *Women Who Love Selfish Bastards* tucked under her arm, title facing inward, she thought she saw Max reading a book in the Witchcraft & Occult section. Looking closer, she saw that it was, in fact, Max.

Feeling slightly guilty that it had been partly due to his misfortune that she was now on daytime as opposed to overnight (of course, the fact that she was romantically involved with the head of broadcast production probably didn't hurt things), along with the fact that she had always really liked Max, she decided to walk over and say hello.

Spells and Incantations for 2000 and Beyond nearly flew out of Max's hands when Leigh tapped him on the shoulder.

"Oh, Max, I'm sorry. I didn't mean to startle you, I just saw you and thought I'd say hello."

Tapping the book against his chest and closing his eyes for a second, Max then smiled warmly, genuinely pleased to see her. "I guess I, I just wasn't expecting to be touched, that's all."

Then he added, "But hey, it *really* is great to see you. How have you been? How's Sellevision?"

Leigh faked a smile. "Everything's been okay, you know, same-old, same-old."

"Yeah? Well I'm glad to hear stuff's going well for you."

"Max, I feel awful about what happened to you. I really think Howard totally overreacted."

"Nah, don't worry about it. It's probably going to turn out to be the best thing that ever happened to me. I mean, my agent is talking with the Discovery Channel and Lifetime, plus there's some anchor spot open at KRON in San Francisco, so . . ."

"That's great, Max, really great. How exciting."

"Yeah, exciting. You know, change and everything. Change is good."

Noticing the title of the book in his hands, Leigh said, "I didn't know you were interested in . . . the occult."

Fumbling to put the book back on the shelf, Max said "Uh, well, I'm not actually. I was just, you know, sort of . . ." He watched as the Italian in bicycle shorts he had been tailing for the past twenty minutes left the aisle and began heading toward the front exit. ". . . just looking around. For a gift. Anyway, what's that book you've got tucked under your arm?"

Immediately realizing it had been a mistake not to ditch the book before approaching, Leigh sheepishly held up the title.

Max laughed. "I've read that."

Leigh's eyes widened and she smiled. "You read *this?*"

"Uh-huh. Last year." Confessing, Max told Leigh, "I got involved with my chiropractor who was divorced from his wife. And then not really divorced, but separated. And then not really separated, but expecting their third child."

"Oh, Max, how awful. I'm sorry."

He brushed the memory away with his hand. "Nah, don't be, I'm over it. Thanks to this," he added, tapping Leigh's book.

Not wanting to go into the details of her own relationship, Leigh decided on a small fib: "Yeah, my sister is involved with something really similar, and it's just killing me to see all the pain she's in."

Max gave Leigh a knowing look. "Sure, I understand. I hope it helps . . . your sister."

"Anyway, I guess I should get running, I have to go over to Mr. Spotless and pick up my dry cleaning."

"Yeah, I should get moving along too," Max agreed.

As Max headed for the exit and Leigh for the checkout, he stopped and turned. "You know, it'd be really great to stay in touch. I mean, I don't know about you, but these days my best friend is the television."

Leigh thought of Valerie Bertinelli, of sobbing into the cushions on her sofa, and said, "I would really love that, Max."

They exchanged phone numbers and said good-bye, promising to get together for lunch sometime soon.

When Max arrived home to his condominium, he saw that the red light was blinking on his answering machine. Tossing his keys and wallet in a bowl on the kitchen counter, Max pressed play.

It was a wrong number, a bass player looking for some guitarist named Ned.

nine

"You didn't think I was crazy? You didn't think it was too much?" Eliot asked Bebe over dinner on date number two.

"I didn't say I didn't think you were crazy, I just said that you were incredibly romantic."

Bebe was wearing the sheer black dress she'd purchased at Henri Bendel. Around her neck was an eighteen-karat gold Stampato necklace that she had ordered during Trish Mission's live show from London.

"Well, I just wanted to let you know that you made a really big impression on me," Eliot said, breaking off a piece of bread from the small loaf on his bread plate and dipping into the little bowl of olive oil in the center of the table.

"You made a big impression on me too, Eliot," Bebe said. She took a sip of wine. "I just really feel like you're so easy to be with, so funny, and, I don't know . . ." She didn't finish the thought.

"I was thinking," Eliot began, "that maybe we should do something *different* for our third date." Then, immediately correcting himself, he added, "I mean, assuming you would want to go on a third date with me."

Bebe smiled. She reached across the table and touched Eliot's hand. "I would love to go on a third date with you. What do you have in mind?"

"Well, I was thinking we've done Italian both nights we've gotten together, so maybe we could do French."

Just as Bebe was about to tell Eliot that she loved French food, he added, "I mean, in France."

Bebe looked at him, unsure of what he was saying.

"No, don't get me wrong, I'm not suggesting we go on vacation or anything, I was just thinking that we could take the Concorde to Paris—it's only three hours—and have dinner at my favorite restaurant on the Left Bank, and then I could have you back home just after midnight." He looked down at his plate, feeling like an idiot for suggesting such an extravagant third date.

Bebe burst out laughing. She wadded up the crust of bread on her plate and threw it across the table at Eliot's chest. "You are certifiably crazy. I mean it: *crazy.*"

Eliot grinned, plucked the bread bullet off his lap and popped it into his mouth. "Is that a yes?"

"I'm probably the most gullible woman on the face of the earth but I've never been known for my common sense."

"So it's a yes?"

"Oui." Then she added, "You know, I thought you were going to say something like we should go to the aquarium or, I don't know, to a monster truck rally."

"The monster truck rally was sold out," Eliot said, smiling.

Because of her Navaho Indian heritage (no matter how distant or slight), Adele Oswald Crawley had already hosted two American Indian theme shows. Both had been raging successes. Although operating full steam ahead, Sellevision's search for a recognizably ethnic show host had thus far produced no candidates. As such, any minority bloodlines among the hosts were being fully exploited.

Although raised all her life as an Irish Catholic, Adele had fully embraced whatever Navaho blood she may have had. Her medium-length red, wavy hair was now a much darker reddish-brown. And she blew it straight before each show, parting it in the middle, as opposed to sweeping it back, like before. Even her freckles were less obvious, as she'd begun wearing more makeup, and dramatically highlighting her cheekbones.

On camera, Adele answered a viewer's question, "I actually don't know what my given Navaho Indian name is, but if you'd write this question down and send me a letter, I'd be more than happy to ask around my family and get back to you with the answer. Just remember to please include a SASE." Adele smiled.

Adele thanked the caller and then immediately took another call. As of that night, Dream Catcher Jewelry was going to become a permanent show on Sellevision. Adele had hit a nerve with America's Indian community, and they were embracing her by the thousands.

"My very own great-great-grandmother may have crafted a belt buckle just like this with her very own hands. Think of the *history* and *pride* involved in making such a piece. I really believe that it's so important to respect and honor the *original* Americans, because we are all connected, and by claiming our past, we claim our*selves*. Once more, this is item number J-7330, it's sixty-eight dollars and thirty-four cents, and it's the Running Wolf simulated turquoise cabochon belt buckle."

A SOLD OUT graphic appeared on screen.

"Another great show, Adele—congrats," the assistant producer said. "And those beaded moccasins are darling," she added, pointing to Adele's feet.

"Thanks, Amanda. I added the beads myself. I'm just really getting into my whole heritage thing, it's like *Roots* or something for me."

"I wish I had some Indian blood in me, but no such luck—Wisconsin bred through-and-through."

Adele waved good-bye to the various cameramen, stylists, and backstage crew. Before leaving the set and heading to her office, Adele paused to thank a lighting technician.

"I just wanted to let you know that I really appreciate what you've done for me in terms of lighting. The overhead thing for my cheekbones is great."

He smiled at her. "Sure, Adele, no problem. It's always fun to do something different."

She walked through a set of double doors that led from the soundstage to the hallway where all hosts' offices were located, along with the lounge.

"Hi, Trish, what's up?" Trish was checking Leigh's hours on the hosts' schedule.

"Oh, nothing." She spun around.

"Oh my God, is that the ring? I haven't even seen it yet, let me have a look," Adele said, tucking her hair behind her ears.

Trish automatically extended her hand for Adele to admire the ring.

"It's incredible. Have you set a date yet?" Adele asked.

"Oh, I don't know. No, not really." Then an image of brown leaves scattered on the ground, dried grass, and bulky, unflattering sweatshirts entered her head. "Maybe the fall."

Adele smiled. "Oh, the fall is my favorite time of the year." She thought of Thanksgiving and maize. "Well, I better get back to my office, I have tons of research I need to get started on."

After Adele walked away, Trish looked back at the schedule, silently tallying the hours that each host had on-air.

Adele sat down at her desk and did an Internet search. Keywords: Unusual American Indian Artifacts.

Peggy Jean kept a chart on her refrigerator door, a chart with the names of her three boys, the days of the week, and the numbers one through ten. It was their Behavior Chart, an easy way for her to keep a motherly eye on her children. At the end of the week, she reviewed the chart with the boys and they talked about any dips. As a concerned parent, Peggy Jean kept a close watch on her boys' emotional well-being. It seemed so many children these days were ignored, became violent, brought guns to school, and performed mass executions. Not to mention drugs and premarital sex. And each time the parents of these deviant children were interviewed on television, they said the same thing over and over: "I had no idea." Peggy Jean was determined not to lose touch with her children.

So on Thursday evening, the evening she had agreed to take them to a movie, she saw on the chart that each boy had exhibited an exceptionally good level of behavior all week long. Nines across the board. Behavior deserving of a treat.

"Tonight at the movies," she told them as they were sitting on the living room sofa, all three in a row, "you may each have a special treat." They looked at her, and she was struck by how beautiful they were, how precious they looked in their overalls, six sweet little eyes so pure and vulnerable. "Any treat you want, popcorn or a chocolate bar or a diet soda, anything!" she said, beaming. "And do you know why?" she asked them. "Do you know *why* you get an extra-special treat?"

They shook their heads, having no idea whatsoever.

"I'll show you why," she said, and walked into the kitchen to take the chart down from the refrigerator. She carried this, along with her second glass of cherry cordial (which, she thought, tasted exactly like expectorant) back into the living room. She displayed the chart for them to see. "Not since April have you boys had such an exceptional chart! This one goes into the family album," she said almost tearfully, hugging the chart to her breast.

"Can we see *High School Slaughterhouse 2*?" asked her oldest boy, Ricky.

The dreamy expression left Peggy Jean's face and was replaced by one of alarm. She set the cherry cordial down on a daisy coaster atop the mirrored coffee table and swallowed. "Most certainly *not*," she said. "We will see nothing of the sort." Then, resting the chart on top of a copy of *Modern Woman* magazine, she announced, "We are going to the seven P.M. showing of *Gone With the Wind*. It was one of my favorite pictures as a young girl."

The boys looked at the floor. The middle boy, who seldom spoke, asked, "Can we just stay home instead?"

Peggy Jean laughed and took a dainty sip of her cherry beverage. "Of course not! You boys *deserve* a treat!" Then glancing at her watch, "Now go put your sneakers on, we don't want to be late."

In the car, all three boys sat in the back as usual. The eldest made a gun with the fingers of his right hand and pretended to shoot their mother in the back, through the seat.

The other two boys covered their mouths and tried not to laugh.

At 7:30 sharp the doorbell rang, and John Smythe bounded down the stairs wearing a T-shirt and a pair of shorts, which he hoped showed off his muscular legs to their best advantage. Nikki was wearing jeans and a little white top. She looked fresh, as if she had just come from a nap on a bed of violets.

"Hi, Mr. Smythe," she said when he opened the door. "I hope I'm not late."

John invited her inside. "Not at all, Nikki. Perfect timing. But there's been a change of plans, and it's all my fault."

She looked at him with big eyes.

"My wife screwed up and took the kids out to a movie. She must have forgotten that I told her I had a surprise."

Nikki looked disappointed. "Gosh, Mr. Smythe, that's awful. And it sounded like it was going to be so romantic."

"Ah, well, another time," he said, scratching his leg, drawing her attention to it.

"Do you run?" she asked.

"Now and then, just to, you know, keep in shape." His face felt hot, flushed. "Well, since you're here, can I get you something? A Pepsi or maybe some milk?"

"Do you have any wine?" she asked.

"Young lady, you aren't even eighteen years old," he said, smiling, flirting.

"I'm almost eighteen," she said, shrugging. "Pepsi's okay, I guess."

She smelled, he thought, like springtime.

"One Pepsi coming right up. Go ahead and make yourself at home." His heart was beating so hard in his chest that he was worried she could hear it. He walked into the kitchen and got two glasses from the cupboard and two cans of Pepsi from the refrigerator, and filled the glasses with ice.

"So tell me, Nikki," he said as he handed her a glass, "how's life?

"Good, I guess. Why is your hand shaking?"

He sat down on the couch, putting his glass on the coffee table. "Oh, just the ice from the drinks, that's all."

She took a sip.

"So, ah . . ." thinking of something to ask her, "what are your plans when you finish high school?"

"Well, actually, I was kind of hoping to be a model," she said bashfully.

He smiled. "Yes, yes indeed, I could see that. You do resemble Bridget Hall."

"Oh my God!" she exclaimed, turning sideways on the sofa to face him. "You *know* who Bridget Hall is?"

"Well, of course I do, everyone knows who Bridget Hall is."

She widenend her eyes. "I cannot *believe* you know who she is, that is like, *so* cool. God, my father has no clue at all."

Why would he, John thought, *with a daughter like you?*

"But I think you're a lot prettier than she is. You're kind of Bridget-Hall-slash-Kirsty-Hume."

"Kirsty Hume! I love Kirsty, I would die to look like her, God, *her hair*." Then, "Do you know that new girl, oh what's her name, she's like fourteen . . . really tall . . . long red hair . . . oh, what's her *name?*" she whined, squeezing her eyes shut, trying to think.

"Heather Sands," offered John immediately. "But she's *thirteen*, not fourteen."

She slammed both hands down on the couch between them. "Yes! Exactly! Oh my God, you are so totally cool, I wish you were my father."

Good thing I'm not, John thought.

"It's really hard to be sympathetic toward somebody who is so tan," Leigh told Howard on his first day back from St. Barts. They were having lunch together at a restaurant forty minutes from Sellevision, a small, unremarkable establishment where there was no chance of being seen together.

"Well, I'm telling you, Leigh, it was hell, just hell. Can you pass the salt?"

"You didn't answer my question," she said, placing the salt shaker in front of his plate.

"Yes, I told her."

"Oh, Howard! You did? You really did?"

"Yes," he cleared his throat. "And no. I mean, I started to."

She glared at him, dropping her fork on her plate. "Howard, cut the b.s., okay? Did you tell your wife you want a divorce or not? I want to know where we stand."

"All right, I started to. I started talking about making changes, evolving as people, and then I realized that it was just too heavy. Way too serious a conversation to have in an airport in San Juan."

"Wait a minute, wait a minute, I thought you went to St. Barts. Are you just physically unable to tell the truth?"

"We did go to St. Barts, Leigh, but we changed flights on the way home in San Juan."

"Okay, whatever, I don't even care about that. I'm just really confused. You told me, you promised me, that you were going to tell your wife as soon as you got back."

"I know what I promised, and I'm going to keep that promise. I love you, Leigh."

"God damn it, Howard," Leigh said, blinking back tears. "Why are you doing this to me? Telling me you love me, telling me 'oh, I'm going to leave my wife for you,' and then nothing ever happens, nothing changes?"

"Sweetheart," Howard said, reaching over and placing his hand gently against Leigh's cheek. "It's just timing, that's all it is, it's just a matter of finding the right time."

"I hate how much I missed you," she said softly, almost under her breath.

"I missed you too, Leigh, so much, so very, very much."

Leigh stared at the poached blowfish on her plate. "You know, I bought this book while you were away," she said, poking her fork at the fish. "It's about women who love people they shouldn't." She decided not to tell him the *exact* title.

"Leigh, why? Why are you reading trash like that, huh? I'm not the wrong man for you. I'm the right man for you, because I love you."

"No, wait. Just listen."

Howard exhaled and set his fork down. "Okay, I'm sorry, tell me about your little book."

"Well, it just really made me feel upset, because in the book they talk about the warning signs, what to look for in a bad relationship. And it was like they were describing you. Everything they said, it was all you." Leigh dabbed her pinkie under each eye and sighed.

"Sweetheart, I just want to hold you. You need to be held. Let's get out of this place and go somewhere where we can be close for a couple of hours." Howard raised his hand and wrote his signature in the air, signaling the waiter to bring the check.

After making love on top of the garish bedspread at the Ramada Inn. Howard rolled over, said, "I'm just gonna grab a quick shower," and went into the bathroom. Leigh stared at the heavy pleated drapes over the window that matched the hideous bedspread. Though it was midafternoon, the room was dark, except for what light leaked out from under the bathroom door. *In the dark, that's me,* Leigh thought to herself.

This was Leigh's day off, so Howard drove her home. "I'll see you tomorrow, sweetheart, and don't forget that I love you." He kissed her cheek.

Leigh managed a weak smile, stepped out of the S-Class Mercedes and walked into her apartment building.

Howard pulled away and headed for Sellevision. As he merged onto the freeway, he caught a glimpse of his aquiline nose, slightly sunburned, and hoped that it didn't peel. He also thought, *What excellent rhinoplasty.*

With a grave expression on his face, the news anchor read the Teleprompter. "In other news, killer teens continue to terrorize schools across the country. The latest massacre occurred yesterday in rural Alabama, where a twelve-year-old boy executed seventy-two of his classmates with an Uzi subma- chine gun. The youth, now in police custody, is said to have lis- tened to music by the recording artist Celine Dion. And now for sports."

"Cut," the director shouted. He folded his almost *carpeted* arms across his barrel chest and walked over to the news desk. "Max, ya gotta *sell* the news. What's with this sour face?"

Max swallowed and cleared his throat. "Um, well, I just thought, you know, since this is about a kid killing other kids, it should, you know, be sort of on the serious side."

The director, a large, balding man with one thick black eye- brow running horizontally above his eyes, was losing patience. "Look, this shit happens all the time. Americans are bored with killer teens. Maybe in the nineties it got under people's skin, but not anymore. This stuff is so *over*."

Max nodded his head.

"Jazz it up! You know? Put a wink in it."

"A wink," Max said. "Okay, I'll try that."

The director exhaled and turned around. "All right, okay, let's take it again from the top." He clapped his hands. "Every- body quiet now, and . . . *action!*"

Again, Max recited the news copy, this time trying to impart a certain edge of restrained wit to the delivery. He even smirked slightly when he mentioned Celine Dion.

"Cut! Cut! *Cut!*" the director shouted. "Okay, this isn't working, but I have an idea." He spun around and started yelling. "Mitch, hey Mitch! Where the hell is Mitch?"

"I'm right here!" shouted one of the guys wearing jeans and a T-shirt, a half-eaten croissant in his hand.

"Mitch, buddy, I want you to throw a key light on Max's chin. Maybe something a little off to the side, something to really emphasize the cleft. Do that for me, buddy?"

"Sure thing," Mitch said, tossing the rest of his croissant into a nearby trash can and running off in search of a key light. The director then stomped back over to Max. "Here's what we're gonna do. Forget what I said before. This time, I want you to be sexy."

"Sexy?" Max asked, unsure.

"Yeah, I want you to think Brad Pitt meets Dan Rather. The fact is, fifty-nine percent of our viewers are women." Then, liking his own idea more and more, the director said, "Yeah, yeah, yeah," and rubbed his hands together fast. "This could be good, so just really *seduce* the camera. Forget you're reading about killer teens. Pretend it's poetry."

After the audition, Max phoned his agent, Laurie.

"She's in a meeting," the receptionist said after putting Max briefly on hold. "Any message?"

"Tell her I just got out of the audition with WXON for the anchor spot."

"Mm-hmm-hmm," the receptionist mumbled into the phone as she wrote. "And a phone number where she can reach you?"

"She has my number. I'll be home in a couple hours, have her call me there," he said, then added, "when she gets a chance."

Max walked down Broadway, thinking about his chances with the station. He thought that what he may have lacked in journalistic appeal, he made up for in personality, believability, and looks. Plus, he was just so natural in front of the camera. It was difficult to read the director, though.

Then, as he was walking, he saw a $50 bill, right there on the sidewalk. He bent over and picked it up. It *looked* real. He grinned, stuffed the bill into his pocket, and continued walking. *So much of life is luck*, he thought.

ten

The flight attendant aboard the Concorde approached Bebe and Eliot with two tall crystal flutes of champagne balanced on a silver serving stray. "Veuve Cliquot?" she asked.

"Yes, thank you very much." Bebe took one glass for herself and handed the other to Eliot. This marked the first time since the sonic boom a few moments ago that the two had acted like adults.

Not wanting to establish a precedent for such behavior, Eliot sipped his champagne with a loud, childish slurp.

Laughing, Bebe challenged him. "I dare you to be normal for five minutes." Then looking at her watch, "I'm going to *time* you."

"Okay, time me," Eliot grinned. After a pause of about three seconds, he turned and asked, "What do normal people talk about?"

"God, how would I know?"

"Okay, let's talk about our jobs, normal people talk about their jobs, I think."

"Terrific, you're doing good so far. You go first."

Eliot raised his eyebrows and said seductively, "There's no stain on earth I wouldn't eliminate for you, my dear."

Bebe smiled at him.

Then remembering, he said, "Oh, I almost forgot, I brought you a surprise."

"You mean like a trip on the Concorde to Paris for dinner isn't enough?"

He reached into the breast pocket of his jacket. *"Voilà,"* he said, presenting her a long, black velvet jewelry box.

Startled, Bebe said, "Oh no, Eliot, no, whatever that is, it's way too much, I can't."

"Please, I wanted to—please, Bebe."

Feeling that she had already been rushing things by agreeing to this crazy Concorde trip in the first place, Bebe was now feeling like this might have been a mistake, that Eliot was moving a little too fast.

"Eliot, that's so—I don't even know what—sweet, generous, but I just don't feel comfortable."

Eliot shrugged nonchalantly. "Okay then, if that's how you feel, I'll eat it myself." And he popped the jewelry box open, revealing a colorful candy necklace.

Bebe burst into a fit of laughter, snatched the necklace from the box, and gave the elastic a little stretch. "Oh my God, I haven't seen one of these in years," she cried. She doubled it and slid it onto her wrist.

"It's lovely," he admired.

She extended her arm in front of her, as though wearing something by Harry Winston. "You failed your normal test," she told him.

"I had you really worried for a minute there, didn't I?"

"Maybe a tad," she admitted. "But thank you. I mean it, this is like the sweetest—no pun intended—thing."

She leaned over slowly and kissed him on the cheek, then pulled away slightly and paused, lips parted.

Gently, tentatively, he moved his lips to hers, closing his eyes.

And they kissed.

He brought his hand around to the back of her neck and she placed her hand along the side of his face.

For an instant, her eyes opened, and then suddenly she pulled away from him. "Oh my God, Eliot, look!" she cried, pointing out the window beside him.

Eliot turned quickly.

Almost breathless, Bebe whispered, "Oh Eliot, have you ever? It's so beautiful. I feel just like Jodie Foster in *Contact*."

Out the window of the Concorde, from an altitude of over eighty-five-thousand feet, the curvature of the earth filled the lower portion of the window. Blackness and stars filled the rest.

"I thought you said you spoke French," Bebe said, punching Eliot playfully in the shoulder.

They were sitting in the back of a taxi, en route to an address that Eliot gave to the driver by pointing to it in a travel guide. "If I told you I didn't speak French, you wouldn't have come."

"The ugly Americans go to dinner," she joked.

"Ugly?" he said, looking at her and smiling.

She came fairly close to blushing, turned away, and looked out the window.

Although the early-evening sky was overcast, there was still a pinkish hue around the edges. Two bicyclists sped past the taxi. On the river, a group of swans bent their graceful necks to take pieces of bread an old woman on the bank was tossing them. Bebe had been to Paris before, but it felt new.

The restaurant was a tiny bistro on a narrow, twisting side street, down a few moss-covered stone steps. Inside the floor was slate, with ten tables each blanketed by crisp white tablecloths. Three beeswax candles sat on each table. A row of tall topiary trees lined the far wall. Bebe thought it truly looked like a place out of a fairy tale. "Eliot, you almost get the feeling they have gnomes in the kitchen."

"Yeah, either that or they serve gnomes for dinner."

Over an appetizer of paté, capers, mustard, and fresh, crusty bread, Eliot and Bebe had the inevitable Past Relationships from Hell conversation.

Bebe told Eliot of the Gay Weatherman ("I just thought he really happened to like Cher. Then I found the Bob Mackie").

Eliot topped her with Tales of Theresa, including her infamous I-slept-with-my-brother confessional weekend.

The waiter arrived, waited for a break in their laughter, then offered more wine.

"We've both really got to stop dating guests from the Jerry Springer show," Bebe said.

"Speak for yourself. I'm strictly a Sally Jessy kind of guy."

Dinner was braised medallion of duck with vegetable confit and, of course, more wine.

As Bebe watched a bite of duck fall from Eliot's fork and land on his tie, she thought, *Is it possible that he becomes more handsome by the minute, more charming?*

Removing the stained tie, rolling it up, and slipping it into the outside pocket of his jacket, Eliot told Bebe that although it was only their third date, "I really feel like I've known you forever, and I don't throw my clichés around lightly."

Bebe admitted that she felt exactly the same way, that the flight over had been magical, and so was dinner—right now.

"I know it's too early to tell you I'm in love with you, but is it okay if I tell you that I'm very much in *like* with you?"

"I'm very much in like with you too, Eliot," she said, unaware that she was absently playing with the candy necklace on her wrist.

For dessert, they shared a cream puff drizzled with Armangac. Two spoons and one plate sat between them on the center of the table. Bebe felt flushed. She couldn't believe she was in Paris *for the evening* with this wonderful guy who for some unknown reason owned the Mr. Spotless dry-cleaning chain. She couldn't believe how quickly her emotions were making themselves known. Three dates. Three dates? How was it possible? Was she that desperate? Or was she that lucky? But why shouldn't he like her? She was attractive, funny, sane. And it's not like she was after him for his money. With a salary from Sellevision of well over $600,000 a year, Bebe could have easily afforded to take them both to Paris on the Concorde for the evening. As she sat thinking, eyes focused on the flickering candle flames on the table, she was unaware of what Eliot was doing—which involved a spoon, a small dollop of whipped cream, a bit of physics, and excellent aim.

The whipped cream hit her neck with a splat that startled her out of her thoughts. It took her a second to understand what had happened. She ran her finger across her neck, wiping off the whipped cream. She looked at Eliot, who was beaming mischievously. Had any other man done such a thing on their third date, Bebe would have simply thrown her glass of wine in his face and stormed out of the restaurant, never to speak to him again.

But since it was Eliot, and she, after all, had been Bozo Bebe in college, she simply plucked the sweet red cherry from the top of the dessert, popped it into her mouth and then spat it across the table, directly onto his clean white shirt. The cherry slid down down his shirt, leaving behind a red trail.

Eliot picked up the cherry and ate it.

Bebe laughed.

Eliot told Bebe that she was especially beautiful when she laughed and that that was the only reason he flicked the whipped cream on her in the first place, scout's honor. To see her laugh.

"No wonder you're single," Bebe teased.

Eliot polished off the last of his dessert wine. "That's funny, I don't feel very single."

As the Concorde flew against the rotation of the earth, Bebe rested her head on Eliot's shoulder. Then she noticed the in-flight duty-free shopping catalog and she immediately reached for it. "Can I borrow a pen, Eliot?"

"I don't have a pen, but I can prick my finger and you can write with my blood, if you like."

Bebe rolled her eyes and signaled for the flight attendant. Once she had a pen, she began circling items in the catalog.

Eliot watched her, amused.

Bebe leafed through the magazine, writing down item numbers.

"You smoke?" he asked, when Bebe selected a carton of Dunhill menthol cigarettes.

"Not me," she said. "But I'm sure I know someone who does."

The box arrived via certified mail, so Peggy Jean signed for it, personally. "Close the door behind you," she ordered the mailboy on his way out.

Under his breath he muttered, "Sure thing, bitch."

What could this be? she wondered. A thoughtful gift from her husband? Perhaps she had ordered something herself and simply forgotten?

Opening the thick paper revealed a simple, flat white box, wrapped in plastic. Sometimes chocolates arrived in such a box. She smiled at the thought, but silently warned herself against eating more than two. If they were chocolates, she would place them in the hosts' lounge for others to enjoy, along with a little note: "Enjoy! God Bless, Peggy Jean."

She placed the box squarely on her lap and opened it. But it wasn't a box of chocolates.

It was a crucified rat.

The tiny little paws were thumbtacked to a homemade cross, Jesus style. The rat's neck had been cut so it sported a collar of dried blood. And then there was the smell.

Peggy Jean let out a high-pitched scream and leapt up, sending the box tumbling onto the floor. She dashed out into the hallway, and ran screaming for the exit.

In the parking lot, a heel snapped off one of her Easy Spirit pumps. Frantically she tried to open her car door, but it was locked, and she'd left her keys and purse in her office. Tugging on the door handle caused the car alarm to begin wailing, the horn honking, and the lights flashing.

When the security officer arrived, she was hyperventilating. He handed her an empty Taco Bell Express bag to breathe into. "Just calm down, Ms. Smythe. Breath into the bag, then tell me what's going on."

Peggy Jean placed the bag over her face and breathed. The bag inflated and shrunk against her mouth.

"I thought it was a box of chocolates," she said, heaving into the bag. She was aware of the scent of nachos . . . or was it a Burrito Supreme? She pulled her face out of the bag and waved it in front of her open mouth, as if to fan more air into her lungs.

Then she limped alongside the security officer back to the building. She led him to her office but refused to step inside herself.

"Well, how about that," the security guard remarked upon seeing the crucified rat. "Poor little thing." An older man, near retirement, the security officer seemed genuinely saddened by the fate of the rodent. "Sure are a lot of crazies out there."

"Just get rid of it," Peggy Jean cried. "Get it the hell out of my office." Her arms were folded tightly across her chest. She was shivering.

Once the security guard and the rat were gone, Peggy Jean sprinkled Giorgio perfume on the floor where the rat-box had landed. Then she took two Valium and washed them down with one of the little bottles of Frangelica.

"I don't like the taste of liquor, so it's okay," she said aloud.

A moment later, Trish appeared in Peggy Jean's doorway. "What's this I hear about someone sending you vermin on a stick?"

Peggy Jean started, and immediately tucked the little empty bottle in the pocket of her jacket. "Tic Tac?" She picked up the small plastic box and rattled it at Trish.

"Sure, thanks."

Could Trish have . . . ? Peggy Jean wondered. *No.* She had to stop thinking like that. It was a sin to suspect her cohost and friend. "Oh, Trish, it's just awful. It's that Zoe woman, she's terrorizing me, and I'm going absolutely out of my mind." Peggy Jean's hands were visibly shaking as she popped a mint into her mouth. She was sweating profusely.

Trish sat against the edge of the desk. "I know it's not my business, but have you considered seeing someone?"

Peggy Jean perked up. "You mean, like a federal agent?"

"Actually no," Trish said. "I was thinking more along the lines of a therapist. You know, someone you can talk to who can help you deal . . . with the stress."

"I beg your pardon?" Peggy Jean asked, incredulously. "Are you suggesting that *I* see a mental health professional?"

"It couldn't hurt," Trish said, crossing her legs at the ankle.

"But I am not the one mailing crucified rats to people."

"Yes, true. But you are the one receiving them."

Peggy Jean licked her lips. She just *hated* Frangelica.

"And, well, you do seem awfully stressed out lately." Then Trish turned around and picked up the box of Tic Tacs. "And, Peggy—I've seen you taking the pills. I don't know what they are, but I've noticed."

Peggy Jean's face flushed red with humiliation. "They're natural—homeopathic pills, like *vitamins*," she said, a bit too defensively.

Trish set the Tic Tacs back down on the desk. "Well, I still think it might be a good idea to see somebody, just until this whole thing passes over."

After Trish left, Peggy Jean waited until her hands stopped shaking before she phoned her other, secret doctor for a Valium refill.

Inside Control Room 1, the producer directed her engineers. She faced a wall of monitors, and was surrounded on all sides by sophisticated technical equipment: title generators, switchers, a stack of nine Sony Beta video players, an audio mixing console. There were also three Avid editorial stations in the room where editors could cut together promos. Not to mention the all-important "G-spot," a nickname for the red button that allowed producers to speak to hosts while they were on the air. It was *Broadcast News*, without the news.

"Five, four, three, two . . . *and* now!" she said.

Somebody threw a switch.

Cut to ten-second prerecorded program promo.

"I am so sick of pizza. Three nights in a row, God I hate this job," Rob, one of the engineers complained.

"Camera Two, we're gonna open with your wide shot . . . ready . . . set . . . three . . . two . . . and . . . *Trish*."

"Hi, everybody, and welcome to the O-mazing Oriental Ring Spectacular! My name is Trish Mission, and you're watching Sellevision."

"Camera Three, stay as you are—we're gonna grab that medium shot."

"We have a lot to talk about this evening, so I want to just jump right on in and start."

"Doing great, Trish."

Trish was radiant, her blond hair piled atop her head in an elegant updo. She wore a sleeveless black satin dress that hung gracefully from her shoulders by two spaghetti straps. "Let's talk bold. Let's talk solid fourteen-karat gold. Let's talk—are you ready?—jade. And gold. Together. Mystery and magic, gold and jade." As she said this, she moved her head from side to side. Already the phones were ringing.

"You're rockin', Trish, love the drama."

"This is item number J-5114—and it's *brand-new* tonight." Trish stared into the camera and let that fact sink in.

"Jeff, gimme some graphics. Camera Three, stay on Trish."

"This is the double-cross jade signet ring, and it's introductory-priced at just one hundred and seventy-nine dollars."

"Camera One, go in for an extreme closeup."

"Measuring it for you, it's almost a quarter of an inch across . . . and almost half an inch long."

"Camera Two, we're taking that medium shot again. Trish, gimme some more ring-talk."

Trish rested her elbows on the glossy black table in front of her and clasped her long fingers together. "Gold is a material of the material world. Jade is a material of the spiritual world. And that's what we have here tonight, this absolutely stunning ring that joins two important worlds together. So whether . . ."

"Great, Trish. Camera One, we're going extreme closeup again—move frame right."

". . . you're wearing jeans or you're all dressed up, this ring can take you anywhere. It can make you feel good about yourself, because you know that you're really treating yourself to something special, and that is so important these days. Because honestly, who is not under pressure? I mean, we all see the news."

"Camera Two, going medium—standby."

"And if you think about it, one seventy-nine is a very reasonable price when you consider how much this ring can offer you in terms of different looks. And of course, there's the . . ."

"Wow, she's really *on* tonight. I mean for somebody who was just told two hours ago that she had to fill in for Peggy Jean, she's like, amazing," Rob commented to the room, then wiped his pizza-mouth on the back of his hand.

". . . spiritual importance, because as we all know, angels and the life *beyond* are all very important fashion trends. Now, let's take a caller. Millie from San Francisco, welcome to Sellevision. Do you love this ring?"

"Oh yes, Trish. It's beautiful. And I love what you were saying about angels, because I collect angels and love anything that has something to do with them."

"That's terrific, Millie. And this ring really does have a certain *something* about it." Trish paused, stroking the jade stone of the ring. "It's like wearing it, you can feel there's something almost mystical about it, that it has an internal power."

"Yeah, Trish, go, go go. We're getting really limited, less than two hundred, so wind this up and let's get on to the next thing."

"Oh, my. I can't wait to receive this ring. I mean, I can almost feel that energy you're talking about over the television set, like there really is . . ."

Trish interrupted Millie from San Francisco. "I'm sorry Millie, but I'm going to have to say good-bye. The ring is just about sold out." Then, holding up a delicate pearl ring, Trish asked, "Think pearls are just for grandmothers? Think again! I'm going to show you a brand-new pearl ring that's going to change the way you think about pearls and glamour in general."

eleven

Max took the elevator to the seventeenth floor reception of Goodby Silverstein Grey advertising and told the receptionist that he was there for a voice-over audition.

"And whom shall I call to inform that you're here?" she asked pleasantly.

"Buzz Davidson."

"Certainly, have a seat and I'll inform Mr. Davidson of your arrival."

Max walked over to one of the many black leather Knoll chairs and took a seat. The wall of floor-to-ceiling windows to his left presented a spectacular view of the Hudson River and uptown. The raw, unfinished ceiling with exposed pipes and electrical cables was a nice juxtaposition to the clean, highly polished wood floors. The place reeked of money. This made Max feel hopeful. Television commercials played silently on a large HDTV screen directly across from him. As he stared at the commercials, he thought back to his most recent conversation with Laurie.

"Well, he said that he felt you just really didn't understand modern news, that you didn't know how to 'work' a story."

"Great. I don't know how to 'work' a story, whatever the hell *that* means. So anything else? Did you get a hold of anybody at KRON in San Francisco?"

"I did, they're only interested in serious journalists. You know, it's the whole CNN, MSNBC thing. I mean, they've just made all the local stations panic. Now everybody needs a journalist. It's a shame because that eliminates a lot of really attractive, charismatic people."

"That's so unfair," Max agreed. "What happened with QVC? Did you call them?"

"Penis-thing is still too fresh. They said we could check back in a year."

"Home Shopping?"

"Same story."

"This is just awful, Laurie. I'm getting really depressed."

"Look, Max. Commercial voice-over work pays a lot of money. We'll get you some jobs, the money will start coming in, and pretty soon you'll forget you were ever on Sellevision."

"You think?" Max said, wanting to believe her.

"Of course. Ad agencies are just filthy rich. And they don't care about controversy—in fact, they love it. Ad people are morally bankrupt. You'll see."

"Yeah, but . . ."

"Sweetie, I've got to run, I have a gazillion messages I have to return. Listen to me: You've only had two interviews so far. There are a lot of ad agencies in New York and I have plenty of cable shows to contact, so perk up."

The conversation had lifted his spirits. And she was right, he had only been on two interviews. Why not do some advertising voice-over work until he could get back on television?

A tall, handsome man that Max pegged at about forty-five walked toward him across the expansive lobby. As the man walked, he gave Max a smile. Then he stuck his hand down the front of his pants, tucking in his shirt and, Max noticed, *adjust-*

ing himself. He then took that same hand out of his pants and extended it for Max to shake.

"Max Andrews? I'm Buzz Davidson, nice to meet you."

"Nice to meet you, too." Max found the man attractive, for an older man. He had all his hair, and a really good body for someone his age. The man was wearing tan slacks and a pink-and-white striped shirt. He looked like somebody who grew up sailing and might have gone to school with one of the older Kennedys.

Buzz led Max back to the elevator banks.

"My agent told me you're auditioning for some art gallery or something?" Max said.

The elevator arrived with a pleasant *bling* and the men stepped inside. Buzz pressed *fifteen.* "That's right, we just won a new account. It's small but there's a chance to do some really good work, maybe win some awards."

"Great, that's great. Congratulations."

As he followed Buzz through a maze of hallways, Max looked at all the framed print advertisements on the wall, many of them familiar. *It must be cool to be in advertising,* he thought. *Just sitting around all day thinking up fun ideas.* "Wow, you guys did that?" Max asked, pointing to one of the ads. The photograph featured a tree with melting pats of butter instead of leaves.

Buzz paused. "We sure did. TreeOla's a great product. Ever try it?"

Max nodded. "Yeah, it's the best." He leaned forward and read the copy beneath the butter tree. "Only TreeOla is made from the natural goodness of trees. Cholesterol-free TreeOla tastes remarkably like your favorite margarine but without the aftertaste of guilt. Plus, it may help prevent cold sores. Tree-Ola. Another breakthrough from the maker of America's favorite retrovirus inhibitor."

"Clients these days believe in diversification," Buzz commented as they walked down the hall.

Max thought, that's all voice-over work is. Diversification. He smiled, pleased with his evolution as a professional.

Then Buzz gave Max a look. *The* look. And Max smiled back at him, giving him The Look in return. Hey, he was dealing with ad people now, and business is business.

Buzz led Max into a professional recording studio. The main room had all sorts of technical equipment, huge speakers and padded walls. A long table divided the room. On one side of the table was all the recording equipment and a place for the audio engineer to sit, on the other a row of ergonomically designed chairs for the ad people. On the table itself, telephones in front of each chair, pads of paper, each with a pen rested on top. On the far wall was a window, through which was another room, also padded, but furnished with only a microphone and a music stand.

Buzz handed Max a script and motioned for him to walk through a set of double doors into the soundproof recording booth. Max stepped into the room, approached the microphone and grabbed the earphones, which were slung over the music stand. He looked out the window at Buzz.

Buzz nodded and Max put the earphones on. He rested the script on the music stand in front of him. A technician entered the main room, settled into his chair, and pressed a button. Max then heard the man's voice in his headphones.

This is just like recording a voice-over at Sellevision, he thought.

"Hi, Max, I'm Donny. Listen, I need to adjust the sound levels, so just speak into the microphone for me."

"What should I say?"

"It doesn't matter, anything. Tell us about the last person you fucked," he laughed.

"Okay, um, testing, testing, one, two, three . . . testing, one, two . . ."

"That's fine," the engineer cut him off. "We're all set, ready whenever you are."

Then he heard Buzz's voice in his earphones. "Okay, Max. Hi, it's me. Listen, just read through the script, real natural—not too announcer-y. Make it very conversational, but also give it a slightly *important* edge, like this is really a big deal, very high class. But don't make it snotty. Also, we're talking to very well educated people here, with a lot of money, so don't make it *too* important."

Max nodded his head, pretended to understand.

The engineer said, "And this is take one."

Max cleared his throat and was shocked by how loud and detailed it sounded in his earphones. He took a deep breath and let it out, then he read.

"His name was Pogo. And he was the Killer Clown. Executed for his heinous sex and torture crimes, John Wayne Gacy was himself tortured—a tortured artist. Now the Weidenbacher gallery is pleased to announce the exclusive world premier of his work—Gacy: The Death Row Retrospective. Join us next Friday at the Weidenbacher gallery for a champagne debut. Prices for the artist's most infamous works begin at just ten thousand dollars. Gacy: The Death Row Retrospective, only at the Weidenbacher gallery. Where art is brought to life."

Max looked out the window, saw Buzz on the phone. He waited.

The engineer's voice filled his headphones. "Nice, Max. That was good. Hold on a sec while I get Buzz." He turned, said something, and Buzz looked up from the phone.

Then the engineer told Max, "Okay, that was great, you can come out now."

That's it? thought Max.

When he entered the main room, Buzz hung up the phone.

"Thanks for stopping by, that was great." Then, standing, he said, "Here, let me walk you back to the elevators."

As they walked through the twisting hallways, Max asked, "So was I okay? I mean, is that it?"

"You were fine, absolutely. We've got a lot of people to audition, so it's gonna be a crazy day."

Max stopped. "No, I'm serious. I mean, I didn't get the job, did I?"

Buzz stopped, looked at Max. "The thing is, your voice is a little too—how should I put this—*soft* for this spot. For something else, I'm sure it's right. But it's not right for this. Sorry, but that's the truth."

They reached the elevators and Buzz pressed the down button. Then Buzz looked at Max. "Personally, I like your voice. A lot. It's just that, well, you know how clients are."

Max hid his disappointment and smiled. "Sure, no problem," he said. And wondered, *Soft?*

"But I wouldn't mind getting together again, maybe talking about some other projects, if you know what I mean. You like sushi?" he asked, and then raised one eyebrow. "Or do you prefer beef?" Buzz was actually leering.

The elevator arrived and Max stepped into it, pressed L and said, "Actually, I'm a vegetarian."

No matter how desperate, he was not going to fuck his way into a voice-over.

After the family came home from church, Peggy Jean's husband went directly into his office to work. The boys headed upstairs to their rooms and Peggy Jean took two Valium. The funny thing about Valium was that sometimes it worked, and sometimes she had to take two. Lately, it seemed she always had to take *at least* two.

That day's sermon had been especially meaningful to her, and she thought about what Father Quigley had said as she unloaded the dishwasher.

Family is what gives us strength. Sometimes we may feel the world has turned against us. Perhaps our health fails. Or perhaps we are struggling financially. But it is with our family that we can find strength and comfort.

How true, Peggy Jean thought as she placed a spatula in a drawer. Without her own family, how would she ever have coped with all the stress from work? The thought of having to face that Zoe monster, her own hormonal problems, and then that awful rat on her own was just beyond comprehension. Thank God she had a close and loving family to turn to. And thank God she had her faith.

Taking the silverware basket to the drawer, she placed the forks, knives, and spoons in their proper places, admiring how spotless each piece looked. "And yet with all of this—a family, a demanding career, and a stalker—I still have time to be a good homemaker." She said this out loud, because it felt good to say it out loud.

Then at the bottom of the silverware basket, she saw something strange and dangerous: a pocket knife, opened. Her oldest boy's pocketknife. Carefully removing the knife from the basket, she folded the blade back into the handle. Kids.

"Sweetheart," she said, leaning her head into Ricky's doorway.

"What?" he answered, not looking up from the computer.

She walked over to his desk and set the knife down next to his keyboard. "I found this in the dishwasher."

He glanced at the knife, then back to the computer. "I put it there. It got dirty."

"Dirty?" she said.

He looked up at her. "Yeah, remember we had to carve Virgin Marys for bible study? It got pine sap all over it."

Peggy Jean was charmed by the mere thought of such a thing. "I'd love to see your Virgin Mary."

"It's not done yet."

Peggy Jean noticed a wad of Silly Putty on the desk and picked it up. "You know, I used to love Silly Putty, too. Some things never change. Although mine wasn't this ugly gray color, it was fleshtone."

"It's not Silly Putty, it's plastic explosive," he told her, tapping on the keyboard.

"Don't even joke about such a thing," she said, placing the Silly Putty back on the desk. "Did you enjoy the sermon today?"

"Very much."

"Yes, I did thoo."

He looked at her, puzzled.

"*Too*, I mean, I did *too*. Goodness, sometimes these pills the doctor prescribed for my health make my speech a little futhy—err, *fuzzy*."

He continued to stare at her.

She started to lean in and give his head a little kiss, but then stopped herself. She'd pestered him enough while he was busy with his school work.

On the way down the stairs, she almost tripped. Then she thought maybe she had better have a little something to even her out, just sort of cut the Valium. Maybe a small glass of something. Because she didn't want to take a chance that she might slur that evening on air.

"Howard, do you have a moment?"

"Of course, Trish. Please, come in and make yourself comfortable."

Trish took a seat on the sofa and Howard came around from behind his desk and sat in the chair directly across from her, crossed his legs, and smiled. "What's on your mind?"

Trish clasped her hands and placed them on her lap. "I feel a little awkward. I mean it's really not my business, but I'm just a little concerned."

"What's the matter, Trish? Please speak freely. I promise you nothing you say will leave this room."

"Thanks, Howard, I really appreciate that. Like I said, I'm a little uncomfortable mentioning this, but she's my friend—as well as my cohost—so I feel like I have to say something."

Howard uncrossed his legs and leaned slightly forward.

"It's Peggy Jean. I'm a little worried about her."

A look of surprise crossed Howard's face. "Peggy Jean? Why?"

"Well, that's just it, I don't know exactly. But something doesn't seem right—she seems a little off, you know? Maybe it's just me, maybe I'm too close to her, but I've noticed the last couple times she's been on air, she seems almost nervous, a little . . . choppy."

Peggy Jean, nervous? Choppy? It seemed an impossible notion. Peggy Jean had been with Sellevision for ten years. Next to Bebe, she was the most senior host. If anything, Peggy Jean could be a little *too* polished. But he had to admit, he didn't have a close, personal relationship with her. And he hadn't seen her on air recently.

"Last night when she was on, she was slurring."

"Slurring?" he repeated, his voice lower.

"And she had a problem with the ruler, finding the right end of it to measure a necklace."

"Go on."

"Well, I've noticed that she takes a lot of pills. She says they're vitamins, but I don't know."

Howard developed a twitch near his eye. "Is this about the rat? Or is there something going on in her personal life? Is her marriage okay? Her kids?"

"As far as I know, everything's fine in her personal life. But the rat is just the latest thing. She's been getting some creepy letters from somebody—she feels that she's being stalked."

This was not a good thing. The last thing he needed was to lose another host.

"There's another thing, Howard," Trish leaned in. "She's been eating Tic Tacs like crazy, but you can still smell the alcohol on her breath. Even in the morning."

"Oh my God." Howard wiped his hand across his forehead. "Do you think I should say something to her?"

Trish waved her hands in front of her. "Oh, absolutely not, no. *Please*. I just think, well, let's see what happens. Maybe you could cut her hours down, a hair. I mean, to give her a little extra space. I wouldn't mind taking them on. I covered for her that day she got the rat."

Howard smiled at her. "That was very good of you on such short notice, by the way—thanks. And that's an excellent idea, I'll do that. Not such a cut that she worries, just enough so that she has a chance to spend more time with her family."

Trish stood to leave and Howard added, "Please, keep an eye out, let me know if there are any developments. Hopefully, whatever it is will pass."

She made a point to touch Howard's arm, to thank him for his understanding. And she made a point to do this while standing very close to him.

twelve

"I thought you'd be happy. I thought . . . well, I just thought this is what you wanted," Howard told Leigh. She sat in the chair across from the desk, legs crossed. Her bright red skirt and jacket contrasted sharply with her mood.

"I am happy, Howard, it's great," she said, rolling her eyes. "I mean I'd be lying if I told you that I'm not excited about having my own jewelry showcase, it's just that I wish things between us could be moving along as fast as my career."

"Sweetheart, we've talked about this again and again—it's just a matter of time. I'm just waiting until the right . . . moment."

"But, Howard, you've been waiting for the right moment for months. I feel like my life is on hold. I really hate it."

Leigh uncrossed her legs, then crossed them again. She felt edgy, uncomfortable. She had been having a hard time sleeping lately, and she'd lost her appetite. A good thing, she supposed, because she'd lost the four pounds that had plagued her since last Christmas.

"Tell me something, Howard," she said, looking into his eyes. "Is that why you're giving me so many more hours? Is this some sort of tactic to keep me occupied?"

Leigh had learned of her jewelry showcase from Trish, who had stopped by to congratulate her. Leigh had been genuinely shocked. Jewelry showcases normally went to the blond women, except for Bebe.

Howard gave her a soft smile, his eyes compassionate. "Of course not, Leigh. Our professional relationship is just that—strictly professional. Viewers love you, that's the bottom line. It makes sense that you should pick up some of Peggy Jean's hours. You deserve them."

"Why me? Why not Trish?

"Trish has some, you have some. You have a little more, because I believe you deserve them."

"Yeah, but I don't deserve you, right?"

"Oh, Leigh, I wish you'd stop doing this to yourself. To us."

Yeah, Leigh thought, *that makes two of us.*

Glancing at her watch and seeing that she had less than an hour before going on air, Leigh stood. "Well, I have to get going."

"You okay?"

"Yeah, I'm okay. I'm fine. I'm always fine."

Howard smiled. "That's my girl."

For the next three hours, Leigh smiled, laughed, and spoke with viewers who called in. She measured the diameter of white-gold panther-link bracelets and fingered bold-hoop earrings. She informed viewers when an item sold out, and asked viewers to stay tuned for the next show, Candle Creations. To the twenty-four million viewers who tune into Sellevision at any given moment, Leigh simply appeared to be a happy, attractive young woman who enjoyed her job as a host for America's premier retail broadcasting network.

One would never guess just by looking at her that inside, her heart was being ripped in half.

After her show, Leigh stepped into her car and made the thirty-minute drive home to her apartment. By the time she'd taken off her work clothes and slipped into a pair of sweats and an oversized T-shirt, it was almost 8:30 P.M. Opening her freezer, she saw a selection of Lean Cuisine frozen entrées and a couple of veggie burgers. Either choice would have been the perfect compliment to an evening spent on the sofa, alone, watching the episode of last week's *Ally McBeal* that she had recorded. Of course, she *should* have been getting ready to meet her boyfriend—or better yet, fiancé—for a romantic dinner somewhere. Hell, even a pizza somewhere. But no, her boyfriend happened to be her boss. And he happened to be married. And the reason he was her boyfriend despite these facts was sitting on her bedside table, every other page dog-eared: *Women Who Love Selfish Bastards.*

"I'm not gonna do this to myself," she said, closing the freezer door and walking over to the stack of take-out menus she kept in a neat pile next to the phone. "If I'm going to be pathetic, at least I'm going to be pathetic over a carton of take-out butterfly shrimp."

Then she thought, *I should call Max. He could come over and we could be pathetic together. I could tell him what's going on.* After all, they had said they wanted to keep in touch.

"Hi, Max, it's Leigh."

"Hey, Leigh. How's it going?"

"Awful. You?"

"I just bought a box of razor blades."

"That bad, huh?"

"Oh, I don't know, let's see: So far, I've managed to blow an E-Z Shop interview, a news anchor interview, and an interview I had yesterday for E!, not to mention all the voice-over auditions."

"Oh, Max, I'm so sorry. What does your agent say?"

"Well, when I reach her, she tries to tell me it's okay. But I'm getting a little freaked out because I'm running out of money and the thing is, it's really tough. I mean, being a Sellevision host is just such a weird, specific thing that you can't just run over and start doing the news on CNN. I don't know. It's too depressing to talk about."

"I have an idea," Leigh said, fingering a menu. "Why don't you drive over here to my place and we'll have some Chinese or something? I'll run over right now and pick it up."

Max thought, *There's a new and interesting idea: human contact.* "Yeah, that sounds like a good idea, thanks. Should I bring anything?"

"Just that box of razor blades."

After hanging up, Leigh phoned Ming Ling's and placed her take-out order. She ordered the butterfly shrimp, spring rolls, and sautéed eggplant with peanuts and hot peppers. She grabbed her jacket, purse, and keys and headed out the door. There was another Chinese restaurant closer to her apartment, but Ming Ling's was one of the better Chinese places in the area, and she would still be back before Max got there.

As she drove, Leigh told herself that she should be happy about her new, expanded role on Sellevision. She told herself that it was only a matter of time before Howard left his wife and they could begin their own life together. She told herself that her life was really not so bad, that it could be a lot worse.

On the radio was the new single by Celine Dion, *I Can't Believe We're Together Again*, from *Titanic II*. Leigh sang along, and by the time she pulled into Ming Ling's parking lot, she was actually feeling a little better.

That is, until she stepped out of the car and happened to glance through the window. Howard was sitting at a table with his wife. She looked even prettier than she did in the photo on his desk. And here they were, laughing, holding hands across the table, with what looked like a Peking duck between them.

For a moment, she just stood there, watching. Then she got in her car and drove straight back to her apartment.

About twenty minutes after she was home, Max arrived. He had a bottle of wine with him. She explained that there had been a slight change of plans. That they would be having pizza and ice cream instead.

Then she told him everything.

And by the end of the night, and one and a half bottles of wine later, the two were sitting on the floor, leaning against Leigh's sofa, and laughing so hard that both of them were clutching their stomachs.

A good plan can do that to a person.

Today's Super Value, a combination desktop cigar humidor and telephone, had sold out and been replaced with a Just for Now Value, a revolving, battery-operated tie rack. Six times a year, Sellevision dedicated twenty-three hours to Gifts for Guys.

After presenting the revolving tie-rack, moving on to a sixteen-piece socket wrench set, and ending her on-air appearance with a presentation of a pocket fishing rod called, questionably, the Pocket Rod, Peggy Jean Smythe exited the set and walked directly into her office.

She had one new E-mail.

To: PG_Smythe@Sellevision.com
Fr: Zoe@ProviderNet.com
Subject: Big Guy

I couldn't help but think how appropriate it is that you are hosting the grand finale of Gifts for Guys. You Big Guy, you.

Don't think your arm hair went unnoticed while you were demonstrating those socket wrenches.

Oh, did you like my gift?

Zoe

Peggy Jean took four Valium to stop the shaking. She had been off air not even ten minutes, and already an E-mail commenting on the show. Zoe was clearly obsessed.

She considered having a little bottle of something because her mouth was dry. She decided, *no*. She'd already had some *before* the show to even her out.

Then she glanced at her arms and saw the dusting of pale, almost pure white hairs. A dizzying amount of them, no matter how fair. *My own body is turning against me.* She took three small bottles of peach schnapps from her desk drawer.

It just didn't make any sense, none of it.

Peggy Jean: a leading figure of her church, a loving wife, the mother of three beautiful children and a top host with America's premier retail broadcasting network. She had once been Junior Miss San Antonio! She received fan mail on a constant basis asking her to reveal her hair coloring, makeup, and manicure secrets.

"I'm a good person. I sponsor two AIDS babies at St. Mercy. I even *held* one of them!" she cried to the computer screen. *"Just like Princess Diana!"*

This monstrous Zoe person was making Peggy Jean out to be some chromosomally damaged, testosterone-pumping beast. She was attacking the one thing Peggy Jean prided herself on: polished femininity.

As if dealing with a terrible medical condition wasn't bad enough, she had a stalker. But who? A dangerous stranger? An obsessed cohost? Trish? Leigh? Don? Adele? It could be any of them. More and more Peggy Jean was actually being affected by this mystery monster. She was edgy, anxious.

Just the other night when she was hosting a Crafter's Quilts show, she'd become dizzy gazing at the geometric pattern on one of the quilts, taken a step backward, and tripped on the edge of the rug, falling onto the floor, the quilt landing on top of her. And to make it worse, the camera had *zoomed* in on her.

It was the single most mortifying experience of her on-air life. It had been her own fault, because she had neglected to have a sip of something before the show to smooth out the Valium. But she wouldn't even have to take the little pills if it weren't for Zoe.

It was even affecting her marriage. The other night she had exploded at her husband when he suggested they try a *new position* during an increasingly rare moment of intimacy, that position being one with Peggy Jean on top, *where the man belonged*.

She had recoiled from him instantly, climbing out of bed and cursing, then locking herself in their bathroom where she turned the faucet on and sobbed, looking at her breasts in the mirror. And she couldn't help but think they looked just fine. Especially when she turned profile and lifted her arms above her head.

And yet what was she to do? If she dared write back, asking to be left alone, the Zoe person would only be fueled in her personal attack. Yet it seemed that the form letter was only serving to make the stalker angrier and angrier.

What she needed was advice from a Stalking Survivor. A celebrity, like herself, who could help her manage the situation before this Zoe person finally and completely deteriorated, sending Peggy Jean a letter bomb disguised as a pretty bouquet of flowers.

Surely Debby Boone had experienced a stalker. And the two *had* hit it off during Debby's recent appearance on Sellevision. In fact, they'd even exchanged personal phone numbers and promised to stay in touch.

Peggy Jean decided that although these were not the ideal circumstances under which to forge a friendship with the multi-platinum recording artist, she simply had no other choice but to call. After all, wasn't it quite possible that God had put Debby on Sellevision for a purpose much larger than simply introducing America to Dolls by Debby?

"Who's calling, please?" the voice on the other end of the phone asked.

"This is Peggy Jean Smythe. I'm a host with Sellevision and recently shared a show with Ms. Boone."

"One moment please." Peggy Jean found herself placed on hold, listening to a recording of Debby singing her legendary hit, "You Light Up My Life." It calmed her slightly.

"Peggy Jean?" the familiar voice said.

"Hi, Debby. I hope I'm not disturbing you."

"No, of course not. What an unexpected surprise!"

Oh, thank God, Peggy Jean thought. Then, as calmly as possible, she explained the situation to Debby, beginning with the first, seemingly innocent earlobe letter, all the way to the shocking on-air event, including the crucified rat and the recent, sinister *Cut Cut* note.

"Debby, I'm afraid it's getting out of hand and quite frankly, I have no one else to turn to."

thirteen

"There's nothing like a microorganism to bring two people together," Eliot said, carefully lowering the tray of chicken noodle soup and chamomile tea onto the plush comforter on Bebe's bed.

"Eliot, you're an idiot to be staying with me when I'm sick. A sweet idiot, but an idiot. You're going to catch my cold, and you know I can't cook."

"I'm not going to catch your cold. Besides, you can cook, I've seen the can opener."

"Very funny."

Bebe sipped the chicken soup that Eliot made from scratch the night before, occasionally removing a small piece of cartilage and discretely folding it into her napkin. As she stirred the soup to cool it, Eliot set a fresh box of tissues on the bedside table and glanced at the television. Yet another Amtrak had derailed, this time colliding with a bus of circus clowns.

"Poor clowns," Eliot sighed, shaking his head.

Bebe nodded. She sipped another spoonful. "The soup is lovely, thank you Eliot."

"You're most welcome." Then, "You know, we usually end up at my place. It seems I'm hardly ever over here."

"It's cramped here, that's why."

"It's because you've got so much stuff. I mean, what on earth do you need that wet-vac for?" He pointed to the corner, next to several Nieman-Marcus bags.

"In case I have a spill," she said.

"What about the drafting table in the living room?"

"Someday I might want to take up drawing, that's all."

He looked at the chair across from the bed and saw five boxes of shoes, but decided not to say anything.

"Did the mail arrive yet?" she asked.

"No, why, are you expecting something?"

"No, not really."

"Let's see what all your friends are doing this fine day." He reached across her chest for the remote control and aimed it at the TV.

"Hi, everybody, I'm Leigh Bushmoore. Welcome to Sellevision. I've got a great show for you tonight that I guarantee you are not going to want to miss. Stay tuned for Simulated Ruby Sensations, because I promise you, this is going to be one sensational show."

The prerecorded intro to the show played and Leigh took a sip of water from the bottle of Evian discreetly tucked under her chair.

She was wearing a deep-blue velvet dress, with a lower neckline than she would normally wear on the air. The dress, Howard's favorite, took on a rich, luscious sheen beneath the studio lights. Backstage, she blew some of the curl out of her hair so that it fell voluptuously across her shoulders. When she first entered the stage, one of the grips had whistled at her.

Because this was going to be her last night on Sellevision, she wanted it to be special. She already knew it would be memorable.

The first item Leigh was to present that evening was a choice of Simulated Ruby Pendants, each three carats. Emerald cut, pear shape, or trillion cut. All on an eighteen-inch fourteen-karat gold chain, included in the $39.79 price. The pendants had sold out on their last three appearances.

When the intro to her show was over, and Camera Two opened with a medium shot of Leigh sitting at the elegant black table, she smiled boldly into the camera and asked, "Ladies, how many of you would enjoy having a handsome man tell you how beautiful you look? Take you to dinner, gaze into your eyes, maybe even tell you how much he loves you?"

Amanda, Leigh's producer for that evening's show, urged her along. "Really nice opening, Leigh, but get to the item number ASAP so we can put the graphics up on the screen."

Leigh smiled and continued. "If you would like to have a man promise you the world, you're going to want to write this number down."

Inside the control room, Amanda shouted to one of the engineers, "Okay, she's giving the number, throw on the graphics."

A graphic box containing the item number for the pendants appeared on the lefthand side of the screen.

"His home phone number is 917-555-5555, and his name is Howard Toast. He's the head of broadcasting production here at Sellevision and I don't want him anymore, because I don't believe he really is going to divorce his wife. I think he's just fucking with both his wife and me and I'm tired of being both fucked and fucked over by Howard. Because I am through with selfish bastards!"

At first, nothing happened. Amanda simply stared at the monitor and remained motionless. Which gave Leigh the chance to continue.

"If you'd buy a simulated ruby, why not a simulated man? His phone number again is 917-555-5555."

Just then, Sellevision cut to a prerecorded promotion for

Adele Oswald Crawley's upcoming American Indian Pride Home Furnishings show.

And even though Amanda was screaming into Leigh's earpiece, Leigh didn't hear it, because she had already taken the earpiece off and thrown it out onto the set behind her, where it slid across the highly polished floor and bumped to a stop against the model's glossy left pump.

I t had been Howard himself who insisted that he and his wife watch that evening's Simulated Ruby Sensations show. Suzette had wanted them to go to the movies, but Howard had explained to her that it was important for him to see Leigh's performance as he had just given her many additional on-air hours, and he would very much like his wife's opinion on her presentation style.

So, moments before Leigh's show began, the two had sat side-by-side on their white sectional sofa. Because the sofa was upholstered in an exquisite raw silk, the couple had never even entertained the notion of Scotch-guarding it.

And that is why his blood would never be fully removed from the fabric.

Suzette had simply taken the closest available object and blindly swung it in her husband's direction. The closest available object had been a solid-brass coffee-table sculpture in the shape of a dolphin.

Swinging in Howard's general direction, the dolphin had made solid contact with the left side of his face, including his eye, cheek, nose, and lips.

Yet despite his needing thirty-two stitches at the emergency room, the biggest blow to Howard was actually delivered the following morning.

Leigh's improvised, forty-three-second appearance on Simulated Ruby Sensations had made not only *The Philadelphia Tri-*

bune, but also *USA Today*, *The New York Times*, and *The Washington Post*.

It was also a top news story on all the major networks, pushing the Barbra Streisand vice-presidential nomination scandal into third place.

He was phoned in his hotel room just after breakfast and terminated from Sellevision.

"Um, okay, um, hold on a sec," the twenty-three-year-old advertising copywriter told Max. "We're gonna listen to a playback."

Max was standing inside a small recording booth wearing earphones, a microphone inches from his mouth. On a music stand before him was a voice-over script for a Tender Tasties cat food radio commercial.

Sitting behind a long engineering console, the copywriter pushed a talk button that allowed him to communicate with Max through the thick glass. "Okay, here's what we need you to do. Just pick up the pace of everything, and try to give a smile to the word 'Tasties.' "

Max nodded.

"Also, when you say 'safe for all cats, even long-haired breeds,' don't make that sound so serious, just lighten it up a little bit."

Max nodded again, scribbling a note on his script.

"One last thing, 'not available in Florida' should be really fast. Just kind of throw it away."

"Okay," Max said, and cleared his throat.

The copywriter leaned back in his chair, took a sip of Diet Pepsi and said to the agency producer, "I think this guy's gonna work. He really seems to *get* the script. This is gonna be pretty cool."

The engineer pushed a button on his console and said,

"Tender Tasties, take twenty-four." He pointed at Max and mouthed the words, "You're on." Max again recited the advertising copy.

This was Max's fourteenth voice-over audition. So far, he hadn't landed a real spot. But so far, nobody had made him do more than three takes. Maybe this would be the break he needed.

"You just have to be patient, it's nothing personal. It's all about finding the right voice for the right product. Eventually you'll land something," Laurie had told him on the phone the other day.

"Yeah, but Laurie, what if it doesn't happen? I mean, if I can't even land an advertising job, what chance will I have of ever getting back on the air?"

"Just go to the audition and do your best."

After Max read the spot, he saw the copywriter beckoning him to come back into the main room. Max removed the earphones and walked through the two soundproof doors into the main room.

"Dude, that was great," the copywriter said. "Really great—you *rock*."

Relieved, Max smiled. "Yeah, I was okay?"

"Totally."

The producer slid a contract in front of Max and handed him a pen. Max would get paid $250 for his demo, and thousands of dollars if he was chosen. He filled out the contract, providing his name, address, and social security number, along with his agent's name and address.

"So, do you think it's gonna happen?" Max asked. "I mean, do you think it's really gonna air?"

"Gotta split, I'm already late for an edit, take care, man," the copywriter said as he got up from his chair and left the room.

The engineer tapped at his computer keyboard, removing breaths and pauses from Max's reading. The producer shrugged his shoulders. "I think it'll probably air, yeah. Of course you never know with these things until it's actually on the air, but I don't see why it wouldn't."

Max handed the contract and the pen back to the producer, extending his hand. "Great, well, thanks a lot, it was really nice working with you."

"Same here. Take care, Max."

"Okay then. Well, I'll see you around."

"Uh huh," the producer said, looking over the contract.

Once he was outside the ad agency, Max smiled broadly. *"Yes!"* he shouted, raising his fist in the air. His luck was finally turning, he could feel it. Standing on the corner of Third Avenue and Forty-sixth Street, Max closed his eyes for a moment, feeling the sun on his face. He exhaled deeply, a huge sense of relief filling him. As he walked toward Grand Central Station, Max could not help but imagine what his life might be like if he continued to get work as a voice-over talent. Regular trips into New York City, royalty checks, perhaps even a big, national television campaign—maybe for someone like Burger King or Kmart.

For the first time in weeks, Max felt excited, not depressed. As he walked, he repeated the ad copy he had just read: "New Tender Tasties, the first cat food that protects cats from fleas by working internally with the natural digestive process."

"I was pretty good," he admitted with a smile. "I really did okay."

As she sank down into the steaming hot bath, inhaling the soothing aroma of Mandarin Orange and Cedar, Peggy Jean smoothed the rich lather of Joyce's Choice Mid-Life Oasis Foaming Bath Purée over her arms, enjoying the luxury of the moment. For the first time in weeks, thanks to Debby Boone, Peggy Jean felt calm, centered, and *feminine*.

As it turned out, Debby had in fact been stalked. It was 1977, and "You Light Up My Life" was the number-one song in America for the ninth straight week. Debby's life was a dream. Until, as she told Peggy Jean, the nightmare began. Through a series of terrifying letters, her stalker made threats of unspeakable rudeness. Somehow, the stalker even obtained Debby's home telephone number and repeatedly called, swearing into the phone and singing a perverted version of Debby's hit single that confused and frightened Debby's broken-English-speaking maid. Poor Nellie quit, fearing the phone calls were from immigration officials who were going to tell her they had scored her test wrong and she was now going to be deported. "Alone and forced to answer the telephone myself, I suddenly smartened up," she told Peggy Jean. By involving the local authorities, and by virtue of her celebrity, the stalker's identity was revealed to be a harmless fourteen-year-old boy in Pasadena with a cleft palate and little parental supervision. And although she had never actually been in any real danger, Debby had learned a very important lesson. She would never again play the role of victim.

Facts were facts: The Smythes' home telephone number was unpublished. All articles of mail sent to Sellevision hosts were now X rayed. And Peggy Jean's address was known only to friends, coworkers and relatives. In truth, E-mail was the only way this Zoe person had of contacting Peggy Jean. And the odds were that in real life, this Zoe person was a confused, lonely, and sad individual who had, for whatever reason, focused on Peggy Jean. Debby even suggested that it could quite possibly be an adolescent girl who was suffering from a distorted self-image and was projecting her own fears and inse-curities onto the celebrity host. Debby had been quite clear with her instructions: "Ignore her E-mails, and eventually they'll go away." She had told Peggy Jean that "a stalker is like a fire; if you stop feeding it wood, the fire eventually dies out."

As for taking Zoe's personal comments to heart, Debby had laughed, saying, "Peggy Jean, if I listened to every terrible thing people have told me over the years, I would have just buried my head in the sand long ago."

Even the crucified rat didn't worry Debby. "It's time for a little tough love, Peggy. You're a celebrity; that's what happens. People have sent me used underwear, bags of fingernail clippings—you name it. What you do is you throw it away and move on."

How foolish Peggy Jean had been to let this confused person interfere not just with her own self-image, but even her marriage. Tonight, she had decided, she would show her husband not only how much she loved him, but how much she desired to please him, and how confident she was in her own femininity. Tonight, Peggy Jean would get on top.

Beginning to feel a bit like a prune from the long bath, Peggy Jean climbed from the tub and gently towel-dried, using a plush England's Rose Palace Collection bath sheet.

Wearing her pink robe and kitty-kitty slippers, she walked into the kitchen and mixed herself a gin and tonic, because she'd read that the quinine in tonic water was actually healthful. Just as she was about to take the health drink and the latest copy of *Soap Opera Digest* into the living room to catch up on her reading, the telephone rang.

"Hello?"

"Hi, Peggy, it's Tina from next door."

"Well hello, Tina. How are you?"

"Listen, Peggy. I don't want to alarm you or anything, but I'm looking out my window and it seems like one of the neighborhood kids has played a dirty little trick on you."

"A dirty little trick?" Peggy Jean asked, confused.

"Well, maybe you should just go and look for yourself."

"Tina, what is it, has somebody knocked over the mailbox or something?"

"Not exactly—look, Peggy Jean, I really think you should just open your front door and take a look."

"Well, all right, but I can't imagine any of the boys' friends playing a prank. But I'll go see for myself. Thanks for letting me know."

Peggy Jean hung up the phone and padded across the mint-green wall-to-wall carpeting in the living room, sipping her beverage. She paused to straighten one of the white rococo arm chairs. What on earth had Tina been talking about? The kids in *this* neighborhood were good kids. That Mexican family moved away months ago.

Peggy Jean opened the front door and looked outside.

Then she screamed, slammed the door shut, and called 911.

"That's fantastic, Max. I mean it, congratulations."

"Well, it's not official yet. But I have a really good feeling about it, you know?"

Leigh took a sip from her iced tea, then lowered her head. "Shit, I think it's a reporter. Don't turn around."

They had gone to the darkest, most unhip place they could find for lunch, but even here, she wasn't safe from the tabloids. Leigh seemed a little strung out by the whole thing, but Max found it kind of exciting.

She peeked up, surveyed, then raised her head. "False alarm."

"I can't even imagine what it's been like for you."

"I'll tell you how it's been. It's been worth it." She gave Max a kick under the table. "I feel so much better now, it's amazing. I mean, I never thought I was a vengeful person, but you really made me feel I could be."

Max laughed. "So this is all my fault now?"

"It was your idea," Leigh teased.

"Yeah, but you actually did it."

"God, what kind of monster have I created?" she asked, taking another sip from her iced tea. "I mean, you would not believe the amount of people calling me, the talk shows, the magazines, it's fucking insane. I had no idea it would have had such an effect. I was on the Internet last night, and there are all these sites about it, talking about how many selfish bastards there are out there." She raised her chin in the air. "I've become something of a modern feminist icon."

He dipped his fingers in his water and flicked them at her face.

She laughed, wiping her chin. "You'll become this big celebrity voice-over and I'll have my own little woman's show on CNN or something. What a riot."

"So when are you going to write a tell-all book?" he teased.

The waiter set the check down on the table, and she snatched it up before Max had a chance. "Don't joke, five New York literary agents have already called me."

"You're kidding," he said, wondering what he could ever do that would draw so much attention.

She placed a $20 bill on top of the check, and then set the salt shaker on top as a paperweight. "Thanks for coming out today. I really needed to be around somebody who wasn't holding a camera or microphone."

They stood up from the table and walked through the restaurant, each taking a mint from the dish beside the cash register on their way out the door and into the unknown.

Sitting at her desk, Bebe opened her latest American Express bill. A mistake, it seemed, had been made. It showed the amount due as $19,287.64. How, she wondered, was that possible? What had she purchased in the past month besides a few basics from the catalogs and a couple of early Christmas presents? She spread out all seven pages of the itemized bill on the desk. Nothing unusual: shoes, sheets and such, hair products, projection TV, restaurant charges, etc.

Oh. She had forgotten about the bronze gong from eBay. But of course, that was really more of an investment.

Still, the amount due on her American Express card was, in fact, correct. It seemed clear that she was on the verge of having a shopping problem.

She'd always been a shopper. When she was a girl and feeling a little blue, her mother would say, "Let's go shop 'til we drop." Shopping was her form of therapy, a relaxing thing to do.

It seemed obvious to Bebe that she needed to remedy the situation, curb her spending. So she put away the bill and logged onto Amazon.com to look for a book on the subject. She did a search and found *ShoppingStoppers: The Breakthrough Best-seller that Can Help You Curb Your Compulsive Shopping*. She clicked on it. The book jacket appeared on her screen. Beneath the book jacket the text said, "Customers who bought this book also bought . . ." and then listed seven other titles. So Bebe purchased them all, along with a book about investing in Chinese artifacts. She logged off feeling tremendous relief.

fourteen

"I don't know what to tell you, Max. I can't create a job for you
out of thin air."

Slumping down into the couch, Max pressed, "Are you *sure*
Discovery Channel has nothing? Did you actually *talk* to
Radio 102?"

"Yes, Max, I'm sure and I did. The programming director at
Discovery was familiar with the penis incident, and he—"

"Jeez," Max interrupted, "do you have to keep calling it
that?"

"I'm sorry. Okay, anyway, he knows why you were terminated from Sellevision and he's just uncomfortable becoming
involved with the situation."

Max pounded his fist on his thigh repeatedly. "Well, what
about Radio 102?"

"They feel—and this was said to me in the strictest of confi-
dence—that they already have a sufficient gay male presence on
the air. They're looking for either an Asian or a lesbian."

"A radio station doesn't want me? *Radio?* God, well, what
about something else?"

"Look, Max, so far I've been able to get you an interview,

even an *audition* for the news anchor spot. That was a no-go. We tried the other shopping channels—nada. And that thing with E! I've run out of advertising agencies to contact for voice-over work."

"I still should have gotten that cat food thing."

"Well, that wasn't your fault and you know it. They didn't get FDA approval. Or maybe it's PETA approval. Whatever. It's just bad luck."

"So what are you suggesting I do? What are you saying?"

"Well, didn't you tell me you had a possible lead on Donny Osmond's new show?"

"Donny Osmond? What are you talking about Laurie? I said *Denny's*. I said I didn't want to end up a waiter at *Denny's*. Jesus."

"Oh. Okay, that's right, I'm sorry."

"Well . . . ?"

"Well, Max, I've run out of options as far as what I can do for you as an agent. I think it's probably the best use of our time if we part ways."

"Excuse me?" Max said, running his fingers through his hair, changing the phone to the other ear.

"Well, I just don't feel that I have any options left, and I need to focus on my other clients."

"But you can't just—you said . . ."

"Listen, sweetie, I've got to run now. I've got Lou Ferrigno's publicist on the other line. Keep in touch. I'll be thinking of you."

Max hung up and sat for a moment, absorbing the reality of the situation. Without an agent, there would be no chance of work. Now he wouldn't even be able to *fail* auditions for voice-overs because there would be no more auditions.

Running down his list of options, Max realized just how dire the situation really was. There just wasn't a whole hell of a lot that a junior college drop-out, Barbizon School of Modeling graduate, and former Sellevision host was qualified to do. God, why *hadn't* he just borrowed Miguel's underwear?

At 33, Max was too old to return to his modeling career, which had never taken off anyway (unless you counted the JC Penney men's briefs ad that appeared in a few newspaper circulars more than twelve years ago.)

But he *belonged* in front of the camera. He had a certain *something* that *worked* on air. Well, until it fell out.

Maybe he wasn't thinking big enough. Why couldn't he be the next Greg Kinnear? Hell, he was as good looking and funny as that guy. And look what happened to him—from *Talk Soup* host to three-time Oscar winner.

Max decided to drive over to South Street and pick up a copy of *Backstage* magazine. Maybe he'd even pick up some forbidden Kentucky Fried Chicken on the way home. As he gathered his keys and wallet then put on his leather bomber jacket, Max felt a small sense of hope and excitement.

Until he realized the hope and excitement wasn't really about finding a job in *Backstage*, but about the Kentucky Fried Chicken. And the thought that such a simple pleasure could actually make him happy made him depressed, because there was no one around to appreciate the fact that Max appreciated the small things in life.

Peggy Jean sat on a chair in the living room shaking uncontrollably as a policewoman sat on the sofa across from her with a pen and pad, asking questions. Blue and red lights from the cruiser outside flashed across the walls, making the entire scene feel like something out of that terrible show her husband insisted on watching, *COPS*.

"I told you, I told you everything I can think of, *oh my God, she's going to kill me—she's going to hurt my babies*." Peggy Jean wept, long streaks of black eyeliner staining her cheeks.

Sitting in the chair next to Peggy Jean's, Tina placed her hand on her friend and neighbor's arm. "She's only trying to help. Why don't you go through it again, maybe you'll remember something new."

Sniffling and thanking the officer for the tissue she was handed, Peggy Jean recounted the entire story, just like she had told it to Debby Boone, right up to the point where she opened the front door and saw what she saw.

What Peggy Jean saw had, at first glance, looked like hundreds and hundreds of yellow flowers had suddenly bloomed throughout her yard. But then she saw that they were not flowers, but rather plastic disposable razors with yellow handles. And they were everywhere—blanketing the grass, the brick walkway, sprinkled across the hedges beneath the living room window—everywhere. Hundreds upon hundreds of disposable razors, their sharp blades gleaming.

It was only after the police arrived that Peggy Jean saw the words *hairy* and *bitch* and *cut cut* sprayed across the front of her home with what the detectives tentatively said was Nair hair-removal foam. (But to make absolutely certain, laboratory tests would need to be performed.)

"No fingerprints so far, not one," a police officer said as he passed through the living room to continue with the investigation outside.

"She knows where I live, she's been to my home—I've got to call Debby Boone." Peggy Jean's central nervous system was collapsing. She felt at once overheated and freezing cold. She could not stop shaking and perspiring. The seven Valium she had taken immediately after calling 911 had done nothing. Neither had the schnapps. Her husband wouldn't be home for another hour, and the boys were with him.

"What exactly is Debby Boone's involvement with this crime? Are you saying you think she might be somehow connected to it?" the officer asked, pen and notebook poised.

"Yes, yes, Debby . . . I need Debby . . ." Peggy Jean was unable to focus her eyes on anything except the shiny silver badge on the officer's uniform. She thought about taking out a ruler and measuring it.

"So, Debby Boone—you're telling me that the singer Debby Boone—you're saying that you believe she has something to do with this?"

"What?" Peggy Jean snapped out of her hypnotic gaze. "What? No, no, Debby Boone's not involved with this, are you crazy? This is Zoe, I told you, it's a crazy woman named Zoe. Debby is a friend, she was helping to calm me down."

The officer and Tina exchanged a glance. "Ms. Smythe, I know that this is a very traumatic event and that you're frightened and confused, but I'm gonna have to ask you to please, for your own sake, try and focus."

"What?" Peggy Jean asked vaguely.

Tina leaned over. "Peggy Jean, you've got to pull yourself together. This lady is trying to help you."

Shaking the fuzz out of her head, Peggy Jean regained her composure. "I apologize, I'm back, I'm here."

The officer continued with her questioning and Peggy Jean did her best to answer and be helpful. But inside, she felt a dreadful sense of doom.

After two and a half hours, the police left without any fingerprints, suspects, or leads. As far as they were concerned, all that could be done was to wait and see. And hope that if the stalker struck again, he or she would make some sort of identifying mistake.

"Listen, Peggy, I've got to run home real quick. My tuna casserole must be in flames by now."

"No, that's okay, I'll be okay, you go . . . you go . . . and . . . did you sprinkle crushed potato chips on top like I told you to?"

"Yes, I bought a bag of Lay's and then crushed 'em all up."

Peggy Jean looked at Tina and yet also through her. "Oh,

that's good. The potato chips are a very nice touch. You know, a fan sent me the recipe." Peggy Jean brought a hand up to her forehead. "Or did I get it from a magazine? I can't remember, Tina. I just can't remember," she cried.

Alone in her home once more, Peggy Jean shuffled over to a cupboard in the kitchen and pulled out a box of Saltines. She opened it and removed the emergency bottle of potato vodka. Then she reached in her bathrobe pocket for the Valium. "Hold my hand, Jesus," she mumbled as she downed the pills.

Eating a cold, leftover drumstick for breakfast while watching the *Today* show and hoping that some of Katie Couric's enthusiasm passed through the television into him, Max told himself not to panic, at least not until *Donny and Marie* came on.

Max's fantasy of perhaps becoming the next Greg Kinnear evaporated the night before last while he was reading the classified ads in *Backstage* and working his way through a sixteen-piece bucket of Kentucky Fried Chicken. Without membership in either SAG or AFTRA, and with no TV commercial credits, no summer-stock theater experience, and no knowledge of show tunes, it seemed to Max that his future was uncertain at best. His future was bordering on iffy.

As a very desperate last resort, Max decided that he could probably secure a retail sales position with Macy's—though that would mean stepping foot, on a daily basis, inside the Woodlands Mall. He felt fairly confident that given his retail broadcasting experience, he could probably start out immediately in the lucrative audio/visual department or perhaps men's furnishings, as opposed to working his way up from, say, cashier. But until eviction and starvation forced him, he would not entertain this scenario.

Tossing the drumstick bone in the trash, Max grabbed a Diet Coke from the refrigerator and settled into the couch, gripping

the remote control. Certainly he could spend his days of unemployed limbo more productively: paint the bathroom, do squats
at the gym, maybe even build a terrarium. But why? His
depression was now his pet, a pet that required constant feeding, daytime television being the food of choice.

The instant Marie's maniacally perky face popped onto the
screen, Max switched to MTV. *Road Rules IV* was on. But the
adventurous twentysomethings with their whole lives and
careers ahead of them, parasailing off the coast of Bali, were
simply too grim to watch, so he flipped over to the Food Channel. *One Fat Lady* was making a cake out of bacon and ground
pork. He went to CNN and for a few minutes watched live
footage of children fleeing a high school, as usual. Switching to
Sellevision he saw Trish Mission hosting Jewelry of Faith, a
show that normally belonged to Peggy Jean.

The Jewelry of Faith set was pale blue. Behind Trish a giant
cross was projected onto the wall, a cross made of light. Phil,
the lead set designer and the most sarcastic queen Max had ever
known, probably dreamed up the whole cross made of light
thing while he was sitting in a bar watching beefy go-go boys
with shaved chests and scars from their laser tattoo removals.

Max hit the remote again. The History Channel was doing
something on Nazi Germany, the Discovery Channel had a
winking zebra vulva, Comedy Central featured a fire-eating
dog, and HBO was playing *Titanic II*, yet again. *It's all a wasteland*, he thought, *but I belong in that wasteland.* He switched back
to the Discovery Channel and the zebra vulva was still winking.

Max got up off the sofa and went into the kitchen to stare at
the phone. After spending five minutes psychically directing his
agent to unditch him and call with a job offer from *20/20*, Max
tossed the empty Diet Coke can into the trash, ignoring the
city's recycling ordinance. *Outcasts make their own rules.*

He made his way back to the couch and the remote control.
Zap, zap, zap, zap, zap—until he saw Leeza Gibbons. On stage

was a handsome blond guy wearing jeans and a sweatshirt, sleeves pushed up. Underneath him was a title that read "Porn Star and Proud of it."

". . . So your mother knows what you do. Let me ask you this, then: Has she seen any of your movies?" Leeza asked, and the studio audience broke into nervous laughter. The porn star smiled. "Nah, my mom doesn't have a VCR, and believe me—I'm not about to buy her one." More laughter. Leeza smiled.

The porn star said that he just accidentally fell into the porn industry when he was twenty-two. Tired of waiting tables at a Mexican restaurant in L.A. he had answered an ad in the back of a newspaper that requested actors for "adult movies."

"I really liked the attention, to be honest with you, and I loved the money."

"How much money are we talking?" Leeza asked.

"In the beginning it wasn't all that much, maybe a thousand dollars per movie. But after I began to make a name for myself—which didn't take long—I was making upwards of seven, eight grand per flick, and doing maybe three to four a month." The studio audience ooohed.

"What about diseases? Are you afraid of catching AIDS?"

"Not really, we're all very careful, all the actors. And we get tested on a frequent basis. We use protection."

"How long do you think you'll continue to make porno movies?"

"As long as, uh, the equipment holds up." Laughter from the studio audience, and a smile from Max.

"What makes for a successful adult actor?" Leeza asked.

The porn star thought for a minute, then answered, "I think part of it is physical, just, you know, the way you look. And another part is, like, having this exhibitionist side."

Max thought back to the conversation he had with Howard after the Slumber Sunday incident. ". . . You make it sound like

I did it on purpose, like I'm some kind of *exhibitionist* or something." He had said *exhibitionist* like it was a dirty word. And yet there on *Leeza* was a handsome, normal-looking guy who was making a great living *because* he was an exhibitionist.

At the end of the show Max watched the credits roll by:

Ms. Gibbons's wardrobe provided by Ann Taylor.

Catering by Mari & Co.

Guests of *Leeza* stay at the luxurious Parker Meridian Hotel, located just blocks from beautiful Central Park and convenient to everything.

Then, at the very end, Max read, "Special thanks to Eagle Studios, San Bernadino, California."

Seven or eight thousand dollars per movie? Three or four movies a month?

You exposed your penis on national television.

Max shut the TV off and got up off the couch. He went to the phone and pressed zero. When the operator came on the line, Max asked, "Yes, what's the area code for San Bernadino, California, please?"

"Peggy Jean, you've got to get out of bed. You can't stay here forever," John told his wife. Peggy Jean moaned, but did not move from the fetal position she had motionlessly occupied for almost three straight days except to get something out of her cosmetics case or take a One-a-Day.

When John had come home from the mall with his kids the evening of the disposable-razor attack, he had found his wife crouched beneath the kitchen table, an array of Henckel knives and an empty bottle of potato vodka at her side. Her eyes were wild and she was panting like an animal, snapping at the air with a pair of scissors. It had taken him the good portion of an hour to coax her out from under the table, and once he did, she would not stop clinging to him. Nor could she explain what had happened. Instead she mumbled incoherently, *"Cut cut . . . she knows . . . I need to be waxed . . . where's Debby? . . . hide my babies . . . I was Junior Miss San Antonio . . ."*

Realizing his wife was perhaps in the midst of a nervous breakdown, John had phoned a coworker whose own wife was in psychiatric treatment for a mild self-mutilation disorder and asked for the name of the psychiatrist. The coworker gave John the name, and before hanging up he warned, "Christ, man, whatever you do, don't let your wife anywhere near a fork. Take it from me." John phoned the doctor and explained the situation. The doctor had told him that if Peggy Jean's condition did not improve within a matter of days, it would probably be best to have her admitted to a local psychiatric hospital for observation.

"You mean lock her in a nuthouse?"

"No, not a nuthouse. A psychiatric facility with trained professionals who can help her."

"Well, for how long? How long would she have to stay?"

"That all depends on your wife."

John pictured his wife upstairs on the bed like an embryo. A time-lapse movie played out in his mind, a movie in which his wife's position on the bed did not change, but her fingernails grew long and her hair went gray. In the movie, nobody ate and the house was a mess.

He had phoned Sellevision to let them know that Peggy Jean would be unable to come to work for an unspecified amount of time. He had found the Amanda person he spoke with to be extremely compassionate and understanding. She sounded very young. He had also spoken with the police, who had no leads whatsoever.

But now, with his wife showing no improvement, John was left with no other option than to follow the psychiatrist's advice and somehow have his wife admitted to a hospital.

"Peggy, c'mon, I need you to get out of bed and get dressed. We're going to go for a little ride."

No response.

"Peggy, please, you need help, you need to be with people who can help you."

More moans.

"Jesus, Peggy, please. You've got to get up out of this bed. Life has to go on. No one's going to hurt you, I promise. You're being ridiculous."

When nothing he said got a response, John decided he would call in sick, take a quick shower, and literally carry Peggy Jean into the car and deliver her to the hospital himself.

Stripping down to his boxer shorts, he stepped into the bathroom and examined his face in the mirror. Dark circles under his eyes, three days of beard, hair a mess. If he ever got his hands on this Zoe person that Tina said was responsible for all of this, he swore he'd strangle her.

Where was his shaver? The vanity was so crowded with Peggy Jean's toiletries, it was impossible to see even a square inch of surface area. Then, hidden behind a collection of Joyce's Choice bottles, he saw the Norelco GlideFlex his wife had stuffed into his Christmas stocking last year. Powered by a rechargeable battery, the electric shaver did not need to be plugged in, allowing modern fathers to shave while they poured coffee, chose a necktie, or visited an Adult Check site on the Internet.

When he switched the shaver on it immediately made a steady buzzing sound. The sound caused Peggy Jean to gasp, cry out "Shave shave shave," and leap from the bed, ripping the electric shaver from his hands.

"Jesus fucking Christ, Peggy Jean, what the hell?" Too stunned at first to even move, John watched as his wife crazily ran the shaver back and forth across her forearms with frantic speed while she screamed, "*Hairy bitch, hairy bitch, hairy bitch!*"

He wrestled the cordless shaver from her and tossed it on the floor behind him where it buzzed into the thick pile carpeting. "It's okay, it's okay," he said, holding her, trying to stop her from thrashing. And then just as suddenly as she had exploded, she collapsed, unblinking eyes focused on the white ceiling above her.

"She tried to slash her wrists with my razor," John Smythe told the admitting psychiatrist of the Anne Sexton Center.

"But Mr. Smythe, we didn't find any lacerations on your wife's wrists during the physical examination," the doctor said, peering over the tops of his round, wire-framed eyeglasses.

"No, I mean it wasn't a razor, it was a cordless shaver. But still, she grabbed it right out of my hands and started going at her wrists like she was insane, just like this." He made a fist and rubbed it hard and fast across his forearm.

The doctor made a note on the pad that sat on his lap. "I understand," he said. "She had the intention, but not the means. Does your wife have a history of mental illness?"

"Not at all. Up until three days ago, she was perfectly normal. She's one of the top hosts on Sellevision, you know?" John said, as though this somehow provided evidence of her psychological stability.

"What about drug or alcohol abuse?" the doctor asked.

John opened his mouth to answer, but then thought of the potato vodka bottle and all the pills she seemed to be taking lately. "I don't think so, I mean not that I really know of. Although lately, she's been taking an awful lot of vitamins or something. Plus, I found a bottle of vodka next to her. Actually, when I think about it, I have noticed that I smell alcohol whenever she's around. But she says it's her perfume."

"Excellent. So there's a possible unrecognized chemical dependency issue. We'll do a blood workup on her. Now, this state she's in, you say it was caused by a recent event involving a stalker?"

John told the doctor everything he knew, which wasn't much. He explained, "For the past month, she's seemed to be under a lot of pressure, just very tense—and then after the disposable razor thing, she snapped."

"Now this disposable razor incident you mention, finding all those razors scattered about the yard, do you believe there is any connection to those razors and her sudden reaction when you began using your electric shaver?"

John shrugged his shoulders. "Like I said, I don't have any idea, all I know is that she was stabbing the shaver against her arms and she kept screaming 'hairy bitch' over and over again."

"Hairy bitch?" the doctor asked, looking up from his notepad.

"Yup, 'hairy bitch.' That's what she was screaming."

"Interesting." The doctor made another note and asked, "Now, you mention Debby Boone. Is this the same Debby Boone who sang that song—"

" 'You Light Up My Life,' yeah, that's her."

"Ah, that's the song I was thinking of. Lovely song. In any case, what exactly is your wife's relationship with Ms. Boone?"

"Again, I have no idea. She kept saying she needed to talk with *Debby*. I had no clue what she was talking about until our next-door neighbor, Tina, who was there when the police interviewed my wife, explained to me that my wife had recently been, I guess, in contact with her, with Debby Boone."

"Mr. Smythe, please don't take offense at this next question, I'm just trying to explore all the options here."

John nodded.

"Well, do you believe there is any chance that perhaps your wife and Ms. Boone were involved in some sort of *physical relationship* that perhaps didn't work out and this is what could have led to your wife's suicide attempt?"

Peggy Jean . . . a lesbian? It just wasn't possible. Was it?

"No, I don't think that's it at all. My wife is not—my wife—

she loves me. I mean, we have three children, boys, you know?"

"I understand, Mr. Smythe. Like I said, I'm just exploring all possibilities here in order to understand and help your wife."

"I can't imagine . . ."

"That's fine, Mr. Smythe, we don't need to continue with this right now. The important thing is your wife is here and she's safe and we can begin to help her." The doctor rose from his leather desk chair and extended his hand for John to shake.

"So is that it? I just . . . wait?"

"That's all for now. We'll keep you abreast of any developments, of course, but you must understand that for the first thirty days, your wife will not be allowed to have any outside visitors. She may make phone calls, though, if they are approved."

John looked upset. He couldn't cook.

"Here at the Anne Sexton Center, we believe in aggressive, total-immersion therapy. It's important that your wife remain one-hundred-and-ten percent focused on her recovery."

fifteen

"Mr. Palantino?" Max asked the voice on the other end of the line. "My name is Max Andrews. Up until recently I was an on-air host with Sellevision and the reason I'm calling you is because I saw something on the *Leeza* show."

After getting the number of Eagle Studios in San Bernadino, Max had spent a good forty-five minutes on the phone trying to learn the name of the person he should talk to about possibly becoming an "actor" in one of Eagle Studio's releases. He had finally been directed to a producer named Mr. Palantino.

"A host? On Sellevision?" Mr. Palantino asked. "Why would you want to go from that kind of job to this kind of job?"

Max told him about the Slumber Sunday incident. About the many failed interviews and auditions. "I think the fact that I learned about Eagle Studios while watching *Leeza* pretty much sums things up."

Max answered his questions as best he could. No, Max hadn't had any previous experience. Yes, he was considered good looking. And yes, he was well equipped. ("Ask almost any housewife in the country.")

"And you're sure you have no prior experience, nothing at all?" Mr. Palantino had asked.

"None. I'm sure I'd remember."

"Fantastic, just what we like. Here's the deal, send us a head shot along with a couple of nude pictures, Polaroids are fine, and I'll get back to you as soon as I get them."

After hanging up, Max worried that perhaps he had over-promised when he had said, "Sure, I've got a great body." So he walked into the bathroom, took off his shirt, and stood before the mirror. Although lacking grapefruit-sized pecs or biceps as large as thighs, Max thought he looked pretty good for thirty-three—tall, lean, a muscular chest, a hint of abs, good arms. He had a hairy chest, and the hair had a nice, natural pattern to it, across his chest and then a trail down his stomach, a T. It could be shaved, or not. Max thought, *I'm good raw material*. Plus, he had a full head of Brad-Pitt hair, thick and gelable. And although his face was handsome, it was not so perfect as to appear plastic. It was a friendly face. "I'd date me," he said to his reflection.

Hunting through the hall closet for his Polaroid camera, Max thought, *I can't believe I'm really doing this*. Yet, instead of ashamed, he actually felt excited. The idea of being a porn star like that guy on *Leeza* was just so outrageous, so completely out of character, that he found it very intriguing. It was almost like going into hiding. He could make some good money, and nobody would ever even know. Besides, why serve eggs to cops at Denny's when you can have sex with them on a soundstage?

Max set the Polaroid camera down on top of the television set and stripped off the remainder of his clothing. Standing in his condo, naked, midafternoon, in the presence of a loaded camera, had a somewhat decadent feeling. He picked up the camera and set the self-timer button on the back, then depressed the shutter. Rushing to stand far enough back so that all of him was in the kitchen, he watched as a small red light blinked steadily on the front of the camera. Then the blinking sped up significantly and was followed by the sound of the shutter and a bright flash. The instant picture was ejected from the camera. Before even waiting for it to develop, Max took more pictures, five in all: standing at a 3/4 angle to the camera, flexing his abs, looking casual (as casual as one can look while nude in front of a Polaroid camera), and finally one last shot of his equipment. Just to seal the deal.

After the shots were finished developing, Max laid them out on the coffee table and sat on the sofa, making his selections. He chose a flattering shot of himself standing with his arms behind his back, as well as the one where he was flexing his abs. He also included the equipment photo.

Then he retrieved a head shot from his filing cabinet, a black-and-white photograph in which he was wearing a suit and tie, smiling into the camera. Although the picture was more than two years old, Max felt he still pretty much looked the same, except that the new, unemployed Max no longer needed to wear a tie. It also showed that he could be lit professionally with good results.

He sat at the computer and wrote a quick note to accompany the pictures. Nice talking with you, look forward to hearing from you, really excited, blah, blah blah. He printed out the letter using the Epson Stylus he had purchased from Sellevision last year when it was featured as a Today's Super Value ($81.66 in three easy payments of $27.22).

Reading the letter over for spelling errors and/or idiotic comments, Max felt satisfied enough to stick the letter, the head shot, and the three Polaroids into a manila envelope.

Grabbing his keys, wallet, and bomber jacket, Max headed out of the condo, care package in hand.

"Gee, Nikki, you don't have to do that, I can do it myself later on," John told the girl.

She set the yellow plastic laundry basket onto the table

beside the washing machine. "Really, Mr. Smythe, it's no problem at all. I want to help," she said as she placed a load of whites in the machine.

He leaned against the dryer, noticing the care that she took while placing the garments into the Kenmore. Unlike Peggy Jean, who wore Playtex gloves when she did the laundry, always complaining about pee stains.

"Are these yours?" she asked coyly, taking a pair of John's Calvin Klein boxer briefs in her hands, dangling them in front of her by the waistband.

"How embarrassing," he said, turning slightly red in the face.

She let them fall into the washing machine and smiled, closing the lid and pressing the start button. "Oops," she said. "I forgot the soap."

He pointed to a family-size jug of Tide on the floor next to the machine.

She slowly bent over and picked it up. He could see no pantyline beneath her tight jeans. And this could only mean one thing.

Upstairs in the kitchen, the two sat at the table, each with a Diet Pepsi. "So when you dropped Peggy Jean off this morning, did they say how long she'll have to stay?" she asked.

God, the girl had beautiful lips; full and perfectly shaped. "Uh, the doctor said she'd be there at least thirty days," he told her, wondering what flavor her lip-gloss was. Peach? Maybe strawberry?

"That's such a long time. And this is such a big house. Please don't be afraid to ask me for help, whenever you need it." Nikki looked into his eyes. "Your eyes are a beautiful brown," she told him.

He blinked. "Peggy Jean keeps telling me to get blue contacts. She thinks they'd go better with my hair color."

Nikki tilted her head slightly down, allowing a few stands of her long hair to fall against her cheeks. "Well, she's wrong." Nikki rose from the table and rinsed her glass in the sink before placing it in the dishwasher.

John trembled slightly, as if from a chill.

Then she walked behind him and placed her hands on his shoulders. "You're so tense. Your shoulders are like rocks," she said as she began to massage. "My father stores all his tension in his shoulders, too," she said kneading his muscles between her fingers with expert skill.

He moaned softly, and she applied more pressure.

"This must be so hard for your sons. What have you told them? Are they okay?"

He sighed. "Oh, they'll be fine. They're good kids. God, you're good at this."

She began softly pounding on either side of his spine with her fists. "See? Already you're relaxing." Then she ran her hands gently across his back; over his shoulder blades, across his deltoids and down to his lower back just above his buttocks. "You have such a strong back. You must go to a gym," she said in a soft, breathy voice.

"I try to keep in shape," he said, his mouth suddenly very dry.

"My father never does anything to stay in shape," she said. Then Nikki leaned her face next to his ear, placing her lips so close he could almost feel them. "You know," she whispered, "this would be a lot easier if you were lying down."

Immediately after making love, Eliot announced, "I'm hungry."

Bebe laughed. "My God, the male of the species is so primal and need-driven."

He gave her his hurt puppy look. *"What?"*

She lay back on the bed in mock despair. "You mean you'd rather eat cold pizza than bask in the afterglow of love with *moi?*"

Eliot had forgotten about the pizza that was in the refrigerator from the night before. He gave her a kiss on the cheek and leapt from the bed.

Bebe smiled and looked at the clock on the nightstand: 4:30 P.M. She'd have to be at work in an hour and a half to prepare for her Sunday night Dazzling Diamonelle show. She lay back and watched the shadow of a tree outside the window play against the ceiling. What funny thing had she and Eliot done that she could talk about tonight? Of course she would absolutely love to talk about the burly judge who brought plus-size Victoria's Secret nighties into Eliot's dry-cleaning shop all the time. But that probably wasn't such a good idea, in case she ever appeared before him.

She heard the microwave beep, and a moment later Eliot was standing naked before her, eating mushroom pizza off a paper towel decorated with puppies and kittens. Her little dog was between his legs, looking straight up.

"Want a bite?" he asked as he chewed.

Bebe burst out laughing. "Now I know what I'm going to talk about tonight."

He grinned, cheeks plumped out with pizza. "Gote ewe air," he said, then after swallowing, *"Don't you dare."* He had learned that nothing he said or did was off limits when Bebe went on the air. Just last week, the entire country learned that he couldn't pee unless the faucet was running. He finished the pizza except for the crust, which he automatically handed to her. For some reason, the crust was Bebe's favorite part and he always saved it for her.

"Oh, I forgot to tell you—guess who called me last night?" he asked.

Pepper jumped up on the bed and Bebe scratched behind

his ears. "What a good boy, *yes.*" she looked up at Eliot. "Who?"

"My mother," he said, slipping into a pair of boxer shorts.

"Your mother? Your mother's dead." Pepper licked her hand.

Eliot pulled his head through a T-shirt. "I mean my biological mother, the one I never knew."

Pepper jumped off the bed and Bebe sat up, pulling the covers over her breasts. "Eliot, you were adopted?"

He nodded his head. "Yeah, when I was a month old."

She couldn't believe he hadn't told her. "Why didn't you ever mention this to me?"

He shrugged. "It just never seemed important. I mean, I don't really even think about it much. I don't *feel* adopted." He licked some tomato sauce off his thumb.

She thought this made sense. "So what did she say? Why did she call?"

"She said she'd always wondered what happened to me, that she never really got over giving me up, and that it had taken her all these years to find me. It was weird. She's a stranger to me."

"Well, did she tell you anything about her? Do you have brothers and sisters? What about your father?"

"Shit!" he cried and hopped on one foot. "Bebe, what the hell do you need this roulette wheel for? And why'd you put it on the floor?

Bebe rolled her eyes. "Eliot, I told you—it's an investment. It's from the original Sands Hotel in Las Vegas. Someday, it'll be worth a lot. I just haven't found a place to put it yet."

He rubbed his big toe and frowned.

"Anyway, tell me more about your mother. Do you have brothers and sisters?"

"She didn't mention brothers or sisters, but she did mention my father." He pressed on his toenail and a small amount of blood appeared at the edge of the nail.

She looked at him, waiting for him to say more.

"She said they were living in Brooklyn at the time. He was with the NYPD. Imagine, I'm the son of a cop." He limped into the bathroom and opened the medicine cabinet. "Haven't you got any Band-Aids?"

She froze. A chill went through her entire body; her arms sprouted goose bumps. "Eliot, what's your biological mother's name?"

"Never mind, I found them," he said, walking back into the room with the box. He handed it to her. "Here, can you open one of these? You've got fingernails."

"What was your mother's name, Eliot?" Bebe asked again.

"Rosalind," he said as he walked over to the chair and picked up his jeans.

Bebe thought she was going to pass out. She closed her eyes and placed her hands over her ears to make sure her head didn't fall off her shoulders. And then it hit her in waves. The heaving came before the actual tears, but soon enough the tears came.

She sobbed into her hands and he ran over to the bed. "Bebe, what is it, what's the matter, what?" There was panic in his voice. He'd never seen her like this, ever.

She was able to control the sobs enough to ask him, "Don't you see?" But then the sobs took her over again.

He placed a hand on her shoulder, and she pushed it away. "Bebe, what's going on? What did I say?" He scolded himself for snapping at her about the roulette wheel.

"Eliot." She looked up at him. "*Rose* is short for Rosalind. That's my mother's name," she said.

He raised his eyebrows: *So what?*

"My parents lived in Brooklyn before I was born. My father was a *cop*." She inhaled. "And they gave their first baby, a boy, up for adoption."

His mouth fell open. He blinked once.

"Eliot, you're my *brother*."

sixteen

"Yes. Mr. Smythe, yes, yes, *oh God!*" Nikki cried, as John pounded into her from behind, drops of sweat falling from his forehead onto her back. "Oh, I've been such a naughty little girl, punish me. *Harder, harder!*"

John thrust into her, groaning loudly, like an animal, his fingers pressed tightly into her buttocks. "Oh, Nikki, I'm getting close, I'm getting so close," he cried out, eyes rolling back in his head.

Just then she pulled away from him and he fell out of her. She turned over on her back. "On my face, Mr. Smythe, all over my face—just not in my hair."

When it was all over, Nikki asked for a tissue. John brought her a box of pink ones from the bathroom.

"How long did you say your wife's going to be in the hospital?" she asked.

He smiled wickedly at her. "Thirty days and *thirty nights*."

Nikki crawled under the covers. "Let's take a little nap."

He climbed into bed next to her, wrapped his large arms around her small, perfect body. She closed her eyes.

"Mmmmm, you're so warm."

"It's all my hair," he said. "It's like insulation."

Nikki ran her fingers through the hair along his arm. "My father's smooth all over, like a porpoise. It really grosses me out."

He nibbled her earlobe. "You never, you know, *did* anything with your father, did you, Nikki?" he asked.

"Just once," she said. "When I was fourteen."

John opened his eyes in alarm. "Your father raped you when you were fourteen?"

Nikki laughed. "I'd hardly call it rape. I was curious so I climbed into the shower with him one morning."

He stuck his tongue in her ear. "You're such a bad girl, Nikki."

She giggled. "That tickles." Then she got philosophical, gazing at the curtain rod. "I'm the Fashion Café generation, you know? I mean I just believe that if something feels good and it's not hurting anybody, you should just go for it!"

Oh yes, he thought, *you little treat.*

"We're all gonna die eventually, so why not have some fun?" Then she turned to him. "Hey, you don't have any handcuffs, do you? I know a good trick."

He brought his mouth to her small breast, sucking on the nipple until it stiffened.

"I'm not really seventeen," she said.

He moaned.

"I'm sixteen. *Almost.*"

He moaned harder. His mouth moved hungrily along her neck. "I don't care if you're twelve. If I can have thirty days with you, it's worth rotting on death row for the rest of my life."

John ran his fingers across Nikki's tight, flat stomach. "Jesus, you don't have a single stretch mark. Peggy Jean is covered with them. It's repulsive."

Nikki tensed. "I swear, I will never have stretch marks. I'd kill myself first. If I want to have a baby someday, I'll just hire some surrogate cow."

John flicked her navel ring with his tongue. "Kids just get in the way."

She reached down between his legs. "Hey, what's this, Mr. Smythe? Already?"

"*Yo, Dad!*" Ricky called out, bounding up the stairs.

"*Shit,*" John said. "Quick Nikki, hide in the closet or get under the bed."

But it was too late. Ricky threw open the door. "Can we order pizza tonight since Mom's—oh, hi Nikki, how's it going?"

She shrugged. "Okay, I guess."

He looked back at his father. "Anyway, since Mom's in the loony bin now and everything, can we order a pizza?"

He stared in astonishment at his son. "Uh, yeah, sure, I guess."

Ricky smiled. "Cool." Then he dashed down the hall and went into his room.

After John and Nikki dressed and Nikki had gone downstairs to move the clothes from the washer to the drier, John, his three boys, and Nikki shared three large pizzas.

"You don't have to call your father, let him know where you are?" John asked.

Nikki slid the point of a slice of pepperoni pizza into her mouth. "Oh no, I do whatever I want. He's sort of scared of me."

John and Nikki sat together on the couch, her leg over his knee. His three boys sat on the floor directly in front of the television. The boys drank Diet Pepsis while John and Nikki sipped from a mutual tumbler of Absolut. John had found a bottle stashed in the vegetable drawer of the refrigerator when he was looking for a cucumber.

All three boys laughed at the part of the movie where Patrick Bateman plugged in his nail gun. But Nikki set her paper plate on her lap and covered her eyes.

"Oh my God, this part is so gross, I can't even watch." She peeked through her fingers.

As *American Psycho II* played out ghoulishly on the television, John thought to himself that this was the first time he'd had such a relaxed family dinner. Normally, the family would sit in stiff chairs and his wife would quiz the boys about their school projects or Bible study class. All the while, John himself would daydream about some girl he'd seen in *seventeen* or *Jane*. Peggy Jean would insist that the boys drink all eight ounces of one-percent milk. And after the boys were excused from the table, Peggy Jean would turn to him; "Darling, tell me about your day."

But here with Nikki and his boys, John was actually present in the moment. Just today, just hours ago, he'd been worried about how he would run the house while still having to work. But Nikki had made it perfectly clear that she'd "take care of the house 'n' stuff, if you take care of me." And it seemed the boys were more than happy to have pizza or drive through McDonald's. So far, the boys didn't seem at all traumatized that their mother had been placed in a psychiatric hospital. And they certainly didn't seem to mind having Nikki around; it was as if she'd always been there.

In fact, when Nikki had suggested they watch *American Psycho II* on Pay-Per-View, all three had squealed with delight. "You're awesome," Robbie had said.

When the movie ended at eleven, John told the boys, "You guys should probably get to bed now." Satisfied with pizza and gore, they agreed without a fuss and said goodnight before going upstairs to their rooms.

"I could sleep over," Nikki offered.

"You could?"

"Sure, I sleep over at friends' houses all the time."

John looked at her as one might look at a winning lottery ticket, with an equal sense of disbelief and greed.

"I do sort of have Kirsty Hume's hair, don't I?" Nikki said, holding a few strands of her hair in front of her face.

■

"Please, enough with the Mr. Palantino stuff, you're makin' me feel like an old man. Call me Ed." The sixty something pornographer with the soaring triglyceride level extended his hand to Max. After they exchanged a firm handshake, he motioned Max over to the sofa, and then sat in the chair across from it.

"Getcha something? Coffee, soda, anything?"

"Oh, no, thank you, I'm fine," Max said, glancing around at all the enlarged and framed video covers that lined the wall: *Rocky Horny Picture Blow*, *Midnight with the Beaver of Good and Evil*, *Titanic Tops II*, *You've Got (Fe)Male!*

"Ahh, so you're checkin' out the goods, huh? But those are only a few of our bestsellers; we do maybe thirty films a year," Ed said, rubbing his hand across his large belly as though he had just finished a huge meal.

"Wow, that's really . . . prolific."

"Oh yeah, we're very open-minded; pro-straight, pro-gay, pro-tits. Eagle Studios can't be pigeon-holed—we're out there makin' movies for everybody." He lit a cigarette. "Hell, last month we wrapped production on this great chicks-with-dicks diaper thing. Bizarre as you can fuckin' imagine. But hey, there's a market for it."

"That's, um, really great." Max noticed that the carpeting was worn away in places from foot traffic. The walls were paneled and the ceilings low. There would be no mistaking Eagle Studios for MGM.

"So, Max, we could sit here all day shooting the bull 'til the fucking cows come home, but what I wanna know is: How serious are you?"

Max wiped his hand on his knee, then ran his fingers through his hair. "Oh, I'm very serious; I mean I'm very serious in terms of learning, you know, more."

"Well, I'll tell ya, I thought your pics were fantastic. And now sitting here with you in person, I like the energy. I like your vibe."

"Okay . . . well, great, I guess. That's really great that I come off good in person."

"And I gotta also tell ya, I'm crazy about your story."

"My . . . story?"

Leaning back in his chair and crossing his hands behind his back, Ed explained, "I like the whole 'boy-next-door Sellevision host' thing. It's a great plot."

"A plot?" Max watched as Ed became increasingly excited.

"Sure is. I can see the whole thing right now in my head. By the way, you gay, straight, or bi?"

Max shifted awkwardly on the sofa. "Well, I guess I'd be considered gay."

"You guess? What does that mean? I'm asking 'cause I need to know what sort of films I'd put you in."

"I'm sorry, no. What I meant was, or you know, what I mean is, that I'm gay, like all the way. I'm not into women, I'm into men. So, that's kinda how . . ."

"No problem man, no problem—shit. I love gays; we do almost forty-seven percent of sales from the gay flicks."

"Okay."

"Yeah, so sure, I think that's fantastic. Helps me see a clearer picture: *Home-Shopping Hunk*. That's the title right there." He flicked his cigarette ash onto the floor.

"So you mean like a movie based on, like, me?"

"Not 'you' personally, but what you used to do. The whole TV thing, the whole shopping thing. It rocks."

"Oh. Okay, I guess I know what you mean."

"So here's what the deal is in terms of next steps. If you're interested, I'd like you to do a little screen test for me. Nothing major, just you and one of the fellas, see how well you perform on camera."

"Oh, I'm very comfortable in front of the camera, more comfortable on camera than off, as a matter of fact," Max said, smiling.

"That's great, yeah, I'm sure you are. But I just want to see how comfortable your *dick* is on camera. Because you know, a lot of guys have trouble getting wood the minute the camera starts rolling."

"Wood?" Max asked.

"Wood, you know, a hard-on."

Well, Max thought, *what did I expect?* He was, after all, interviewing for a career in porno movies. He'd had to audition for the news anchor job, hadn't he? This was the same thing, pretty much. "So when would you want to do this screen-test thing?"

Ed rose from his chair, dropped the cigarette on the floor, and squashed it with his foot. "We're shooting a film right now, in the sound stage across the parking lot. We could just walk right on over and take care of it this minute."

Part of Max felt paralyzed from the neck down. But another part of him felt like, *sure.* As if there were an internal audience in his head chanting, *Go Ricki, go Ricki!* "Sure, no problem."

"Follow me, then."

And Max did.

seventeen

By her third day at the Anne Sexton Center, Peggy Jean was no longer shaking or crouching over the toilet to vomit. The electroshock therapy sessions had ceased. And she was not on a twenty-four-hour suicide watch, which had been automatic, given the attempt she made on her life with her husband's cordless shaver. She'd been told that the first three days of withdrawal were the most difficult, and it had been true. For the first two nights, she'd seen spiders creeping along the ceiling of her room, yet when she turned on the light, they were gone.

"Hallucinations are very common with alcoholics," she'd been told by one of the chemical dependency counselors.

Alcoholics.

Peggy Jean had become an alcoholic. *And* a drug addict. At least that is what they told her.

"No, Mrs. Smythe. Kahula is *not* just like coffee and it *does* count."

They'd even taken her Giorgio perfume away from her. "I'm sorry, but you're not allowed anything containing alcohol."

Did they really think she would drink her perfume?

"You'd be surprised," one of the chemical dependency counselors had said.

When asked how much Valium she took, Peggy Jean replied, "Oh, just five or six little pills a few times a day."

So here she was, in a hospital. A mental hospital. True, it was named after a poet, but it was just as much of a hospital as the one where Peggy Jean had held one of the AIDS babies she sponsored. Harsh, unflattering fluorescent lighting, cold tile floors, bathrooms equipped for the handicapped. It was just awful. One long hallway of hospital rooms, at the end of which was a "community room" with utilitarian sofas and chairs, tables piled high with year-old magazines. There were two classrooms, both of which were filled with beige padded banquet chairs arranged in a circle. There was no art on the walls, only white marker boards and red fire extinguishers. Three times a day, for breakfast, lunch, and dinner, all the patients were led into a large elevator that was operated by a key. It stopped at only one floor: the cafeteria. A grim, linoleum-tiled room that smelled of Pine-Sol and grease.

Just like common cattle, Peggy Jean had thought on her first day as she stood in the rear of the elevator, a skinny black man and a girl with bruised arms pressed up against her.

At first Peggy Jean had been repulsed by the meals: dry pancakes for breakfast, a grilled Velveeta cheese sandwich for lunch, and Swedish meatballs for dinner. But by the third day, she'd begun to look forward to the meals. There was usually a deep-fried fish option for dinner (if you asked) and always plenty of tarter sauce.

Most of the patients had roommates, but Peggy Jean was fortunate enough to have an entire room all to herself, although she wasn't allowed to close the door. This small bit of privacy had made the first three days bearable. And she began to think of it as a luxury.

But the core of the program was not the menu options or the luxury of a private room, no matter how unluxurious that room was. As Peggy Jean learned by the third day, her stay at the Anne Sexton would involve intense therapy. Therapy unlike anything Peggy Jean had ever seen on *The Bob Newhart Show*.

"Please, I really don't want to get glue all over my finger-nails. I'll ruin my manicure," Peggy Jean protested when instructed to create a "pain portrait" out of elbow-macaroni noodles, construction paper, Elmer's glue, and glitter.

"I think healing is more important," Stacey, the art thera-pist, had said. "You can always get another manicure, but how many recoveries do you have in you?"

She didn't know how many recoveries she had in her, but she did know that her manicure had cost $32, including a gen-erous tip. Not to mention the fact that she had to book her manicurist, Nina, two weeks in advance.

Peggy Jean dutifully drew a picture of a sunflower with the glue and then placed the noodles, one at a time, on top of her glue outline. She placed each noodle carefully. At the end, she sprinkled glitter randomly.

"Very interesting," Stacey commented, leaning over Peggy Jean's shoulder to peer at the artwork. "Most interesting to me is that one noodle there." She pointed to a noodle with a crack in it, a noodle that helped to form a sunflower petal.

"Oh, thank you for pointing that out, I didn't notice," Peggy Jean said and reached for a fresh, uncracked macaroni noodle to replace it.

Stacey paused Peggy Jean's hand, placing her own hand on Peggy Jean's wrist, and then knelt down beside her chair, speak-ing almost in a whisper. "I think you *did* notice. I think you're making a statement with that noodle. I think that noodle is the very crux of the piece."

Peggy Jean looked at the heavy-set woman with the short haircut. "You do?"

Stacey nodded very slowly, pointed at the artwork. "What do you see?" she asked.

Peggy Jean cleared her throat and smiled. "Well, I see a pretty sunflower."

The art therapist raised her eyebrows. "And . . . ?"

Peggy Jean looked at the therapist, then at her picture. "Well, it's just a pretty flower, except I accidentally put a cracked noodle on one of the petals."

Stacey smiled and Peggy Jean looked at her. "And what does that make this a portrait of?" she asked.

Peggy Jean again looked at her picture. "A sunflower . . . *with a cracked petal?*" she asked tentatively.

Stacey gave Peggy Jean a knowing smile. "Congratulations. I think you're on the road to recovery."

That evening, Peggy Jean went to the single payphone to call her husband. Telephone privileges were awarded on the evening of the third night. Each patient was allowed to make one phone call during the day. It had been torture for Peggy Jean to be unable to speak with her husband.

"Hello?" a woman's voice said. Had she dialed the wrong number? Peggy Jean disconnected the call and dialed again.

"*Hello?*" said the same woman, this time slightly irritated.

"Yes, who is this, please?" Peggy Jean asked.

"You've reached the Smythe residence," the woman told her.

"Well, this is *Peggy Jean Smythe* calling for my husband. Who is this?"

"Oh, hi Mrs. Smythe, it's Nikki from next door."

Peggy Jean filled with relief. "Oh, Nikki, how are you? What are you doing at our house?"

Nikki covered the mouthpiece of the telephone with her hand, moved John's head up from her crotch and mouthed the words, "It's your wife."

He frowned.

"Oh, I'm over here helping your husband take care of things, laundry and cooking and stuff. But how are *you?*"

It was all Peggy Jean could do not to burst into tears, right there on the telephone. That sweet girl from next door was taking care of her family; making sure they had clean things.

"Nikki, you don't have to do that. John and the boys are capable of taking care of themselves."

Nikki smiled at John, winked, and tickled his penis with her big toe. "Oh no, I enjoy it, Mrs. Smythe. I like helping out. I did volunteer work at the hospital last year and, well, not that this is like that or anything, but I just like to feel like I'm helping."

Peggy Jean closed her eyes and smiled. She made a mental note to purchase Nikki the Double Heart of Friendship rose and yellow fourteen-karat-gold pendant with the sixteen-inch chain from Sellevision, the very day she returned home. Given her employee discount, the pendant would cost less than forty dollars, and yet she would have paid twice that. "Is my husband there, Nikki?" Peggy Jean asked.

"I think he's doing something with the plumbing, let me go see if I can find him." Nikki again cupped her hand over the mouthpiece and laughed. "She wants you," she whispered.

John took the phone from Nikki and gave her a wink. "Peggy Jean?" he said, wiping his mouth on the sleeve of his rugby shirt.

"Hello, darling! I'm calling from *the clinic*. I haven't been allowed phone privileges until now. I hope you haven't been too worried about me."

John watched as Nikki went into the bathroom, returning with a bottle of baby oil. "Uh, no, that's fine, I mean sure I've been worried, but I figured you were in good hands."

Nikki stood in the doorway of the bathroom and tipped the open bottle of baby oil over her chest. She massaged the oil into her breasts until they glistened.

"The boys? How are my babies? Please make sure they eat, I don't want the trauma to wear them down."

"The boys are fine, keeping busy with their studies."

"Thank God. Recovery is so difficult, John, but I believe I had my first breakthrough today. I'm a sunflower with a cracked petal."

Nikki massaged John's toes with baby oil. "That's, uh, great,

Peggy Jean, but I shouldn't keep you on the phone, so I'll talk to you later. Bye." He hung up.

Peggy Jean held the payphone receiver in her hand for a moment.

"Hey, give somebody else a chance, lady," a patient said to her.

She hung up and felt a sudden rush of guilt. It was obviously very difficult for her husband to speak with her right now, his pain so great. How confused he must be. How lost without her. It was because of her own weakness that her family was in turmoil, staying afloat only thanks to the help of a thoughtful neighborhood girl.

"My name is Peggy Jean Smythe, and I'm a . . ." She tried to say the words out loud, but couldn't. Instead, she went to her room and prayed.

"Hello, this is Leigh. I'm not here to take your call right now, so please leave a message after the beep. Thanks." Leigh stood next to the answering machine, screening.

"Please, Leigh, please, I'm begging you. Oh, Leigh, I love you so much, you don't understand. Why won't you call me back? I need to . . ." Leigh picked up the phone.

"Stop calling me, Howard," she said.

"Leigh! Finally! Please, don't hang up. I need to tell you something."

"Make it quick."

"The divorce proceedings are already in progress, it should be final in a month. It's over between me and her."

"No thanks to you," she said, the Peking duck still quite fresh in her mind.

"Leigh, you don't understand, I have nothing without you. Sellevision fired me, the house is in my wife's name, and I can't stay at this hotel forever. Please, what about us?"

Leigh shook her head is disbelief. "Howard, you are a selfish fucking bastard is what it comes down to. And you're getting exactly what you deserve. I loved you, I really did." Then softness entered her voice. "Okay, and maybe part of me still loves you. But that doesn't mean you're right for me and it doesn't mean I'm going back to you."

Howard began crying into the phone. Leigh heard ice tinkle in a glass.

"Please don't do this to me, Leigh. I need you now more than ever."

Leigh pictured him sitting at the desk inside his room at the Marriott. His face was probably still swollen from the stitches, a few bottles of Dewar's from the minibar in the trashcan under the desk. She could see his toiletries lined up on the bathroom counter; his Egoist cologne, his Armani undereye gel and moisturizer, his Todd Oldham shaving mousse. She could see his suitcase on the floor of the closet, and she knew which pieces of clothing were in it. He probably still had the picture of his wife in his alligator wallet, and she was certain he had the tie that she gave him for his birthday last year.

She also knew that the marriage was over, that he was hers now—if she still wanted him. It would be so easy to just get in her car, drive the twenty minutes to his hotel, and be with him. And it was true that she had basically ruined his life with her little stunt; all the papers had covered it. And her own phone was ringing off the hook: *A Current Affair*, *Today*, the literary agents from New York.

"I'm sorry, Howard, I really am. I never imagined this, but I just really think you were wrong to have lied to me and I was hurt, and I did what I did out of anger and hurt. Because I loved you so much."

"And I love you so much, Leigh, I do."

"It's over, Howard. Good-bye."

"No, please don't hang up, *please*."

Leigh hung up. *I do love him*, she thought. *But that's not reason enough.*

She then went back to her computer and put some finishing touches on a letter she'd written to Peggy Jean.

Dear Peggy Jean,
Amanda told me you're at the Anne Sexton Center for a while,
and I just wanted you to know that my best thoughts are with
you. I know that we never spoke much or were close or any-
thing, but I just wanted you to know that I care. You're a won-
derful host, and I've always admired you. My mother was an
alcoholic and she's been clean and sober for fourteen years. It's
nothing to be ashamed of.
I'm thinking of you and praying for your recovery.
Leigh

"Three parts Oil of Olay Age Defying Series Revitalizing Eye Gel, one part sugar, and half a part non-dairy creamer," the prop stylist told Max.

"It looks so real," Max said, leaning over and inspecting the artificial semen in the plastic cup.

"That's the point, honey." The prop stylist had set up his little semen factory on a box right next to the craft service table that was piled with crackers, cheeses, fruits, and various other snacks. A cooler below the table was filled with sodas and bottled water.

"Follow me," Ed said. "I'll give you a little tour." Then, "Obviously, this is the prop area, and over there . . ." He pointed to an illuminated set in the far corner of the soundstage, a set that resembled a pizza parlor. ". . . that's where we're shooting today."

Ed introduced Max to various people, most of whom were dressed in jeans and T-shirts and had crackling walkie-talkies clipped to their belts. A thin, dark-haired boy sat on a folding metal chair reading *Vanity Fair*.

"That's Shaun. He's a fluffer."

"A fluffer?" Max asked as Ed led him over to the boy.

"Hey Shaun, tell Max here what it is you do on the set."

The boy looked up from his magazine, and said flatly, "I help keep the guys' dicks hard while they wait for their scene." Then he went back to his article.

"Here's where we store the lights," Ed said, taking Max over to an area where fifteen or twenty gigantic stage lights on tall metal stands with wheels were parked, their thick black electrical chords wrapped around their bases.

"More set stuff," Ed said, pointing to where various wallpapered, windowed, and fake-bricked walls were leaning against the wall of the soundstage itself.

"Hey, Trixie, how's it going, baby?" Nick said to the naked, oily woman with the largest breasts Max had ever seen in his life. She was holding a cup from Starbucks.

"Hey, Eddy," she said, pausing to kiss him on the cheek.

"This is Max. Max, meet Trixie."

"Hi, Max. I'd shake your hand, but I'm kind of greasy. Just finished a scene. So are you a new guy?" she said, taking a sip from her coffee.

"Well, I'm, uh," Max stumbled.

"He's here for a test, gonna see how much the camera loves him," Ed said, slapping Max on the back.

Trixie smiled. "Well, good luck with it. And just try to forget the camera. I know it's hard, but if you don't forget the camera," she said, then looked at Max's crotch, "it won't *stay* hard." Trixie gave a little wave and walked past them, stopping at the snack table to collect some grapes.

"Trixie Thunderpussy, *the* Trixie Thunderpussy," Ed told Max as they walked over to an area where three naked men sat around watching a television. The men each sat on towels which were draped over folding chairs. They were shouting at the TV.

"Hi, guys. How's it hanging?" Ed said as they approached the men.

They looked over and nodded, smiled. *"Go, go, go, go, go!"* one of them shouted. Then they all screamed, *"Yes!"* and leapt from their chairs, high-fiving each other.

"Man, those Broncos are fucking awesome this season," said one of the men, walking over to Ed and Max. Then the guy looked at Max. "Hey, buddy. How's it going?"

"Okay, pretty good," Max said.

"Max, this is Rocky. He and the other fellas are working with Trixie, who you just met."

"Oh, so you're working with Trixie. Yeah, she seemed nice."

"Listen, Rocky, Max here's gonna be testing today. Think maybe you could be his camera buddy?"

Max gulped. Rocky was at least six-foot-three, all muscle and equipment. A human Rottweiler.

"What, just playin' stuff? Kissin', foolin' around, that sort of thing, just light action?" he asked.

"Yeah, Rocky, you know the drill. Ten minutes—tops."

Rocky shrugged, looked at Max, shrugged again. "Sure, no problem." The other guys started shouting and Rocky ran back over to the TV. *"No way, no fucking . . . aww, man . . ."* He slammed his fist on top of the television.

Ed led Max into a dressing room. "There's a shower in there, clean towels are everywhere, and there's a pile of robes right over there," he said pointing to a pile of thirty or forty white cotton robes folded on a table. "So just shower up, throw on a robe and when you're done, just go back out and find Rocky." Then Ed slapped him on the shoulder, smiled, and left Max alone in the dressing room.

The dressing room was spotless, pleasant even. A long white counter ran along one wall; above it a mirror was illuminated with large white bulbs. On the counter itself was a small stereo, speakers attached, not unlike the stereos Max had presented dozens of times on Sellevision. There was a stack of CDs next to the stereo along with some tall white candles. A shoebox filled with condoms was on the opposite end of the counter, along with a couple of cans of Evian mist. In front of the counter were two white director's chairs. The room also had a small, two-seat white leather sofa and a couple of matching chairs. On the floor next to the sofa stood a small refrigerator. Max opened it and saw that it was stocked with spring water and soda. The bathroom was also spotless, if simple. There was a shower stall and shelves attached to the wall, stocked with fresh towels, bottles of Kiss My Face shower gel, and Pert shampoo. "Well, this doesn't seem too horrifying," he said as he undressed. He walked back out to the main dressing room and tossed his clothes on one of the chairs. Then he went back into the bathroom and took a quick, hot shower before returning to the soundstage.

"Hey, Buddy," Rocky said, as Max appeared in front of him wearing one of the white robes, hair still damp. Rocky himself was dressed in a white shirt and black-and-white checked pants, the kind chefs wore. "You ready?" he asked.

"As ready as I think I can be," he told him.

As Rocky led Max over to the lit set, Max asked him, "So how long have you been doing this?"

"What, making porn? Ah, I don't know. Five years, six maybe." He steered them around some large black plastic crates.

"So you do, like, all kinds of movies?" Max asked.

"Well, any kind of straight or bi thing. I don't do just guys. It's, you know, not my thing."

Max wondered, *Well then, why are you about to have sex with me in front of a camera?*

Seeming to read his mind, Rocky answered the unasked question. "But you know, I don't *mind* it with guys, and if the guy's handsome and not slutty, not some old pro, then it can be fun. You know, like this, with you."

Max felt flattered.

They arrived on the set of *Pizza Parlor Pussy*. Ed greeted them and told Max, "Go ahead and take off your robe, make yourself comfortable." Max noticed that Shaun, the fluffer, was lurking nearby.

"So here's what I want you to do," Ed began. "Rocky here's gonna be standing over there by that pizza oven. What I want you to do is come up behind him and start taking off his clothes, getting him excited. You don't actually have to do anything except touch, play around with each other. I really just want to see how comfortable you are."

Max did not feel comfortable. This was, he realized, a large mistake.

Rocky got into position and opened the oven door.

"Let's go!" Ed shouted, "And . . . *action!*"

Max exhaled and stepped onto the set. The lights were so bright, everything beyond the set was immediately plunged into darkness, just like on Sellevision. Then he saw the camera. It was trained on him. Max was on a set, in front of a camera. He wasn't in a dark sound booth doing a voice-over audition. He wasn't miserable, in his apartment watching MTV. And most importantly, he wasn't on radio.

Max looked into the camera and a smile spread across his face. Then he looked at Rocky, who was pretending to slide a pizza into the oven. He could see the muscles in Rocky's back flexing beneath the crisp white shirt. Max took a step forward. And then another. He reached his hand out and gently touched the nape of Rocky's neck.

Rocky turned. The smile left Max's face, was replaced by something else. Despite the sheer power of him, Max could see there was a softness in Rocky's green eyes. He was *attracted* to Rocky. Max took a step closer and unbuttoned the first button on Rocky's shirt.

Rocky took Max's hands in his, pressed them to his chest. "You're trembling," he said gently.

"A little," Max said softly, still looking into Rocky's eyes.

"Here, let me help," Rocky said, unbuttoning his own button.

First one, then the next, then the next. Max slid his hands across Rocky's exposed chest, felt the strength that was in those muscles.

The shirt fell to the floor.

Rocky unbuckled his belt, slowly. Then unfastened his pants. He slid them down his thighs, stepped out of first one leg, then the other.

Max and Rocky stood naked before each other. Rocky extended his arms, and Max moved into them.

Rocky ran his fingers across Max's back, then pulled him closer. He took Max's face in his hands, cocked his head slightly, and kissed Max on the lips. A gentle kiss, but a real one.

He turned Max around so that Max's back was against his chest. Rocky slid his hands across Max's chest, then down his flat stomach. Max closed his eyes and arched his head back against Rocky's neck. He moaned softly.

"*Cut!*" Ed shouted.

Max's eyes startled open.

There was applause from the crew.

Rocky let go of Max and stepped back. "That was *great*, buddy," he said. "Man, you're really good. I was really getting into it." He gave Max's neck a playful squeeze, the way buddies sometimes do with one another.

Ed approached enthusiastically, extended his hand. "Max, you are nothing less than brilliant. I mean, you could just *feel* the intensity, the raw sexuality. The whole room was frozen. Max, my man, you were born for this, the camera *loves* you. And obviously, you don't have any problem with the camera," he said, winking.

Rocky walked off the set. "See you later, buddy. Hey, maybe we'll work together sometime, that could be pretty cool."

Max just stood there, stunned. And then he looked down. *Wood.*

Someone handed him a robe.

He caught a glimpse of Shaun, sitting off to the side, completely engrossed in his magazine.

eighteen

"I'm sorry, Peggy Jean. But confrontational group therapy isn't supposed to be pleasant. Achieving mental health is never a picnic." Peggy Jean was sitting in her case manager's office having just come from a humiliating group therapy session. She had asked Ms. Guttel, a woman so masculine that Peggy Jean had at first called her "sir," to excuse her from future group-therapy sessions. "Absolutely out of the question. You're a very sick woman and group therapy plays a primary role in recovery." Then the hateful man/woman glared and said, "Don't think that just because you're some fancy-shmancy Home Shopping host from TV that you get special privileges, because lady, you're just another alcoholic, plain and simple."

"*Sellevision*," Peggy Jean spat. "*Not* Home Shopping Network." Then she stood and abruptly left Ms. Guttel's office.

It was getting worse by the minute. How could her husband have put her in such an awful place? She tried to imagine Elizabeth Taylor staying there and she couldn't. Dear Lord, why hadn't he sent her to Betty Ford instead? This was no place for a celebrity.

"I can channel Tammy Wynette," said a raspy voice from behind Peggy Jean. She turned to see a haggard old woman with a wart on her nose like a fairy-tale witch. The wart had a hair growing out of it.

Peggy Jean backed against the wall. "Please don't speak to me," she said to the witch. Thankfully, a nurse appeared, taking the witch by the arm.

"Well, Peggy Jean, I see you've met Mrs. Creenly. She's a new patient." Peggy Jean slid away and went into her room. More than a crème de menthe, more than a Valium, she just wanted to close her door.

And then it hit her. It hit her like a baseball bat across the face. She really *did* want a crème de menthe; she did want a Valium. The feeling was powerful, overwhelming. She sat on the edge of her bed and rocked. What was she supposed to do when cravings hit? What was it they had told her? *Feelings are like the weather, they will pass. Let go and let God. Feel the fear and do it anyway.* Or was that last one for something else?

Just that morning in group therapy she had said that her real problem was not alcohol or pills, her real problem was that she was being stalked by some crazed person, jealous of her fame.

An awful man sitting across from her had said, "Look, honey, denial ain't a river in Egypt."

Somebody else said, "You may have a stalker, but you're not facing the fear, you're drinking it away. You're pill-popping yourself into oblivion."

Peggy Jean had said that she wasn't like "the rest of you people," that she was only "trying to smooth her nerves out a little, for the *camera.*"

Leslie, the group facilitator, reminded Peggy Jean that she had made an attempt on her life, that when she had been discovered by her husband, she was intoxicated.

"I don't remember any of it. I was in a state of complete mental collapse."

One of the patients, a woman too pretty to be an alcoholic,

sneered at her. "It's called a *blackout*. We've all had 'em. And normal people don't have blackouts. Hate to break it to you but only we alcoholics get them."

Peggy Jean was aghast. "You people are . . ." She used a word she'd learned recently. ". . . *projecting* your own problems onto me. I shouldn't even be here."

She stood to leave but was told by Leslie that leaving was not an option. "I'm sorry, but you need to confront these issues."

That was when she burst into tears and somebody handed her a box of tissues. She looked at the box and sobbed even harder. "I can't use these tissues. I can only use the ones with lotion in them. *Don't any of you people understand how close the camera gets?*"

Peggy Jean got up off the bed and went to the sink. She splashed her face with cold water and looked at herself in the mirror. "My name is Peggy Jean Smythe *and I'm an alcoholic and a drug addict.*" It rang true. She walked over to the nightstand and looked at the small pile of letters that people had sent her. She sat on the bed and then picked up the stack of letters. Debby Boone, Bebe Friedman, Adele Oswald Crawley, Trish Mission, and Leigh Bushmoore. *I have friends. People love me. I am somebody. And isn't it true, doesn't everybody have tiny little hairs all over their body?*

Peggy Jean could hear the sound of patients gathering in the hall on their way to the elevator for lunch. Maybe the cafeteria would have the green Jell-O again today. And this thought momentarily perked her up. Of course, she'd have to face all those awful people from group therapy. But she'd just eat and leave as quickly as possible.

"Hi, Peggy Jean," said one of the awful people who attacked her earlier, the pretty one.

Peggy Jean said an icy, "Hello."

The woman came right up beside Peggy Jean and entered

the elevator with her. "You were great in group today. You really got in touch with some feelings. It's hard at first but it gets easier."

Peggy Jean looked at the woman, who was suddenly being friendly. "Hmph."

"I sure hope they have patty melts today, I could really go for a patty melt," she said.

Mmmm, Peggy Jean thought, so could she. The hospital food had really started to grow on her.

"My name's Debby, by the way. I know it's hard to learn all these new names."

Peggy Jean gave her a little smile. "I have a friend named Debby," she said.

"Really?"

Peggy Jean nodded. "Yes, the singer Debby Boone. Actually she's been a tremendous help to me through my crisis." Just then Peggy Jean noticed the witch woman staring at her from the other side of the elevator. *I bet that's exactly what Zoe looks like*, she thought.

Peggy Jean and Debby sat together at a table.

"Oh well," Debby said. "It may not be a patty melt, but I guess turkey loaf will have to do."

Peggy Jean took a bite of turkey loaf and wondered what her family was having for lunch. Maybe Nikki had made them a nice chicken salad. Or maybe something festive, like stuffed tomatoes. "This is actually quite tasty," she told Debby. "I wonder if I could get the recipe. My family would love it."

Debby nodded with her mouth full.

"And I bet it would make great sandwiches the next day."

Debby asked, "How many kids do you have?"

"Three. Three little boys, four if you count my hubby!" She pierced a lima bean with a prong of her fork. "And you? Do you have any kids?"

A pained look spread across Debby's face. "I have two children, Hope and Charity."

Peggy Jean smiled. "What lovely names. How old?"

"They're thirteen, twins."

Peggy Jean paused her fork in midair. "How wonderful. They must be very beautiful. I mean, you're so pretty yourself."

Debby lowered her head. "Thank you." Then, looking Peggy Jean in the eyes, "Actually, my girls aren't just twins, they're conjoined twins."

Peggy Jean leaned in. "Con*what?*"

Debby nodded her head, resting her fork on her tray. "Conjoined. They share major organs; they each have one leg, one arm. They share a chest and they have one vagina."

Peggy Jean bit her knuckle.

"I started drinking right after they were born. It's very stressful because they've never gotten along, and well, there's nothing I can do about it because they basically have one body."

Peggy Jean would not be able to finish her turkey loaf. "My Lord, you poor thing. No wonder."

Debby began to cry softly, reached for a napkin. "If only they got along—but they don't, they just scream and fight all day."

Peggy Jean shook her head in disbelief. "I don't know what I would do, I honestly have no idea. I don't know that I could bear the grief."

Debby dabbed at her eyes with a corner of the napkin. "The only good thing is, they just got a movie deal from Streistar for their life story. So at least they'll have some money for college. Or whatever."

Peggy Jean placed her hands on Debby's shoulders. "There's always a silver lining." And then, alarmed, she blurted out, "I forgot to say grace!"

The two women left the cafeteria and Peggy Jean thought, *Well, if she can survive all of that . . .*

■

"What are the chances? I mean, how many people named Rosalind who were living in Brooklyn and married to police officers in the mid 1950s gave their first son up for adoption?" Bebe asked Eliot as they sat on his sofa.

"It's just incredible," Eliot said. "I mean, we really should do a talk show."

Bebe smiled. "I was so terrified, Eliot." She reached for her glass of wine.

"I knew it couldn't be true," Eliot told her.

She took a sip of wine. "You were scared shitless," she said.

"I knew in my heart that it couldn't be true, because God couldn't be that cruel."

It had only taken a quick call to Bebe's mother, Rose, to clear the matter up. Her mother told her that she had never searched for the baby she gave up for adoption. She hadn't phoned Eliot. There was no way Eliot was Bebe's brother. Bebe was just being crazy. Period.

Bebe wasn't so sure.

"Does he have a large birthmark shaped like an owl on his chest?" her mother had asked.

"No," Bebe had said. She even made Eliot lift his shirt so she could look for a scar. But there was nothing but a normal chest.

Of course, the confusion had made a wonderful story for her to talk about on her Sunday Dazzling Diamonelle show. It had also shown her how much she cared for Eliot and how devastating the thought of losing him was to her. It was a relief to know that her relationship was okay. Unlike, it appeared, Peggy Jean's.

Yesterday Bebe was having lunch with Joyce DeWitt, who was in town for one of her Joyce's Choice shows. Bebe happened to notice John Smythe sitting at a table with a young girl. They were tucked away at a rear table in the restaurant, but it was impossible not to see them. They were practically going at it, right there on the table.

"What are you thinking?" Eliot asked.

"I was thinking if I ever catch you licking a young girl's wrist in public, I'll kill you."

"What?" Eliot laughed.

"I mean it, I'll send you right through that dry-cleaning machine of yours."

Eliot picked up Bebe's hand and licked her wrist. "There's only one wrist I want to lick, I promise." She smiled at him. He studied her face for a moment. "We really do have the same nose, don't we?"

"Oh, that reminds me," Bebe said. "I want to take a quick trip over to CVS and pick up some of those strips that you stick on your nose, you know, for your pores. Actually, maybe we could stop at the Gap along the way. I could use . . ."

Trish slid the post of the gold-finish Diana-Dodi Double Hoop Forever earring through her ear. She gave herself a final once-over in the mirror, then nodded her approval. She had twenty-five minutes before going on air, just enough time to have a quick cup of herbal tea. She walked to the hosts' lounge and said hello to Adele, who was microwaving some popcorn. "Smells good," Trish said.

"Help me eat it?"

"Can't," Trish smiled. "Just brushed my teeth." She took a bag of Earl Grey out of the box and dropped it into a white Styrofoam cup. "Your Kitchen Creations show was fantastic. Is that lobster ice cream really as good as you said?"

"It honestly is, believe it or not," Adele said, straightening the eagle feather in her hair.

Trish filled her cup with hot water. "Well, I'd better be running along."

"Good luck with your show. Love your earrings."

Trish brought the cup of tea back into her office and sat at her desk. Max was gone, Leigh was gone, and Peggy Jean probably wouldn't be returning to the show. She smiled. To top it off, the new head of broadcast production, Keith Everheart, was crazy about her. He'd even flirted with her, and she'd flirted back. And why not? With her Price Waterhouse ex-fiancé no longer calling her in the middle of the night crying, she was a free agent. A free agent whose star was rising.

She picked up the phone and immediately dialed Dallas. "Hi, Daddy," she said when he answered. "Did you see my Greek Key showcase last night?"

Her father told her that of course he'd seen it, had watched every second of it, and had made Gunther tape it.

Trish applied a quick-drying top coat to her nails. "Well, guess what? I'm on *again* tonight!" She held the phone between her ear and shoulder as she waved her fingers in the air in front of her to dry them. "I *know*, and I thought my hair looked really good, too. Well, make sure you watch tonight, okay Daddy?" She blew across her fingernails. "Love you too, bye," she said and hung up the phone. Checking her watch, she realized that she had to get over to the stage.

Trish Everheart, she said in her mind as she walked. *I like the sound of that.*

After Adele's popcorn finished popping, she brought it back to her office, peeled the bag open, and set it on her desk. Three of the kernels tumbled out of the bag, and she popped these into her mouth. She sat down at her computer to check her E-mail when her phone rang.

"Hello, this is Adele Oswald Crawley," she said. "Oh, hi Mom, what a great surprise, how are you?" Adele reached into the bag and plucked a kernel out, brought it to her mouth, and then paused. "*What?*" Adele set the kernel on the desk, pressing the telephone against her ear. "Oh my God," she said. She closed her eyes. "Oh Mom, please tell me this isn't true, please tell me."

But it was true.

Her mother had been mistaken. There wasn't any Native American blood in her at all. None.

Now she'd have to completely redecorate her apartment. The tepee, the birchbark canoe, the feather headdress lampshades—all of it would have to go.

"Speak to the chair, Peggy Jean. The chair represents Zoe. What do you want to say to the chair?" Alice, the drama therapist, had instructed.

For a moment, Peggy Jean was gripped by fear. But she allowed herself to *feel* the feeling and then move through it, thus enabling her to perform the exercise. She approached the chair. "What did I ever do to you? Were you unhappy with a purchase? You could have sent it back—we have an *unconditional thirty-day guarantee!*"

Then feelings began to pour out of her and she pounded on the padded seat of the banquet chair. "I am *not* a hairy bitch and you have no right to come to my house and terrorize me and my family," she screamed. "I do not have a hormonal imbalance—*my endocrinologist said everyone has little hairs.*"

When Peggy Jean collapsed on the floor in tears, Debby offered her a tissue, but Alice intervened. "No, don't, you might interrupt the grieving process."

After a small break, allowing Peggy Jean the time she needed to *feel* her feelings, Alice said, "I'd like you all to stand in a close circle."

The patients obliged, creating a tight, safe space.

"Now, Peggy Jean—I'd like you to stand in the center of the circle, close your eyes and fall backward."

"What?" she cried.

"And *group*, when Peggy Jean falls, I want you to all reach out and catch her; show her that she has support."

"I don't think I can," Peggy Jean whispered.

"I know you can," empowered the therapist.

And so, *trusting the process*, Peggy Jean closed her eyes and, going against instinct, fear and pride, she allowed herself to fall backward; backward into the outstretched arms of the other patients at the Anne Sexton Center.

Tears welled in Debby's eyes.

Then a smiling Peggy Jean was raised to her feet, and as she opened her eyes, the whole room applauded. "I hope I wasn't too heavy, what with all the patty melts and pudding cups I've been eating."

A kind-hearted man who wore a small, reflective codependency awareness ribbon pinned to his hospital smock said, "You weren't heavy at all, Peggy Jean— the only weight you carry is on your shoulders. I wish I could carry it for you."

Indeed, the progress Peggy Jean had made was remarkable.

Not only did she raise her hand and speak at each of the Alcoholics Anonymous meetings she attended twice a week, but she had become an active participant in her group-therapy sessions.

"It's about protecting myself, and it's about *setting boundaries*, and it's about . . ." she had trailed off, unsure, trying to think of the correct word. "And it's about being . . . *angry?*" Pausing long enough to see the therapist smile and nod, she continued. "My stalker violated my self-esteem, and then she violated my home. My security was breached—and I'm very . . . I'm . . . well . . . *I'm just not happy about it.*"

"You're not *happy* about it? one of the members of the group challenged, a man named Edward who claimed to have three testicles.

Clenching her fists and *owning* her anger, Peggy Jean cried, "I'm *Goddamn* angry!"

As a good Christian woman, Peggy Jean immediately felt she should have said, *darn* angry, or *very* angry, or *really, really* angry. But she had simply spoken what was in her heart. Yet God *created* her heart, hadn't he? And her heart had said *Goddamn*.

"But you're a celebrity. You have to get used to those things," another patient argued.

"Tell *that* to Prince William and Prince Harry," she snapped. "You tell *that* to Debby Boone." Peggy Jean calmed herself by concentrating on her breathing; *in for three counts, out for six*.

Somebody else asked, "So what about those ads for milk? You know, where all the stars have milk mustaches? What about them people; they get stalkers and they don't have to go to the hospital."

"The reason I had to be hospitalized was because I used alcohol and pills to *stuff my emotions*, instead of going *through* the feelings." Then she added, "I was asked to do one of those milk ads, as a matter of fact, and I still may." She placed her hands on her lap, noticing the faint hairs on her arms.

And I am okay with that.

Peggy Jean would not lock herself in the garage and turn on the ignition like the namesake of the clinic had done. Oh no. *It can't be wrong when it feels so right. 'Cause you, you light up my life.*

"Welcome to Sellevision. I'm your host, Bebe Friedman, and this is Dazzling Diamonelle." The first item Bebe presented was a pair of teardrop two-karat total weight Diamonelle earrings in fourteen-karat white gold. A quarter of the way through her presentation, they sold out. The next item, a seven-and-a-half-inch Diamonelle tennis bracelet, seven-karat total simulated gemstone weight, set in fourteen-karat yellow gold also sold out quickly.

By now, Bebe's fans knew all about Eliot, much to his horror. Bebe received so much E-mail that she had two assistants to help her answer them. And most of the E-mails wished her good luck with Eliot, telling her how wonderful he was. On air, it seemed she barely talked about the item she was presenting and instead talked about her relationship—yet all of her shows continued to be hugely successful.

On the Teleprompter in front of her, Bebe saw there was a caller with the name Michael. Bebe was presenting a two-karat round Diamonelle solitaire in fourteen-karat yellow gold. "Let's go to the phones and say hello to Michael from Pennsylvania—hi, Michael, how are you this evening?"

"I'm very well, thank you, Bebe," Michael said.

Bebe recognized Eliot's voice. He had used his first name, the name he almost never used. *I'm going to kill you*, she thought. "So, Michael, what made you decide to pick up this ring?" she said, smiling into the camera, pretending not to know him.

"Well, Bebe, the reason I chose this ring is because it's such a classic engagement ring, and the woman I'm going to present it to is anything *but* classic, so I thought it would be a nice juxtaposition. Oh, and I also liked the fact that it's a pretty big stone. I was hoping this would up the odds of her saying 'yes' when I ask her to marry me."

For a few seconds, the estimated twenty-four million viewers tuned into Sellevision at that exact moment saw only Bebe Friedman staring blankly out from their television screens, saying absolutely nothing. Then they heard a deafening scream, followed by a laugh, then a gasp, until finally, Bebe broke into tears; tears and laughter colliding.

Inside the control room, her producer turned to the engineer and said, "What the hell is going on?"

"So, Bebe, what do you say?" Eliot asked.

Bebe waved her hands in front of the camera, "I'm sorry, I'm sorry, oh Eliot, I can't believe you're doing this, I can't *believe* . . ."

"Is that a yes?" Eliot said, excitedly, his face inches from his television screen.

Bebe was able to pull herself together enough to say, *"You crazy insane lunatic, yes, yes, I will marry you!"* Then she sniffled, wiped the tears from her eyes, and explained to her viewers, "I'm sorry everybody, *Michael* is Eliot's first name, that's my Eliot on the phone. I can't believe this. . . . Eliot, why did you do this to me on live television? . . . I'm going to kill you . . . I love you," she said, her words all running together.

Immediately, Bebe was surrounded by cameramen with headphones slung around their necks, assistants dressed in jeans, all the behind-the-scenes people that put Sellevision on the air twenty-four hours a day, 364 days a year. They were smothering Bebe, hugging her, throwing their headphone sets into the air. Somebody bumped against the large prop column and sent it crashing down against the illuminated city skyline at the rear of the set, blowing out some lights.

And above all the chaos on the screen, above the cheering, the hugging, the kissing and the crying, Eliot could be heard over the airwaves loud and clear as he shouted, "I love you, Bebe Friedman, I love you so much. I'm the stain you'll never get rid of!"

one year later

"Hi, I'm Kyle Thunderwood. And you're watching the Shop From Home television network," the host said as he sauntered across the set in black leather jeans and a white button-down shirt, taking his seat in the center of the set. "I hope all you viewers out there tonight are looking for some very exciting *merchandise*, because I've got a great *show* in store for you." Kyle gave a sexy, teasing smile, unbuttoning his shirt down to his waist. "Man, oh man, it sure is hot under these studio lights. I hope you don't mind if I get a little bit more comfortable." Kyle let the shirt fall from his shoulders and rubbed a hand across his smooth chest, which glistened from perspiration. He traced a line from the center of his chest slowly down his stomach, stopping just before the button on his black leather jeans. Then he took the finger and stuck it in his mouth, moaning softly.

The video clip ended and the lights of the Reno Grand Hilton were once again illuminated as the audience applauded.

The scantily clad hostess of the awards ceremony then opened a sealed envelope and announced, "And the winner is: Kyle Thunderwood in *Home Shopping Stud!*"

The audience broke into thunderous applause, cheers, and whistles.

At one of the tables, Ed smiled broadly, clapped, and leaned over to whisper in Max's ear. Trixie Thunderpussy kissed Max's cheek. When Max rose from his table, Rocky slapped his butt and grinned, giving him the thumbs-up.

Max made his way around all the other tables and up the steps of the stage to accept his Golden Phallus award for Best Newcomer in a Gay Feature.

Standing at the podium and holding the nine-inch solid brass penis, Max smiled into the audience, squinting against the spotlights. "Hi, um, thanks a lot for the, ah, this award. I really can honestly say I never expected to win anything like this. So, cool. I guess I'd like to thank the people at Eagle, for giving me a chance; especially Ed. And thanks also to Trixie and Rocky for being really good friends. So thanks, everyone."

More cheers and applause from the audience, and Max shrugged, ran his fingers through his hair, and exited the stage. Behind him, a gigantic projection video screen silently played the scene from *Home Shopping Stud* in which Max made love to a telephone.

Although Max's mother knew nothing of her son's new career—and she most certainly had not seen the awards ceremony, which was televised live on a cable station—she did learn of his success within the adult film industry the next day, hearing the news on an *Inside Edition* exclusive.

"It's been a rocky year for the retail broadcasting network Sellevision. And now, scandal has hit again. Last night former show host Maxwell Andrews accepted an award from the porn industry for his recent role in an explicitly gay male sex video."

His mother had been applying decorative lace to the front of a pillow with her hot glue gun when the report came on.

As *Inside Edition* anchor Deborah Norville stood outside of the Sellevision headquarters, she asked viewers to "Take a look at this exclusive clip from the shocking video, and keep in mind that even though it's been edited for television, it is still unsuitable for young or sensitive viewers."

Mrs. Andrews watched as her nude son, genitals obscured by a black box, unfastened a cameraman's pants with his mouth. The glue gun slipped from her grip, burning her hand and sealing the burn with epoxy. At the same moment, her systolic blood pressure soared to over 180 and her diastolic pressure to 105.

"Andrews was fired from the show last year after exposing his penis to viewers on air while hosting a show *intended* for children."

Then *Inside Edition* replayed the Slumber Sunday incident before cutting back to Deborah Norville. "This hard-core pornography scandal is just the latest in a string of blows the network has suffered."

They showed a brief clip of Leigh during her *Oprah* appearance, the jacket of her book blown up huge behind her. As the clip played, Deborah could be heard saying, "Earlier in the year, former host Leigh Bushmoore publicly ended her adulterous affair with then-head of production, Howard Toast. The on-air revelation created a whirlwind of publicity and sparked heated debates nationwide."

Larry King and Leigh.

Leigh receiving a standing ovation at Smith.

Next back to Deborah, who asked, "The future of the network? That's anyone's guess. But we'll keep watching Sellevision, and you keep watching us. I'm two-time Emmy-award winner Deborah Norville, reporting exclusively for *Inside Edition*."

But Max's mother hadn't seen this portion of the *Inside Edition* report, as she had fallen from her seat and landed on the floor, unconscious.

"I've never had lunch with a porn star before," Adam said in his deep, everyone-assumes-I'm-a-cop voice, stabbing the lime in his seltzer water with the thin straw, sinking it to the bottom.

"Well, I've never had lunch with a hotel maid, so we're even," Max said, smiling at the handsome man across the table.

The two had met the old-fashioned way. Max was coming out of a Safeway grocery store and Adam Rollerbladed into him, causing Max to drop the plastic bag containing the eggs.

"Jeez, I'm sorry about that," Adam had said, seeing the yellow, slimy leakage.

"It's okay," Max told him. "They're bad for you anyway— cholesterol, all that stuff."

Adam had smiled at him and Max had smiled back. And then they both just stood there in that awkward silence that happens when two people are attracted to each other but don't know what to do about it because they are strangers.

"So . . ." Max said.

"Yeah, well . . ." said Adam.

It had been Adam who took the risk. "Hi, I'm Adam," he said, extending his hand. Max, who was crouching down and scooping the contents back into the plastic bag, stood up and shook his hand. "Max. Nice to, uh, run into you."

They exchanged phone numbers. "Maybe we can get together sometime, grab a beer?" Adam had said. Something that, if his hunch was wrong and Max was straight, wouldn't sound too far off the wall.

"Sure," Max had said.

And now here they were, in the garden of Café Left, having lunch on a Tuesday afternoon.

"So, what's it like?" Max asked. "At the hotel, I mean."

"Well, the best part is the snooping."

Max raised an eyebrow. "The snooping? You snoop?"

"Well yeah, sure. Wouldn't you?"

"I don't think so, no. Yes, maybe, I don't know."

Adam took a sip of his seltzer water as the waiter delivered their matching salads. "Freshly ground pepper?" he asked, holding the grinder. Max and Adam nodded.

"Anyway," Adam continued, "the hotel is really chic, beach-front and all that." He stabbed a piece of lettuce with his fork. "Mostly business people, Hollywood producers, New York advertising people, some Japanese tourists. An upscale crowd. No breakfast buffet. The ceilings are low."

"Low ceilings?" Max said over the lettuce in his mouth.

"That says a lot, I think. To have low ceilings you have to be pretty sure of yourself, as a hotel. It's like Julia Roberts always going barefoot at her weddings. You have to be really beautiful to do that."

Max thought, *Why does this make sense to me?* As he attempted to hoist a slice of tomato on his fork, it slid off the prongs and onto his lap. "Shit," he said, blotting the oily stain with his napkin. "It looks like a pee stain."

Adam smiled.

"I'm sorry, go on. Tell me about the snooping."

"Well, first," Adam said, "you need some background information."

"I do?"

"Yes. You need to understand the system."

"Okay, understand me."

"Well, the first three days is pretty intensive training. You learn how to power-clean a room, which is my name for it. Basically, it's all choreography. Efficient hand-swipes with the towel. Dusting as you walk. I never really thought there was technique to cleaning a room. I was surprised." He plucked a crouton off his plate with his fingers and continued. "But it's a science, really. Granted, it's a rinse-the-hot-tub-and-coax-the-pubic-hairs-down-the-drain-while-you-dry-the-floor-with-your-knees science, but still. They teach you how to *do* a room in twenty-three minutes. So you go through a sort of boot-camp, basic-training kind of thing for three days and then you get your uniform. Sea-foam green with scalloped edges on the collar. Everything has to tie in to the ocean there."

Adam saw Max looking down at his crotch. "Am I boring you?"

"No," Max said, looking back up. "I was just seeing if the stain went away. I'm sorry. I tend to have problems with this area of my body."

Adam smirked. "So anyway, they teach you not to make eye contact. This is probably for the benefit of the Japanese tourists. You're supposed to knock three times before using your key. And if you find change on the floor, they tell you to work around it. And then they set you loose."

The waiter popped over, asking if everything was all right. Max asked for another Diet Coke and Adam asked for another seltzer.

"So when do we get to the snooping part?"

"I'm getting there," Adam said, leaning heavily on his words and smiling at Max in such a way that made Max think he was being promised something good.

"I'm responsible for the seventh floor, west wing. Seventeen rooms. Twenty-three minutes each to clean. Plus a thirty-minute lunch and two ten-minute breaks. And that's my day. At least on paper."

Adam shuffled the leaves on his plate around, moved an onion slice over the edge of the plate, and poked at an endive.

"But I've trained myself to clean a room in sixteen minutes—tops. Usually, I can do a room in twelve. I'm a fucking machine.

Except when I open the door to get soap refills or hand towels from my cart. Then I move at a normal swift pace, as opposed to my manic pace, so as not to draw attention to myself from the other maids. I don't want them to know how fast I can do a room. I need my time for investigating."

"Okay, good, this is the snooping part. Where do you snoop?"

"I go through everything. The side pockets in the suitcases. The little secret flap pocket on the top of the Prada bags. I go through pant pockets and desk drawers, I smell the perfumes, I try on the coats and sometimes the dresses. Always the shoes. Oh, but the laptop computer has changed everything. And if there's one in the room, this is what I go to first."

Max liked this guy. He was like a good TV show.

"Right away, I double-click on the hard drive to get a basic overview. Then I immediately open any file called 'personal,' 'letters,' or 'journal.' I also open anything that sounds suspiciously vague, like 'reports,' because I have found that this is often where the good stuff is hidden—cleverly, the owners think." Adam gave Max a knowing look. "I read very quickly. A book a day on the weekend. So I can cover a lot of ground in eleven minutes."

Max grinned.

"I check people's E-mail. Sometimes I reply."

Max rested his fork on his plate, leaned in. "You reply? You reply to other people's E-mail?" As much as he thought this was extremely wrong, he also thought it extremely interesting. "Like what? What do you say?"

"Well," Adam began, "Last week I placed a personal ad."

Max's eyes sparkled.

"I was in this guy's room: Rogain, two baseball caps, *Adweek* magazine, Doc Martens, Obsession, Abercrombie & Fitch underwear, G4 Powerbook. So obviously, the guy's in advertis-

ing. Which means he's too insecure to make it in the film industry. And the Rogain, well, that was pretty funny. I loved that. I
immediately opened it up and poured it down the drain and
refilled the bottle with tap water. Anyway, so I'm looking
around and I see this picture of him and his girlfriend, kind of
slid inside his notebook. He's got all kinds of shit in that notebook—doodles, lousy headlines, phone numbers, and this picture of the two of them, sitting at a table, dressed in black.
They both looked kinda drunk, and their eyes were red from
the flash. They were laughing. And I looked at him, and I
thought, 'This guy is so queer.' I mean, it was just so obvious to
me. He is completely and totally gay. No straight man I have
ever known had a face that well moisturized. You could see it in
the picture. And his body? Perfect. Only he obviously doesn't
know he's gay. Hasn't come to terms with it. Either that, or
does know and the girlfriend is just unwittingly along for the
ride. I started to feel really sad for his girlfriend, because eventually, he's going to come face-to-face with the fact that he's a
fruit and it's just gonna be too damned bad for his girlfriend.
She's a little overweight, I noticed. So there's obviously some
fag-hag stuff going on in this relationship. And it's always the
woman who gets hurt in a situation like this. I looked at this
girl's plump, laughing face and I thought, boy, is she gonna
crash. He's gonna come out and find some hairy-chested, back-
wards-baseball-cap-wearing guy who saw *Showgirls* six times
for the camp value, and the poor girl is just gonna eat." He took
a long sip of seltzer water.

"You are insane," Max said, completely absorbed.

Adam took this as a compliment and continued. "That's
when I decided to help. America Online was just right there on
his computer. I hit return, which immediately signed me on.
He'd already stored his password."

The waiter appeared again. "All finished with these?" he

asked, and then carried the two plates, empty except for onions, away.

"Anyway, I'm quite familiar with America Online, so as soon as I got the main menu, I went right to the gay section. And I placed the ad in the Chicago section, because I'd looked at his return airline ticket and seen O'Hare."

"Oh my God, I can't believe you really did this. What did you write?" Max asked.

Adam smiled, brought one of his big furry arms up and ran his fingers through his hair, then caught himself. "Sorry, I do that all the time, run my fingers through my hair, it's like a nervous habit or something and it drives people crazy."

Max shivered.

"So anyway, I wrote, 'GWM thirtysomething advertising guy, average looks, gym bod, thinning hair, Doc Martens and a girlfriend. Help me out here, guys. I'm just coming to terms with my sexual orientation and would appreciate any support/advice you could give me. I'm real new to this whole thing. If you have a HOT picture, send that too.' Short and sweet."

"I don't ever want to stay in a hotel again," Max said. "I never knew that you people were so . . . *involved*."

"Well, it's like brain surgery in a way, being a maid. Because these people check out, they move on with their lives, and I have no idea what ever happens to them. Like, I'll never know how much my little ad helped this man."

"Or ruined his life," Max added, grinning.

"So tell me about you. What's it like being a porn star? What does your mother say?"

Max thought of his mother, her wrist in a plaster cast from when she fainted, falling and breaking her old wristbones. "Well, I just sort of fell into it," he said.

Adam leaned in. "Fell into it? How does one 'fall into' a career as an actor in porn flicks?"

"Well," Max said, "it started when I fell out."

After going through the entire saga and finishing their entrées, Max and Adam split the check and stood on the sidewalk outside Café Left.

"I had a really nice time, thanks," Adam said.

"So did I."

"So . . . see you again?" Adam asked.

Max blushed. Something left over from his childhood; the inability to conceal his emotions.

"You're blushing," Adam happily pointed out.

"Sorry. Um, yeah, I'd love to."

More silence as the two men stood outside the restaurant, hands in pockets. Max looked at Adam, at his strong Italian features, his cleft chin etched with razor stubble.

"Okay," Max said.

"Okay what?" Adam asked.

"Okay, so I guess I'll see you soon."

"You have beautiful eyes," Adam told Max.

"Don't tell me that," Max said, lowering his head. "You'll make me turn red again."

Adam laughed, reached out, and touched Max's shoulder. "So . . . what are you doing for dinner tonight?"

"Oh, I don't know, maybe order in some Chinese or a pizza or something. I might call my friend Leigh from back East."

"I have a better idea," Adam said.

Max felt his palms begin to sweat. "You do?"

"Yes. Much better. You like roasted quail with garlic mashed potatoes?"

"Well, gosh, yeah, that sounds great!" Max said.

Adam shifted his weight onto the other leg. "Yeah, so do I, but I can't cook. So why don't we rent a movie and order in a pizza over at my place?" Adam's smile was about a thousand watts.

Max was blinded by it.

■

Peggy Jean sat on a folding metal chair in the basement of her church. A ceiling fan turned lazily above her head. On the wall was a large poster: The 12 Steps of Alcoholics Anonymous. Next to it, another poster read: The Promises. The room was filled with about thirty people forming a half-circle around a desk that was placed in the center, in front of the wall. Behind the desk was an alcoholic. The alcoholic had spoken for twenty minutes, telling his own story, his *qualification*. Afterward, the other alcoholics in the room raised their hands and he would call on them, allowing them to say whatever was on their minds.

Peggy Jean raised her hand and the alcoholic behind the desk pointed to her.

"My name is Peggy Jean Smythe, and I'm an alcoholic-slash-drug addict."

"Hi, Peggy Jean," the other alcoholics in the room said in unison.

Peggy Jean squeezed one hand with the other. "I've been clean and sober for a year, and I'm just trying to get on with my life, *one day at a time*."

Many of the alcoholics nodded their heads, understanding.

"But you know, I'm still dealing with the same old . . . *shit*."

There, she'd said it. Her therapist would be proud of her. She would tell him that she said it when she saw him on Friday.

She took a sip of coffee from the styrofoam cup in her hand. "I mean, sometimes I'll be out with a friend having dinner, or on my way to the beauty parlor, and I'll see them together. And it still hurts. It's just so very hard for me to even say the word out loud. I know I'm a modern woman, but I've just been programmed to believe that *divorce* is something to be ashamed of."

A pale, lanky woman with long, stringy brown hair continued to shred a napkin.

"I try to think of Princess Diana and how she was able to lift her head up high. But then my internal tapes start playing. The tapes that say, 'Charles left Diana for an older woman who looks like a Chesapeake Bay retriever, while your husband left you for a seventeen-year-old girl who can do backflips.' "

Peggy Jean went silent. For a moment she thought of Pete, the homeless man she had become friends with at the shelter where she volunteered. He had begun to turn his life around. Recently, he had said to her, "All I could think about was the crack, smokin' the crack. And that's what I became. Just a bum that smoked crack. And somehow, someway, I got it—that flash of truth. I realized that what you focus on, that's what grows, that's what you become." He had taken another bite of her turkey loaf. "Like this here turkey loaf of yours. Best damn turkey loaf there is because you put your whole heart into makin' it, you focus on it."

Peggy Jean looked at the faces of the other alcoholics in the room. "For a long time, I've been focusing on the wrong things. On the things outside. And you know what? To heck with the outside crap. I'm going to focus on my inner garden."

When the meeting ended, the alcoholics joined hands and said the Serenity Prayer together, one of Peggy Jean's favorite things about being *in the program*. Afterward, the lanky girl approached her.

"Hi, Peggy Jean, I'm glad you were able to make it today," she said.

Peggy Jean gave her a hug. "Hi, Nadine. No, I had to come today. I was really feeling anxious, but I'm better now."

"Do you want to get some coffee?"

Peggy Jean smiled and rested her hand on the girl's shoulder, the two-karat Queen of Hearts simulated sapphire ring sparkling on her finger. "I'd like that." She checked her watch. "But we better make it a quick cup. I've got a long drive upstate ahead of me."

Nadine linked her arm through Peggy Jean's and the two walked outside. "I'm proud of what you're doing," she said. "I wish I could be there in person to support you."

Peggy Jean saw a glint of copper on the ground. She bent over and picked it up. "A lucky penny!" she cried.

"It's a sign," Nadine said.

Peggy Jean slipped the coin into her pocket. "The Lord works in mysterious ways."

As Peggy Jean cruised along the highway, she thought to herself, had it really been just a year ago that life changed forever? Sometimes it felt like ten years; sometimes it felt as fresh and raw as yesterday. If only she had not come home from the Anne Sexton Center one day early. If only she hadn't been so eager to be reunited with her loving family. Then she wouldn't have unlocked the front door and seen her husband giving a tongue bath to Nikki, who was handcuffed to the coffee table.

She had screamed, taken the Lord's name in vain, and hurled her pocketbook at his head, missing. He just had laughed and told her to take the kids and move out. Nikki simply giggled and arched her back. The floor was littered with Diet Pepsi cans and tissues.

And in the end, Peggy Jean had done exactly what her husband had told her to do. She had not reached for a Valium or an apertif. Instead, she collected her boys and her wardrobe and rented an apartment for the four of them. But she didn't do it for him. She did it for herself and her babies.

She had almost relapsed when Sellevision fired her.

"You can't expect us to allow you back on air after you've been in a mental institution. You admit yourself that you're an alcoholic and a drug abuser," the heartless new head of production had said.

Those first few weeks had been the most difficult of her life. At times, she had even questioned God's commitment to her. "Remember Peggy Jean, in early sobriety, you will face many challenges, but God will never give you more than you can deal with," they had told her at the center. Peggy Jean had expected such things as spoiled food in the back of the refrigerator, dried leaves on the hanging spider plant in her sewing room, or perhaps an ingrown toenail on one of her boys. Things she could deal with. She had not expected her marriage to fall apart and her career to collapse.

And never in her wildest dreams had she expected that phone call from the state's prosecuting attorney.

"There's been an explosion at your son's school," he had told her. "Nobody was injured, but the damage is significant."

Her relief was brief.

"I'm sorry, Mrs. Smythe, but your son, Ricky, is responsible. He's confessed to the crime and plastic explosive was discovered on his person."

And then Ricky was sent to a juvenile facility for boys in the western part of the state.

Her own son, her firstborn, a potential teen killer. It was simply more than a mother could bear. And then after one month at the facility, he called her on the phone. "There's something I need to tell you" he said. And then in a muffled, high-pitched voice identical to the voice of "Zoe" when she had called her on air, he quoted verbatim from the first letter she received: "Peggy Jean, my ears always perk up when I hear your voice on Sellevision. You are my favorite host. You are so professional and friendly, and I just love your hair! Speaking of

hair, I just want to tell you this, woman to woman: Peggy Jean,
I have noticed many times in close-up pictures how very hairy
your earlobes are."

Zoe was her son.

Hearing this, she had instinctively reached for a Valium.
Then the awful reality set in. The reality that *there would be no
more of that*. And that she had to face this dreadful truth, *stone
cold sober*.

"But why?" she had asked, blinking away the tears.

"Because I had a lot of repressed anger, a lot of self-esteem
issues in terms of feeling infantilized by you. And your lack of
physical affection, well, it just cemented my already latent feelings of inadequacy and failure. I've also got major control
issues."

He'd been undergoing extensive therapy since the bombing.

"Do you hate me?" she whimpered.

"I did," he told her. "But I'm moving through my anger.
And it's something we can work on—together, with a therapist—when I get out."

He also told her that when he got out, he was going to apply
to the Vidal Sassoon Academy in Venice, California. He was
going to become a colorist.

As for her two youngest boys, she no longer charted their
moods and even allowed them to drink nondiet sodas on week-
ends. She didn't force them to go to church. And she was learning to throw a softball. Her therapist called all of it *progress*.

Life was a journey.

Peggy Jean saw her exit up ahead. She moved into the far
right lane and turned on her blinker. The sun had nearly set. She
would have just enough time to check into her room at the Quality Inn and have a refreshing shower and a quick dinner. Being
on tour *was* exhausting, but also very rewarding. Most importantly, what she was doing was God's will. And who was she to
argue with God? After all, they were business partners now.

The blue neon sign in front of the Poco-no-no Motor Lodge in the heart of the Poconos advertised "Heart Shaped Hot Tubs!" and "Free Cable!" The beige shingled building was set back from the street and nestled among tall pine trees. The "no-no" was clean, comfortable, and only $39 a night. Frequent daytrippers, John and Nikki had checked in just after lunch, registering as father and daughter. But even at three-thirty in the morning, the games were still going strong.

"Mr. Smythe, I'm going to need you to take a deep breath and then let it out very slowly," Nikki said, placing the cold stethoscope against his back.

John shivered. "That's so cold," he said.

Nikki smiled and placed the stethoscope in the front pocket of her white L.P.N. uniform. "Now, now, now, I hope you're not going to cause me any trouble today," she warned. She wagged her finger at him.

He licked it.

She slid the finger deeper into his mouth. "Mmmmmm," she moaned, "Nurse Nikki thinks you're just what the doctor ordered."

John reclined on his elbows, knocking the remote control onto the floor. The television suddenly came to life.

Nikki screamed and brought her hand to her mouth. "Oh my God," she cried. Her eyes bulged in disbelief.

John turned toward the screen. He gasped.

Nikki laughed viciously. "Have you ever seen anything so pathetic?"

"Shhhh," John said. "Where's the volume? Where's the remote?" His erection immediately deflated.

"You knocked it on the floor. *Hurry.*"

He reached over and grabbed it, stabbing at the volume button.

Nikki leaned forward with her mouth wide open.

John snickered through his nose. "Jesus, Nikki. Even I never imagined she could sink so low."

Nikki shook her head slowly from side to side, frowning. "Her roots must be half an inch!"

John scratched under his arm and absently brought his fingers to his nose. "She must have stopped taking her medication."

"And look how she's standing! She thinks she's Cindy Crawford with a halo!" Nikki shrieked with delight.

The two then pointed at the screen, both laughing so hard the bed shook.

"Oh, God, this is so priceless. I wish we were taping it," Nikki said, wiping a tear.

John grinned and reached for the ashtray. He put the half-smoked joint between his lips. "Got a light?" he mumbled.

"Yay!" Nikki said. "I forgot all about that." She scanned the room. "But we're gonna need munchies."

John smiled devilishly. "I got your munchies right here," he said, grabbing his crotch.

Nikki slapped him on the arm and arched an eyebrow. "Don't make me give you another prostate exam, Mr. Smythe."

Retail Salvage had the distinction of being the Poconos' very own shop-from-home cable show. It was broadcast live from a small studio in an industrial park. The hours were irregular. The lighting was harsh. And at 4:15 A.M. Peggy Jean was the guest. Although she had visited numerous bookstores and radio stations and had established her own Web site, this was Peggy Jean's first television appearance. Her self-published book was entitled, *Peggy Jean, Jesus and You!* Under the large color photograph of Peggy Jean was a quote from Debby

Boone: "Together, Peggy Jean and Jesus will light up your life—take it from me."

"And for our viewers who are out there watching in these early morning hours, what would you like to say to them?" the somewhat paunchy host asked.

Peggy Jean shouldered her way in front of the host and looked directly into the camera. "Maybe you have insomnia," she began, "or a terminal disease. Perhaps you're older and live all alone. And you're frightened because you know that crime can strike anyone, anywhere, at any time. This book is for you. It offers not just hope, but real-life solutions."

The host attempted to move out from behind Peggy Jean and stand beside her, but she would not allow it. She was much more experienced, and knew how to move on camera.

"Phone call!" someone yelled from off the set.

"I understand we have a caller," Peggy Jean said, smiling confidently. "God has opened a window. Come on through!"

There was a loud crackling sound, followed by a screech. "Hello?" said the caller. "Hello? Am I on the air with Peggy Jean Smythe? Hel—"

"This is Peggy Jean Smythe and welcome to the show." She deliberately did not use the name of the show, *Retail Salvage*, because she considered it too low-class. Wearing a Kathy Ireland sweater from Kmart had been her only concession to the lower-income demographic that this particular television station attracted. But one had to start somewhere.

"Hi, Peggy Jean! I thought that was you. I miss you so much on Sellevision."

Peggy Jean would need to move this caller along. "Thank you very much. But the Lord had bigger plans in store for me. What would you like to overcome?" she asked.

The caller laughed. "Well, I'd like to overcome about fifteen extra pounds I put on after my second baby, but I th—"

"I understand perfectly," Peggy Jean interjected. "You suffer from a poor self-image. And you're understandably worried about the health of your new baby. After all, so many babies have medical problems that go undetected. My book can help. I can point you to the tunnel and you will see the light at the end of it for yourself." She held the book squarely in front of her. The tip of her fingernail resting on the cover, pointing at her name. "Let Jesus and me help you, caller. Order now. An operator is standing by."

"Would you like to save the placenta?" the midwife asked. "For soup stock," she added.

Eliot winced.

But Bebe just gazed into her baby's eyes. "You're so perfect," she whispered. "Yes, you are."

The midwife shrugged. "I'll bag it and put it in the nurses' fridge for later," she said as she carried the warm organ off. It was Holymount Hospital policy to at least offer.

Eliot reached over and stroked his newborn son's head. "You are as beautiful as your mommy," he said.

Bebe looked at him. "Oh, Eliot. This is just a miracle. I . . . I . . ." Tears streamed down her cheeks.

Eliot wiped them away with his finger. "Baby Jake is gonna love his new room back home that mommy fixed up for him. Aren't you, baby?"

Bebe kissed his tiny fingers. "Daddy's right, little one. You have a ceiling full of stars. And a big happy clown in the corner of the room to protect you. And lots and lots of stuffed animals to snuggle up with. And your very own merry-go-round pony to sit on when you get bigger."

Eliot rolled his eyes and smiled. "And don't forget his very own PastaMaster, Jumping-Jack-O-Matic, and stained-glass Monarch butterfly collection. Oh, and let's not forget his brand-new snow blower."

"Eliot," Bebe whined. "I got the snow blower for *you*. So you don't throw out your back."

"Bebe, my love. How could I throw out my back when I have my brand-new Chirochair 3000?"

"Don't be mean," Bebe whimpered. She kissed his nose, then kissed her baby's. "I love my guys," she said. "And I love making a nice home for them."

Eliot couldn't help but laugh. "Soon there won't be enough room in the home for your guys."

"Shhhhhhhh," she said. "He's sleeping. Anyway, I've already decided to get rid of a few things. I think it's time to simplify. Pare down. You know, get a little more Zen."

"Oh, brother," Eliot moaned.

Because the Glade Plug-In shared an electrical outlet with the neon spoon, the room ionizer, the bread maker, and the acoustic rodent repeller, it overheated. The plastic warmed, and then started to melt. The outlet blew and the clock on the bread maker went black.

But a tiny spark landed atop Bebe's brand-new copy of *Zen and the Art of Simple Living*.

The spark burned a small hole in the cover and the page below began to smolder. Before long, the book was on fire. Quickly, the fire leapt from the book to one of the nearby baskets lining the kitchen counter. Soon, all the baskets were blazing, and the fire spread to the cabinets, the walls, and the ceiling. Flames fell from the ceiling and caught on the carpets. The elephant-foot umbrella stand exploded, causing the antique mannequins next to it to become engulfed. Soon, the sectional sofa was in flames and thick black smoke was billowing out from behind the swag drapes. The Venetian glass collection cracked and shattered to the floor.

By the time the fire department arrived, the duplex was a

three-alarm inferno. It had taken nine men to get it under
control.

"Jesus H. Christ," Lt. Brickhouse said to his partner. "I've
never seen a residential fire burn that hot. This is like a fucking warehouse fire. What have they got in that place, anyway?"

"Beats me," said his partner, wiping a gloved hand across his
forehead. "But it's always the pack rats."

Lt. Brickhouse shook his head. "Ain't that the damn sorry
truth."

"At least nobody was home."

The men stared at the smoldering rubble. "I sure wouldn't
want to be the one who comes home to this mess. Poor folks
are gonna have to start from scratch, right down to the can
openers," the lieutenant said.

Because Bebe's next door neighbor had agreed to take care
of Pepper, the dog had a clear view of his home as it burned to
the ground. He whined and circled in front of the living room
window. In his own doggy way he knew something was terribly
wrong. *No more house, no more kitchen table to sit under, no more
Beggin' Strips.*

Trish glanced at her watch. Because she'd stayed on the phone
with her father longer than she realized, she was running
behind. She needed to rush over to makeup and powder her
face quickly. She felt herself begin to shine while she was talking on the phone. As she dashed out of her office she collided
head-on with Amanda.

"Oh no, oh, God. I am so sorry, Trish, look at your blouse.
I keep forgetting that you're in Peggy Jean's old office now.
Oh, no!"

Trish's sheer white top was drenched with chocolate milk-
shake. Trish was furious. But there was no time to reprimand

Amanda now. "Get me another blouse." She checked her slacks. They were clean, thank God. "I don't care what it is, but make sure it goes with my slacks. I'm going to go clean your mess off me."

Amanda scurried away. There was a new blouse she'd bought at Club Monaco hanging on the back of her door. She hadn't even worn it yet. And she and Trish were about the same size. Hopefully, it would do. She grabbed the hanger and dashed back to Trish's office. "Do you like pale pink?" she asked, gently.

Trish snatched the blouse from Amanda's hand. "Yes. Pale pink is suddenly my new favorite color," she said, slamming the door. She changed quickly, breathing through her mouth because the office still reeked of that damn Giorgio perfume.

"Good evening and welcome to Sellevision. I'm your host, Trish Mission, and tonight we've got a wonderful show for all you collectors out there."

Trish sat on a blue velvet armchair in the living room set with her legs crossed. On top of the coffee table before her were three porcelain collectible figurines. "The first item I'm going to show you is wonderful, especially if you have children. It's item number J-1135 and it's called Molly and Her Puppy, introductory priced at just forty-seven fifty."

As Trish started to reach for the figurine, she realized that the prop stylist had placed the coffee table a few inches too far from her chair. She would need to lean forward.

So she did.

But of course, Trish hadn't worn the milkshake-soaked bra beneath Amanda's low-cut blouse. She hadn't worn a bra at all.

So when she leaned over, her left breast fell out.